CRIME IN QUESTION

The nightmare made her start awake, and then she heard a sound. She sat up in bed. A cool draught blew in through the open window. The noise was probably the branch of a tree creaking outside, or the old wood of the house stretching. She lay down again, pulling the covers round her, trying to think of something soothing, but it was useless . . .

She crossed to the door and found it ajar. That was odd. She always shut it when she went to bed, and it was fitted properly, never coming open once it was closed. Then she saw the window was wide open, not latched as she always left it. Audrey barely took these facts in as she switched on the landing light and descended the stairs; she certainly did not suspect that there was an intruder in the house . . .

Also in Mysterious Press by Margaret Yorke

THE COST OF SILENCE
DEAD IN THE MORNING
DEATH ON ACCOUNT
DEVIL'S WORK
EVIDENCE TO DESTROY
FIND ME A VILLAIN
THE HAND OF DEATH
INTIMATE KILL
MORTAL REMAINS
NO MEDALS FOR THE MAJOR
THE POINT OF MURDER
SAFELY TO THE GRAVE
SCENT OF FEAR
SILENT WITNESS
THE SMALL HOURS OF THE MORNING
THE SMOOTH FACE OF EVIL
SPEAK FOR THE DEAD
CAST FOR DEATH
GRAVE MATTERS

CRIME IN QUESTION

Margaret Yorke

MYSTERIOUS PRESS

Mysterious Press books (UK) are published in
association with Arrow Books Limited
20 Vauxhall Bridge Road, London SW1V 2SA

An imprint of Random Century Group

London Melbourne Sydney Auckland
Johannesburg and agencies throughout
the world

First published in Great Britain in 1989 by
Century Hutchinson Ltd/Mysterious Press UK
Mysterious Press paperback edition 1990

Printed and bound in Great Britain by
Courier International Ltd, Tiptree, Essex

ISBN 0 09 970680 6

1

Denis never knocked.

He marched into the house as soon as Yvonne returned from shopping in Leckerton. She was alone. He remembered that the little kid went to a playgroup in the village.

'Come for me cocoa,' said Denis, admitting a blast of raw autumnal air as he stumped along the passage and entered the kitchen.

'You've left the back door open,' said Yvonne. 'And take your boots off.'

The boy raised his eyes to heaven in wonderment at these remarks, but he slouched away to bang the door and leave his boots on the mat. Returning, he did a little jig with his hands over his ears as if he were wearing a Walkman, and capered round the big scrubbed table in a pair of red socks with a hole in one toe before sitting down.

In silence, Yvonne Davies made him a cup of hot chocolate, which was his preferred mid-morning beverage, and fetched a tin from the larder. She cut a slice of sponge cake filled with home-made raspberry jam and put it on a plate before him.

'Ta,' said Denis.

He began to shovel cake into his mouth with one hand, still holding the other over one ear and writhing about as if in response to some ritual beat.

Denis was the jobbing gardener at Ford House. He had applied for the post after seeing it advertised on a card in the village shop, but he did not live in Coxton.

'I'm staying with me gran in Leckerton,' he had informed Yvonne, whose first impressions of the applicant were not encouraging. He had dark, almost black eyes, and a round florid face with a sparse crop of acne. His brown hair was shorn at the back and brushed up in short spikes above his low forehead. He said he was doing casual work before going on a Youth Training Scheme, and that he liked working outside.

Only the last of these statements was true.

'So you wouldn't be staying long?' Yvonne asked.

'No. Sorry,' said Denis.

That suited her. She didn't want the expense of retaining someone through the winter when there would be little to do. Denis's task would be to dig over the vegetable garden, a large neglected area behind a hedge at the side of the house and too much for her to tackle unaided. Yvonne was glad to be living in the country after years in Shepherds Bush, and excited at the prospect of putting things to rights both inside and outside the house, but there was so much to do, and Charles had little time to help. His day was much longer now, with the journey; sometimes she thought he extended it more than he need.

Denis was a stocky, sturdy boy, and digging was straightforward enough. As the only other applicant was a frail-looking man of seventy-three, Yvonne had taken Denis on for the two mornings a week which were all he said he could spare, and today was his third appearance. Yvonne had not been sure he would stay the course, but he was working well, laying the soil in large clods to be broken up by the frost, as she had instructed, and burying all the weeds. If he stayed long enough, she might imprint some manners on the blemished canvas that was his character. The 'ta' this morning was an improvement upon his previous silent grabbing of whatever he was offered.

While he was eating his cake, Yvonne unpacked the shopping and put it away, walking to and from the larder which opened off the old scullery. Ford House had been built near a shallow stretch of the river where there had been a ford before the bridge had been built. It dated from the late eighteenth century, but bits had been added and removed at various times until what was left was a somewhat uncoordinated house. It had been on the market some time before Charles and Yvonne bought it after the asking price was reduced, and it needed renovation which they intended to do gradually when they could afford it. As it was only twelve miles from the motorway, they had thought themselves lucky to have their offer accepted. That was before they discovered that there was an open prison only four miles away to the north.

Buying the house had landed them with a large mortgage to be met from only one salary, and Charles was stretched to his financial limits. They had both been married before, and he had another family to support. Yvonne tried not to resent this drain on their income, but it was difficult. She had never received any money either for herself or for her two children from her former husband, who had disappeared and was thought to be living in Australia.

When she met Charles, Yvonne had been working for an interior decorator for whom she made curtains, cushions and bedspreads. The pay was not very good but she could work at home, travelling back and forth as necessary in her old Mini making deliveries and collecting fabrics. She intended to branch out on her own; there must be local scope for such a service. At last she had plenty of space; a room on the top floor of the house warmed only by a portable gas heater because the ancient central heating did not stretch so far, was her new workplace. She had a large trestle table on which to cut out, and there were shelves for her bolts of material. The ironing board could be kept permanently ready for use, and there was room for Robbie to play with his cars on the floor. In any spare time she could find between commissions, she was making cushion covers and bedspreads to form the basis for her own business.

Denis had finished his cake. Yvonne, as she moved in and out of the kitchen unpacking her shopping, had not noticed his eyes darting about as he wondered what he could pick up which she would not miss. She was too careful; that was the trouble. She never left her purse lying about, nor even the odd coin. He knew where she kept her keys, however; he'd noticed them the first day, hanging openly on the dresser, her car keys and one that opened the front door. They were just asking to be taken.

Denis had not yet decided how best to use them, but he would. You had to take your chance when it came. He'd always done that, ever since he'd seen a pair of brand-new jeans pegged to a clothes line and had liberated them for his own use. He was only twelve at the time. After that he'd done a fair bit of snow-dropping: collecting gear that had been hung out to dry. Some of it he sold to other boys, but most he kept for himself. He liked to look smart, and his mother wasn't too fussy about seeing that he did; when she put on the old washing machine that leaked on to the kitchen floor, she never took any notice of what was in the load and colours got mixed and ran. Denis's sister had sometimes seen to things, but she had gone now, shacked up with a guy who worked as a plasterer. He had his own van and went around working for different builders; self-employed, he was, and Denis admired him for that. Sometimes he went round to see them, and it was Alan who had brought him over to Coxton for the ride on the day that he saw the card advertising this job. That had been in the school holidays when working was a way of passing the time. Denis had told Mrs Davies he was seventeen but it wasn't true. He would be sixteen in November and then he could give up school, where both he and the staff agreed he stood no chance of ever passing an exam. His departure would be a relief on both sides and meanwhile he could simply not turn up sometimes; he'd done it before but not often enough to land himself in serious trouble.

Mrs Davies – for some reason Denis always thought of her in that respectful way – had paid up for new boots for him, for naturally he couldn't go digging in his trainers. Instead of buying them, he'd liberated a pair of wellingtons from a stall in Leckerton market at no cost at all. He'd tried them on when the place was busy and then, still wearing them, had picked up some shoes as if to inspect them while he waited for an opportunity to walk away with his own trainers tucked up under his bomber jacket. The chance had come while the stallholder was busy with two talkative women. He had been tempted to take the shoes too, but that would have been asking to get caught. He had laid them down and walked away.

It was dead easy.

Denis liked that sort of challenge. Why pay good money for things you could get free?

After his first day, when Denis had worn a pair of Charles's boots padded out with extra socks, he was not at all sure that he would come again. It wasn't easy to get over to Coxton without a lift and he was certainly not going to use the bus, although Mrs Davies was going to pay his fare; that was a wicked waste of money. Turning over the heavy soil had been hard work, though there was satisfaction in seeing the area of neatly dug earth slowly increasing. His back had ached a bit, but not a lot. He'd been starving hungry after a very short time, and when she called him to the house for his mid-morning break he had been surprised; he hadn't expected that. For one of her sort, she wasn't bad, and she made great cakes. He supposed she used those packets you got at Tesco's, like his mum had done on good days when he was young. She'd paid him on the nail and advanced him the cash for the boots.

11

Yvonne had had misgivings about that as she handed the money over, having telephoned a shop in the town to ask about prices. She would be waving it goodbye and the boy would never turn up again. But the next week there he was, and he had given her twenty pence back, saying it was the change.

She had accepted it as a matter of principle, and she had found him an old anorak of Charles's to wear while at work, so that his own wouldn't get soiled.

Charles knew nothing about the deal with the boots. He simply paid for Denis's time and his bus fare.

Denis discovered how near Ford House was to the open prison after his second day's work. On his way to hitch a lift at the crossroads, he decided to take a look round the village and walked down a road he had not been along before. Soon he came to the church, where he saw a group of men in overalls repairing the stone wall which bordered the graveyard. He recognized them at once for what they were, although there was no sign of a warder in charge.

As he passed, Denis had his make-believe earphones attached to his head, his hands cupped, and he was listening in his mind to Michael Jackson. This distracted him from immediately thinking of speaking to any of them. Later, he realized that they might be interested in the pickings up at the big house, all those bits of fancy china he'd seen through the window, dotted about on cupboards and stuff, and she'd probably got loads of jewellery. A con would know how to get rid of it the best way without getting caught, and there'd be a good cut for whoever had set up the job. Denis did not see as a flaw in this theory the fact that the men had already proved fallible enough to be charged and convicted.

The four men busy in the chuchyard repairing the wall had seen Denis go by. They noticed everyone who passed. Interested parishioners, including those who never went to church, came to see what they were doing,

12

and the parochial church council was so pleased with their efforts that it was contemplating asking for prison labour to repair the roof.

The men rode to work on bicycles.

Mrs Bannerman, who lived at Ivy Lodge, had asked for a prisoner to help her plant a hedge. Some villagers had reservations about the presence of these men among them, but she had none. Help was difficult to find in Coxton, and by employing a convict she might, in some small way, make up a little for the past.

Denis had been back in the garden for only half an hour after finishing his cake and hot chocolate before it began to rain.

As soon as what had started as a fine drizzle turned into a downpour, Yvonne called him into the house.

'You can't go on in this, Denis,' she said. 'You may as well give up for today. I'll take you down to the bus stop on the way to pick Robin up from the playgroup.'

Denis had never been to a playgroup. When his mother was at work he was left with a child minder, and he had soon learned to fend for himself. The child minder was an unofficial one who crammed ten small children into her small terraced house, where survival was for the fittest. Once, Denis had been shut in a cupboard for hitting another boy over the head with a wooden engine. There were good moments, though, when the child minder had made them all sit down and watch television and had given them buns and milk. His mother worked at a factory in Leckerton packing small plastic objects into boxes. She spent much of what she earned on drink. Denis's father was a warehouseman. He liked drink too. It made him free with his fists and he had knocked them all about, Denis and his sister Tracy, and their mother, but the rows between husband and wife ended in noisy reconciliations when the children were locked out of the house if

13

they had not already chosen to leave until things quietened down.

Sometimes their mother took men upstairs who were not their father. Tracy and Denis were always locked out then.

The grandmother Denis had mentioned to Yvonne did not exist any more. Years ago the children had spent their school holidays with their grandparents near Ramsgate but that had ended when their grandmother died and their grandfather was now in a home.

Denis got into Yvonne's old blue Mini and watched how she started it up. If ever he was in any sort of motor vehicle, he always studied how it operated. He reckoned he could drive Alan's van as easy as wink and begged to be allowed to try, but Alan always refused.

'What, have you out on the road when you've not got a licence? Suppose you crashed? Think again, Den,' Alan had said.

'Where's the playgroup?' Denis asked.

'At the vicarage,' Yvonne told him. It was run by Amy Parker, the vicar's wife, who was a former teacher; two other mothers took turns to help her.

They drove through the village and as Yvonne slowed down to drop Denis at the bus shelter, they saw a man on a bicycle emerge from a gateway further along the road.

'That's one of them cons,' said Denis.

'Yes,' said Yvonne.

'They're working up at the church. I've seen them.'

'So I believe,' said Yvonne, who had heard talk in the shop.

'Must be a cushy number,' said Denis. 'Better than being in the nick.'

'I'm sure you're right,' said Yvonne drily. 'And it's supposed to prepare them for rejoining society.'

Denis always wanted to mimic her when she talked in that lah-di-dah way, but he knew better than to try

14

when she was within earshot. To help himself resist the urge, he cupped his hands over his ears and writhed in his seat.

'We've arrived, Denis,' Yvonne pointed out, and added, 'I'm surprised you haven't got a Walkman; you're always pretending to be listening to one.'

'I did have,' said Denis. 'It got nicked.' His mother had popped it to buy drink. 'I'm getting another.'

'Well, watch out when you're wearing it,' Yvonne warned. 'They're dangerous things in traffic. You can't hear anyone coming up behind you.'

And you couldn't hear rows, either, or people cursing you, or not very plainly.

'Yeah, I know,' said Denis.

He got out of the car, banging the door, and watched her disappear round a bend in the road. He would not admit, even to himself, that he enjoyed the time spent at Ford House. For one thing, no one got at you, and she was all right, handing out food. The silence in the garden had got him down at first and it was a relief when he heard a car or lorry pass in the road, but once you started to listen there were other sounds — birds twittering and dogs barking.

They'd got no dogs at the house. You'd think they would, with all that space, and it would be nice for the kids. Anyone planning a heist would be glad to know about that.

Whistling, Denis stood inside the bus shelter waiting for someone to come along and give him a lift.

He'd get another Walkman that afternoon. He'd find one somewhere, just waiting to be tucked up inside his jacket.

2

Returning from the playgroup with Robin, Yvonne slowed as she passed the gates through which the man on the cycle had ridden. As she had thought, it was Ivy Lodge. That was where the old lady in the tweed hat lived. Yvonne had seen her walking around the district. She went for miles, always alone. Yvonne had met her in the shop and noticed her awkward, gruff manner. She did not know her name, but then she scarcely knew anyone yet, not even the other mothers at the play-group. They all seemed very friendly amongst them-selves, but she was always in too much of a hurry to stop and chat. When she got home, if it was not household tasks that must be done, there was her sewing.

She did not like the thought of those convicts roaming, apparently freely, round the village. It was no wonder Ford House had hung fire on the market so long. People wouldn't want such neighbours, any more than Charles did. He had wanted to withdraw from the purchase when they learned about the prison.

'They'll be escaping. We'll have murderers and rapists at large,' he said. 'And there will be times when I'll be late home from work, or even away. It won't be safe for you or the children.'

'Men like that aren't kept in open prisons,' said Yvonne, with the confidence of ignorance. 'They're all con men and embezzlers. Not violent men. And they don't escape much. It stands to reason, after all. These places wouldn't exist if they did.'

She knew Charles was in many ways reluctant to move to the country, and not just because of the added financial burden of buying Ford House. They would be living much further from his daughters, and visits would not be so easy. Yvonne, however, had never been happy living in town, and now that there was their own small son, Robin, to consider, Charles had conceded that a freer way of life might be possible if they moved.

They soon discovered that some of the prisoners at Lockley had, indeed, committed major crimes, but were considered to have atoned for them and to be no danger to the public. Yvonne had never seen them cycling to or from the prison, which they did unattended. The lone man on his cycle today was the first she had observed actually in the street, where he might encounter Philip and Emily if they went into the village on their own. They had not done so yet; she took them to school every morning and collected them again each afternoon, but she had thought that before long they might at least come back by themselves.

She would never let them do that while the prisoners were working in the village.

That evening she told Charles about the one she had seen. When he came home, Robin and Emily were in bed and Philip was in his pyjamas in his room, learning the words he was supposed to be able to spell the next day. It had been a pleasant surprise to Yvonne to discover that spelling was considered important by the Coxton primary school headmaster, who set high standards for his pupils and achieved excellent results.

Charles had looked in on Robin, who lay on his back, petal mouth slightly open, breathing softly, a small Paddington Bear tucked in beside him. Emily was awake, listening to a story on the tape recorder beside her. Charles pretended not to notice, because it was against the rules; he knew that it meant Yvonne hadn't had time to read to her this evening. He tiptoed away, unseen. Philip began to tell him eagerly about the day at school and showed Charles a drawing he had done in class, but while he was doing this Charles's attention began to wander in the direction of a new line in tooling machinery which his firm was about to produce.

'Off to bed now,' he said, before Philip had finished his story.

Philip did not protest. Charles wasn't his real father, so he couldn't be expected to show the same interest in him as in Robin, for instance. He was pretty good on the whole, however, and had brought them from the small house where they had lived all their lives to this enormous place, where you could do almost anything from climbing trees to riding your bike round and round at top speed and pretending to be in a Ferrari. In Philip's mind there lurked a fantasy figure of a big, tall man in Australia. He rode a chestnut horse with a flowing mane and wore a leather hat while he rounded up thousands of sheep which he proceeded to shear faster than anyone else in the outback. This man, his real father, would have liked to be with him and Emily, of course, but fate had decided that he must live at the far side of the world instead. Philip knew that in some way he had been mean, leaving them with no money and making Mum very sad, but it must all have been due to something he couldn't help. He wasn't really bad, and one day he would ask them out for a very long visit. Meanwhile, Charles was all right. Things were easier for Mum and they weren't so poor, though Charles was always saying they had no money. It couldn't be true, because they were living in a huge house and Charles drove a BMW. They were lucky. Even Rosalind and Celia, Charles's daughters, who had come to stay in the summer, were quite nice, for girls. Before that, they had only ever come for a day as there was so so little room in the old house. Emily, though only seven, liked playing with Celia, who was eleven, and who was always nice to Robin, though both she and Rosalind, who was nearly fourteen, were often rather snappy with Mum. Once, Philip, who would soon be ten, had seen his mother walking off down the garden, very fast, her arms folded across her chest and her head down, and he knew that she was crying. He had gone after her and she'd pretended that she was going to look for late raspberries, a silly excuse because they'd been over even before the move and the canes were in an awful tangle needing sorting out. They had done that, he and Mum and Robin, cleared out the canes, cutting down the old ones and tying in the ones Mum thought would bear fruit next year, that very day while the three girls played some silly game.

He supposed Rosalind and Celia found him and Emily a pain. Why should they like them? They must mind that Charles preferred Mum to their mother.

That evening, when Charles and Yvonne were having dinner, Robin began to cry.

'I'll go,' said Charles.

He had been good at soothing Rosalind and Celia when they were small, reading to them and sitting with them until whatever trouble had woken them had been forgotten, and he had often been the one to get up in the night when Robin was teething. Since then, the little boy had been a good sleeper until the move. Now he had nightmares several times a week and though she ridiculed herself for thinking it, Yvonne had begun to wonder if the house could be haunted. Charles was certain, though, that it was simply the change of surroundings. He did not believe in ghosts. He was always patient with Robin, overjoyed and proud to have a son.

After he had gone upstairs, Yvonne sat for a while amid the remains of their dinner while Charles's black-currant sorbet slowly dissolved on his abandoned plate. A new resolution at Ford House had been to present a delicious meal every evening, with the dining room table properly laid and the children all quietly stowed away in their beds, but she had discovered years ago that being a wife was more difficult than being a mistress. Before the move, she had attributed their worst problems to the cramped conditions in which they were living. Charles had come to live with her and the children after calling Olivia's bluff in one of the hysterical scenes she was always contriving during their marriage. She frequently said that she wanted to resume her career as an actress and that he got in her way. During this uneasy period he had met Yvonne and their affair began. Finally he decided that he had had enough; if Olivia did not need him, Yvonne certainly did, and he moved out.

Olivia had never done more than tiny parts in a few television series and one or two commercials. Now she performed strongly as the wronged wife, accusing Charles of being unfaithful throughout their marriage. This was untrue; Yvonne was Charles's first adventure of that sort. Ironically enough, he met her at a theatrical party; she had made the curtains for the new house into which the host had just moved. After Charles left home, a struggling actor ten years younger than Olivia had moved into the house in Gerrards Cross, but that had lasted little more than a year. Then Olivia had met Hugh, who owned three jewellery shops and was nearly old enough to be her father. Hugh was still married, and it took time for the legal niceties to be arranged, but at last, earlier this year, he and Olivia had married and Charles was freed from the financial burden of supporting her as well as the girls.

Now he had a son, who would draw them all together, but that did not compensate for the partial loss of his daughters, whom Charles saw only once a month. Before, they had come for the day on alternate Sundays. Now, they spent every fourth weekend at Ford House, where each had her own room for which Yvonne had made pretty curtains and bedspreads before she did any others, so that everything was ready when they stayed for a fortnight in August while Olivia and Hugh were touring in France.

After Charles had settled Robin, he went into the small room that had become his study. That meant he had brought work home and did not want to be disturbed.

Well, Yvonne could work, too. There was plenty to do in her attic room.

She went up there as soon as she had cleared away the dishes. Before the move Charles had always helped wash up and then they had spent the evening together. Here, there was a dishwasher.

Charles's mother had died a year ago, and his father had sold the family house. He had given Charles and Yvonne the surplus furniture and was now living in a bungalow near Sidmouth. He had not yet seen Ford House. After Yvonne's father had died, when she was still at school, her mother had opened a guest house in the Lake District. Before Charles had moved in with them, Yvonne and the children had gone there for frequent visits during off-season times, but this had lapsed. Yvonne's mother thought she was making a mistake in throwing her lot in with Charles, and did not disguise her reservations about the marriage.

'I'll look after Yvonne and the children,' Charles had told her. 'Things will be much easier for all of them now.'

Yvonne's mother thought that it would be her daughter looking after Charles. She was pleased, however, about the move to the country, and it was she who had given them the dishwasher as a house-warming present.

While Charles studied sales figures and graphs, Yvonne sat in her attic workroom with the door ajar in case a child cried out. She started drawing together pinch pleats on some gold brocade curtains promised for the following week.

Denis was still in the bus shelter when the prisoners who had been working in the churchyard, also defeated by the weather, started back to Lockley. He had waited, thumb extended when any vehicle approached, for some time. Then he had felt hungry and had gone across to the shop for some crisps and a tin of Coke. While he was in the shop the bus went past, not that he'd intended to take it, but he might have this once, since people were so mean, driving by without even pausing. He returned to the shelter, where he threw down the empty crisp packet and the tin when he had finished their contents.

Four men on cycles rode up, propped their machines against the wall of the shelter, stepped inside and lit up cigarettes. It was raining hard now and they were in no hurry to get back to the prison.

'Hullo, kid,' said one. 'Like a smoke?'

'I don't mind,' said Denis. 'Ta.'

He didn't like smoking much, but this was not the time to say so. The man rolled him a cigarette, sealing it neatly, then handed it over. Denis puffed inexpertly at the result, affecting an air of nonchalance. Then one of the men asked him to go across to the shop, which had a licence, and buy them some beer.

'You got enough cash for that?' he asked, grinning. He knew they got very little in prison.

They had, but shopping by proxy was wiser than spending it themselves since they had been given it by a well-meaning parishioner who had not realized that they were allowed to handle very little cash.

Denis took the money and scampered off down the road again, one hand over an ear. Soon he returned with four small cans. One of the men offered him a swig, which, although he wanted to be friendly, he refused. He never drank. He had seen the effect of alcohol on his parents and was afraid of it.

He told them about Ford House, and what he had seen there, and about the keys that hung on the dresser, and one of them told him how he could make an impression on soap. They could easily cut a key in the prison workshop and it would be simple to enter the house.

'You don't want to bother with that, Len,' said another man, frowning. 'Don't give the kid ideas.'

But the man called Len, who was due out in two weeks' time, thought it sounded an excellent way to get back into business.

'I'll need a bit of this and that,' he said. 'You're on, kid. I'll cut you in.'

Denis was to hide his piece of soap under a loose stone in the wall just along the road from the bus shelter; Len chose a place in the exterior wall of a cottage whose owners both went out to work every day, as the prisoners already knew. A mark scratched on the side of the shelter would be a sign that the job was done.

Denis was delighted with this encounter. He stood looking after the men as they cycled away and almost missed signalling an approaching car. Its driver took pity on him and gave him a lift all the way back to Leckerton.

It was too wet to go looking for a Walkman but, as usual when his mother was out, the house was locked. He had no key, nor was one hidden so that he could get in when the place was empty. His mother thought he was at school, but that made no difference. She might not be home for hours. He could not remember when she had been waiting there, with his tea. He'd been locked out for years.

He had had enough of it. He walked down an alley that separated the rows of terraced houses and along the narrow path that divided it from another row at the back. Some of these places had been smartened up and turned into chic homes for first buyers, but Denis's parents' house remained dark and shabby, with grubby net curtains across the ground-floor windows.

Denis took off a trainer, put his hand inside it and used it to break the glass of the back door, which he then unlocked. He went inside and used up all the hot water in a steaming bath.

He thought about leaving home. It wasn't a new idea, but where would he go? He didn't fancy sleeping rough in the park, or putting himself where the police might pick him up and take him into care. He'd have to wait a while, maybe until that man Len had done the job at Ford House. He'd have money, then.

He'd stick it out till that happened, even if his father beat him up for breaking the door down.

And his father did.

3

Jim Sawyer liked working for Mrs Bannerman. After planting the hedge he suggested re-laying the uneven flagstones on her patio.

'It's a terrace,' she told him sternly. 'Strictly speaking, a patio is a courtyard. It comes from the Spanish.'

'Oh.' It made no difference to Jim. He'd call it the terrace if that was what she wanted.

'People are careless about words,' she added.

'Sorry,' said Jim.

He got on with Mrs Bannerman. She didn't talk a lot, but she told you plainly what she wanted and she took him into the house to sit down in a comfortable chair while he drank his coffee.

'That's good, isn't it?' she said, her craggy face softening into what was almost a smile as he lowered himself into a deep armchair covered in flowered linen.

'Yes,' he agreed. 'I'd almost forgotten.'

'How much longer have you to do?' she asked.

'Eight months,' said Jim. 'If I get full remission.'

'Well, you'll have some home leave, won't you?' she asked.

He shrugged and his face closed up.

'You will, surely?' she said.

'Maybe,' said Jim.

She knew he had been convicted of embezzling funds at the building society where he had worked for nearly ten years.

'Where else have you been?' she asked him, and he told her about the other prisons where he had served the first part of his sentence.

'This place is like heaven after them,' he said.

'I'm sure it is,' she agreed. 'But the worst place of all must be Holloway.'

As she said this, she seemed to shiver. She couldn't have been inside herself, could she? Jim looked at her with renewed interest. She was about sixty, maybe more, and thin, with neatly styled grey hair and a very pale face. She always wore a tweed hat in the garden, but it wasn't an old, shapeless thing; it was made of checked fabric and looked expensive.

She might have done some shoplifting and been sent down for a bit. It wasn't the sort of thing you could ask about, however.

'They fill the women up with drugs when they should be in hospital, not in prison,' she was saying.

'That's true of some of the men, too,' he said. 'I mean, that they shouldn't be locked up. Not me,' he added. 'I deserve what I got. But there are blokes inside who don't really know the time of the day.'

'Why did you do it?' Audrey asked.

'I wanted nice things for my wife and daughter,' said Jim simply. 'More than I could afford.'

Audrey nodded.

'And my wife got into debt. She had a credit card, you see, and it was too easy for her to overspend.'

'Yes.' Audrey, too, had a credit card and constantly received mail shots suggesting she apply for large loans which would be instantly granted. 'How's your wife managing now?' she asked.

'She doesn't visit any more, or write,' said Jim, staring at his hands.

She's found someone else, thought Audrey. It was a familiar story.

Audrey had seen the young woman from Ford House driving through the village in her battered blue Mini and with her little boy in the shop, where one day Audrey had nodded and said 'Good morning'. Then the child had helped himself to a packet of sweets and had to be reproved, so no further conversation resulted.

It was difficult to meet new people. Audrey went to church, not from conviction but because it was part of the pattern and had always been expected of her; she had made some acquaintances in Coxton as a consequence and had even been invited out to coffee and to drinks. Each time she had dutifully asked her hosts back, but that was where it had stopped. Audrey had never been good at making conversation, and no mutual interests were discovered.

She decided to call on Mrs Davies one morning, when presumably, with the children at school, she would not be too busy.

Audrey drove up to Ford House a week after Denis's meeting with the prisoners, and he was the first person she saw as she negotiated the potholes in the drive. He was ambling across the lawn towards the house, his hands in his pockets, occasionally executing a small skip as he progressed.

Audrey parked outside the front door and got out of her Fiat.

'Good morning,' she called to the approaching youth, who did not answer. His gaze was rapt and far away, and she realized then that he had a headset clamped to his bristly skull. 'Is Mrs Davies in?' she asked loudly, in a curt tone.

The boy had seen the car and his attention was diverted from his tape. Taking his time, he freed one ear and said, 'Uh?'

'Is Mrs Davies in?' repeated Audrey. Who could he be? Certainly not one of the family.

'Yeah,' said Denis.

'I'll ring, then,' said Audrey, and stepped forward to the front door. She paused for a moment, staring at it. It was made of solid oak, and she touched it gently, then

27

turned to the bell pull, which she tugged. There was a jangle from within the house.

'She won't hear you,' Denis said. 'She'll be up in the attic at her sewing.'

'Oh.' Audrey wavered. What sewing?

'She'll be down. Comes to get me cocoa,' said Denis. 'Doesn't use this door a lot.'

He stumped off round the side of the house, his earphone back in place, an awkward, sturdy figure. Audrey hesitated, then rang the bell again. Mrs Davies would hear it from the kitchen.

A few moments later the door opened to reveal a woman of about thirty-six with dark hair reaching well below her shoulders and large blue eyes. She wore jeans and an over-washed yellow sweater.

Audrey's instinctive reaction was that her hair was a mess and she was too old to wear it so long; her next, that she looked tired and she had a small spot on her chin.

'Mrs Davies?' she asked.

'Yes.' Yvonne waited for Audrey to explain her presence. She held no collecting box but she must be wanting something.

Audrey was seeking appropriate words.

'I – er – I –' she began.

'Are you collecting for a jumble sale?' Yvonne asked abruptly.

'I – no. No, indeed,' said Audrey. 'I came to call. I used to live here,' she burst out.

'In this house, do you mean?' Yvonne asked, startled. She took a grip on herself. Though her time was precious and strictly rationed, she must not be inhospitable. This old woman, who looked stern, even hostile, could be given a cup of coffee while Denis drank his chocolate, and then swiftly coaxed upon her way. 'Come in,' she said, and smiled. 'I hope you don't mind the kitchen.'

Audrey hoped she often smiled; it transformed her face and made her almost pretty. She followed Yvonne through the large square hall to the back of the house, casting curious glances to right and left. The place looked different: lighter, and more spacious.

'You lived in the house?' Yvonne prompted. 'When?'

'From the time I was thirteen until I married,' Audrey answered.

'Did you?' Now Yvonne sounded interested. They had reached the kitchen, and as they entered, Audrey saw Denis sitting at the table, quite at home.

'This is Denis, who helps in the garden,' said Yvonne.

'We met outside,' said Audrey.

'Do sit down,' said Yvonne, crossing to the old cream Aga. Could it be the original one that Audrey remembered being installed?

Yvonne moved a saucepan on to the hot plate.

'Coffee?' she asked briskly, crossing to the larder.

'Thank you.'

Audrey pulled up one of the chairs that were drawn up to the table and sat down facing Denis. The youth had not attempted to stand up when she entered. Young people were so mannerless these days.

'What did you say your name was?' Yvonne asked, returning with more milk which she poured into the pan. She took a mug from the dresser.

'Bannerman, Audrey Bannerman. I live at Ivy Lodge.'

Denis blinked. That was where the con had come from that he'd seen the week before. He'd checked it, later.

'And you used to live here?' Yvonne tipped coffee powder into two mugs and chocolate into another. The milk came up and she poured it into them, stirring.

'Yes.'

Their drinks made, Yvonne sat down herself, then rose again to fetch the cake. She offered Audrey a slice.

'No, thank you,' Audrey said. 'It looks delicious, though.'

Yvonne cut a wedge for Denis, giving it to him on a plate and waiting for his thanks, which came belatedly.

'Do you hate us for living in your former home?' she asked, astonishing Audrey.

'What a strange idea! Why should I?' Audrey answered. 'Of course not. I'm glad a family with children has come here.'

'We'll put it straight,' said Yvonne. 'But not immediately. We haven't got much money.'

In Audrey's youth it was bad form to discuss finances, but people did it all the time now.

'Employing builders is expensive,' she said.

'We're hard up because we've both been married before,' said Yvonne, who had discovered that it was wise to explain this early to a new acquaintance, before false assumptions were made. 'Now come along, Denis. It's time for you to go back to work.'

'Oh, all right.' Taking his time, Denis finished his chocolate and slouched from the room.

'Denis is doing wonders with the garden,' he heard Yvonne say as he resumed his boots. When the back door had closed behind him, she told Audrey, 'I wanted him to hear that I was pleased with him. He's a funny boy.'

'Is he local?'

'He lives in Leckerton with his grandmother,' said Yvonne.

'He's very young.'

'He says he's seventeen.'

'Hm.' Audrey raised an eyebrow as she drank her coffee.

'I couldn't get anyone else. There was just a very old man who applied when I put a card in the shop. I don't know his name.'

That was a pity. Audrey might have remembered him.

'Old men who have spent their lives digging can

often carry on almost to the end,' she said, in her tart voice.

Yvonne prickled at the implied criticism.

'It's heavy work. It seemed best to have someone young and strong,' she retorted. 'Of course, if I'd known you were in the village, I could have asked for your advice.'

Audrey did not notice her intended sarcasm.

'I would have been very little use,' she answered. 'I've been back here only a year, myself. No one remembers me now.'

'I see.' What a scratchy old woman, thought Yvonne, wondering how to get rid of her since she wanted to get back to work.

'You do sewing, the boy said. What did he mean?' asked Audrey.

'I make soft furnishings,' said Yvonne. 'I've got a workroom on the top floor. Do you want to come and see it?'

It was not a graciously worded invitation, but Audrey, who would have expressed herself in just the same way, took it as kindly meant.

'I'd like to, very much,' she said, and rose. 'Thank you for the coffee.'

'We'll use the back staircase,' said Yvonne.

Audrey followed her up the steep stairs to the main landing, where they walked a little way and then climbed the narrow staircase that led to the top floor.

'I suppose maids slept here in your day,' said the younger woman.

'Yes.' Audrey remembered them all: Daisy and Maud, and the cook, Mrs Truman. 'Do you have any help?'

'No,' said Yvonne. 'Only Denis.'

'I think that's wonderful,' said Audrey. 'Running a big house and bringing up a family. How many children have you got?'

31

'Two of my own. Then we had Robin,' Yvonne said. 'Charles has two daughters who come sometimes.' She opened the door of what had been Mrs Truman's room. 'I often think I don't do any of it very well,' she confessed.

'It can't be easy,' Audrey said. 'Oh, what pretty chintz.'

She had followed Yvonne into her workroom and saw some finished curtains hanging on an old towel horse.

'Yes, I like it too,' said Yvonne. 'Those are for a merchant banker who lives in Islington.'

'Really?'

'Yes. I work for an interior decorator, but I'm planning to set up on my own.'

'Are you? I wish you luck,' said Audrey. She eyed the bales of fabric and trimmings stored on some old bookshelves along one wall. Then she sensed a restlessness in the younger woman. 'I must go. I expect you want to get on.'

'I'm working to a deadline,' said Yvonne flatly. 'And soon I'll have to fetch Robin from playgroup.'

'I'll be off, then. There's no need to show me out,' said Audrey. 'I know the way.' She moved to the door and stood there, hovering. 'I hope you'll be happy here,' she said.

'We must be,' said Yvonne. 'A lot's at stake.' She picked up a piece of material. 'You know all about us now,' she added.

'I'm sorry.' Audrey felt rebuffed and answered harshly. 'I didn't intend to pry. I meant my visit to be neighbourly.' She turned and started off along the passage to the stairs.

Yvonne flung down her work and hurried after her.

'Mrs Bannerman, please don't leave like that,' she said. 'I didn't mean to be rude. It was good of you to come.'

Audrey was hastening on, but Yvonne caught her by

the arm. 'Please come and talk to me while I stitch a hem. It's too noisy to talk when I'm using the machine.'

No one, apart from the dentist and the hairdresser, and sometimes a chiropodist, had physically touched Audrey for a very long time. She turned towards Yvonne, whose expression was contrite, and allowed herself to be led back to the workroom. Now it was her turn to apologize.

'I'm sorry,' she said. 'All my life I've offended people because I'm so abrupt.'

'I'm sure that isn't true,' said Yvonne. 'I was the graceless one. Please forgive me. I'm a bit touchy, I suppose, on the subject of our mixed household. Not everyone understands.'

'It's quite usual nowadays, I believe,' said Audrey. She looked squarely at the younger woman. 'You've both got a second chance, haven't you, and you want to make it work.'

'That's right,' said Yvonne. She still held Audrey's arm; it felt bony beneath her jacket. 'Come and sit down,' she said. 'Tell me about your life after you left here. Have you any family?'

'Not now,' said Audrey. 'I had a daughter, but she died, and then my husband left me.'

Denis, banished from the kitchen, had not hurried back to work. He had loitered near the house and, peering through the window, had seen the two women leave the kitchen.

In seconds he was back in the house, and had seized a piece of soap from the kitchen sink. It was reasonably pliable and he made a clear impression of the key that hung, with Yvonne's car keys, on the dresser. Returning to his digging, he nursed the soap and laid it under a shrub while he finished his morning stint.

Yvonne missed the soap, and, after searching for it for

a while, decided she must have thrown it out with the rubbish.

That evening she told Charles about Mrs Bannerman's visit.

'Fancy her having lived here,' she said. 'She seems a sad sort of person. I gather she and her husband stayed together because of the daughter, and when that reason had gone, bingo! It was over. She told me quite lot about it, once she got going. It was a bit as if a dam had been unstopped.'

'Oh.'

Charles was not interested in this old and cranky neighbour.

'Her husband took off with some woman she'd been at school with,' said Yvonne. 'It had been going on for years. I don't know why the daughter died. She didn't tell me that.'

'Watch out. She could become a nuisance,' Charles warned. 'You don't want that.'

Yvonne did not tell him that she had invited Audrey to tea the following week. She was already regretting the impulse.

4

Len hadn't been very serious when he spoke to the kid about making a key to that house on the edge of Coxton. He'd get into the place without one, if he'd a mind to do it. Even so, being able to open the door without effort would give it to him on a plate. He'd be needing some money when he got out. Len knew his chances of getting a job, even with the help of his probation officer, were non-existent, with his record. Besides, he didn't like regular work. You could pick up enough here and there if you kept your eyes open, and dodging the law was a challenge.

He didn't really believe that the kid would produce the mould, but soon after their conversation, stopping again for a smoke at the bus shelter before returning to Lockley, he saw the agreed signal and there, under the stone, was the cleanly marked soap.

Len pocketed it. He knew several men in the metal shop who would enjoy cutting a key under the noses of the screws.

Denis was delighted when he discovered that the soap had gone. Things were moving. He was in business. But how would he learn when the hit would be made? That man Len didn't know how to get hold of him to give him his cut. He'd hardly come looking for him at Ford House. Denis mulled away at the problem while he continued digging.

The little boy had not gone to his playgroup that day. When Denis went into the house for his chocolate, Robin was sitting at the table doing a simple jigsaw.

'I'll help you with that,' said Denis, sitting down and leaning over the large wooden pieces. 'See, that pig goes in there.' He picked up a section and slotted it in, heedless of Robin's affronted expression. Half the child's pleasure in doing the puzzle was its familiar ease. 'Why ain't you at school today?'

'He had a bad night – bad dreams,' said Yvonne.

'You look pretty rough yourself,' said Denis.

Yvonne knew what he said was true. She had had little sleep for several nights because of Robin's nightmares, which ended with the child coming into bed with her and Charles.

'I sometimes wonder if the house is haunted,' she confessed.

'Course it is, an old place like this,' said Denis. 'Didn't you know?' Memories of something he had seen on television came to him. 'Some kid was murdered here, by its sister or some such,' he declared, biting into his slice of cake.

'That's not true,' said Yvonne, but her already pale face went even paler.

''Tis. Happened a hundred years ago, or so,' said Denis more confidently. 'Smothered with a pillow, he was. Happened in that room that looks out over the pond,' he added.

The story might have been better if he'd said the kid had drowned in the pond, but it was too late to change the script. The pond itself was covered with a strong wire frame clamped into place so that no child could drown there now.

The room Denis had mentioned was the one occupied by Robin. Denis knew that. He had scant opportunity for prowling round the house because Yvonne was always there but last week, after that old girl had come round, she was rattled and had gone to fetch Robin without locking up. Denis had knocked off work as soon as he saw her leave – there was no point in overdoing things – and had sauntered up to try the door.

He'd already made the key impression, so now was his chance for a quick look round. She'd be gone at least fifteen minutes. By the time she came back, he had seen

36

the attic room where she worked, and the children's bedrooms. Each had one to him or herself, and they were huge, with everything clean and fresh, though rather bare. Denis had worked it all out. In a small room on the ground floor there was a photograph of a man with two girls. It stood on a desk with another of Mrs Davies and Robin. She'd said that morning that they had both been married before. Denis saw that these were the two families.

All information was useful. He might get a chance to use this some day. Now, he was pleased with the effect of his words on Mrs Davies.

'You want to watch it,' he suggested. 'Those other kids might have it in for this one.' He left it to her to decide if he meant her two, or the girls in the photograph.

'You're very silly, Denis,' said Yvonne.

But that night she persuaded Philip to let Robin sleep in his bed and the small boy never woke. Philip, however, in Robin's room, did. He did not cry out, simply turning on his light and reading for a while until in the end he fell asleep over his book.

Charles did not object when Yvonne proposed changing the children's rooms. Robin had been given the one nearest his parents because he was the youngest, but it was smaller than Rosalind's, which was across the passage. Would she feel put down if they exchanged?

'No,' said Charles. There was a washbasin in the room now proposed as hers, and Rosalind would like that as there was only one bathroom upstairs. There was another on the ground floor, once used by the staff, Yvonne supposed. She must ask Mrs Bannerman about it. The older children used it now. Eventually, when they could afford to put a second bathroom in upstairs, it would become a utility room.

Charles helped her move the things across. Rosalind

had seemed satisfied with her former room, which looked out over the front of the house, but she would like this one better. It had a much nicer view and when the leaves were off the trees you would be able to see right across to the river.

When he left Ford House that Friday, Denis was elated with a sense of power. All he'd had to do was to agree that the place was haunted, and Mrs Davies had lapped it up as the truth. Thinking of something to tell her that involved a kid was a stroke of genius. If he'd said the ghost was a knight in armour clanking chains, she'd have taken no notice. Now she'd be moving everything round just because of what he'd said. Mind you, the change might stop the kid dreaming. He was a nice little lad and he'd got everything given to him with a golden spoon. No drunk mother for him, just a re-modelled family. Probably the older kids spoiled him rotten as he was the baby.

He went down to the churchyard to look for Len, but the work there was finished. When was Len coming out? If that other man was still working at Ivy Lodge, he might take a message.

Denis wandered back until he came to the house. The gates were open but there was no one about. No cycle was parked in sight, but a con would probably put it round at the back in case someone nicked it. Whistling, Denis sauntered up the path. If the old girl was in, he'd think of some excuse for calling. He could always say he was looking for work.

If she wasn't in, he could have a look round.

Denis rang the bell, pressing it firmly. The sound echoed round the house – a sharp buzz: none of your melodic chimes here. Silence followed, apart from the sound of a car going past in the road. Denis rang again, and when no one answered he walked all round the house looking in through the windows, even trying one at the back. All were secure. She'd got those special window locks recommended by the police. Well, it was useful to know that this wouldn't be an easy place to do over.

There was no sign of the prisoner.

Denis tried the garage. The doors were fastened but not locked, and the car was out. She had a Fiat, he remembered. There was nothing inside the garage that would be of use to him. It contained only a hosepipe coiled round a drum, a plastic pail and rubber sponge, and a long aluminium ladder slung on hooks against the wall. He'd seen a shed in the garden. That must be where she kept her tools, like Mrs Davies, whose garden shed was vast though it let in rain at one end and had a door that had to be tied with string to close it.

He didn't want to get caught nosing about. Denis left.

When he got back to Leckerton, there was nothing to do.

He spent some of his pay at the new Pizza Parlour on a good, filling meal. Then he went home and tried the doors. It was locked up, as usual. Even quite little kids at school had keys, or knew where one was kept so that they could let themselves in. He didn't feel like breaking in again and getting another beating.

The mood of what, in Denis, passed for happiness, which had filled him earlier, ebbed. What was he supposed to do while he waited for someone to come home? Get into trouble? It was a wonder he hadn't done anything seriously bad before now. The fact that he was supposed to be at school went for nothing. Kids got sent home when they felt ill. They could let themselves in, couldn't they?

There was nowhere to go, only the cinema which opened at four and which cost money. You could sometimes get in through the exit doors, though, once the paying customers had been admitted.

Denis tried it, and succeeded. He spent two hours

watching a pseudo-psychological thriller which he found difficult to follow. There were some powerful sex scenes which made him laugh. His sniggers provoked 'Sshing' sounds from the other people in the audience, which was sparse.

That gave him an idea.

When the showing was over, he went to a café nearby and had some beans on toast while the second house audience bought their tickets and filed in.

The nearest telephone box needed a phone card, but you could dial 999 from anywhere. Denis did so, and when a voice asked him which service he wanted, he just answered, 'There's a bomb at the cinema.'

The authorities had to take such calls seriously.

Denis had the satisfaction of seeing the cinema audience trooping from the building and milling about in the mizzling rain which had begun to fall. Police cars came, and sniffer dogs, and it was brilliant. He mingled with the cinema-goers as they were herded to a supposedly safe distance. Some of them decided not to wait until the scare was over, and when they drifted off, he went too.

When he got home, his father was waiting for him. Someone had been down from the school and had said Denis had been absent at least twice a week all term and was not there today.

His father took a belt to him. Denis managed not to make a sound while he was beaten, but, in his bedroom later, he could not suppress a whimper.

He didn't have to stay here. Maybe they wanted him to go and that was why they treated him so badly.

He didn't take a lot, just his new Walkman and his better clothes, in some plastic bags. He found some money, though, in the handbag which his mother had left in the kitchen when she went up to bed. Denis unlocked the back door and just walked away, leaving the place open, hoping someone else would come and take anything they fancied.

He did not think about the beating he had had; there would not be another. Instead, he remembered the commotion he had caused at the cinema, all those coppers out there telling people what to do, the blue lights flashing and the traffic cones and cordons, cars stopped from passing by, and people made to go another way.

That was power.

He spent what was left of the night in a bus shelter and, when first light came, he went round to his sister. Tracy would give him breakfast, let him keep his things there. And she did. When she and Alan had gone off to work – they both worked most Saturdays – Denis, trusted with her key, climbed into their bed. It smelled of various things, some nice and some faintly disturbing, but Denis did not wonder for long what they were. He slept for hours.

5

Jim Sawyer's work at Ivy Lodge was complete after only four visits and he wished it could have been prolonged. After he had finished the outdoor jobs, he painted the kitchen, and Mrs Bannerman had left him alone in the house while he did it. She'd gone off for a walk, and was away more than an hour.

When she came back, she admired what he had done and they had tea in her sitting room. She used real bone china cups and saucers and a small silver teapot.

She asked if his wife had written yet and he said that she hadn't. Prisoners in open prisons were allowed to make telephone calls and in desperation he had rung her several times without getting through. In the end, he had realized that she had changed the telephone number and gone ex-directory. Inquiries made through his probation officer had produced only the information that she was still living in the same house and had a job at a local factory, now that Nicola went to school.

'It's awful, not knowing what's happened,' he said. 'I suppose she hates me. But there's Nicola, too.'

'Shall I go and see her for you?'

Audrey heard herself utter the words and wished them unsaid as soon as they were spoken. She had no wish to travel to wherever he lived and put personal questions to an unknown woman, become involved in what was not her business.

Jim stared at her.

'Would you?'

She could not back off now.

'If you wish.' She spoke grimly, sitting in her wing armchair, knees together, thin legs in ribbed tights.

Jim glanced down at her feet. She wore wide, soft,

shabby brown shoes which had open toes and were loosely laced across feet distorted by enormous bunions. He hadn't noticed that before.

'Where do you live?' she asked.

'In Reading,' Jim replied.

'That's not so very far,' said Audrey, relieved. He might have said Birkenhead. 'Write down the address.' She pointed to a table where, beside the telephone, there was a notepad and ballpoint pen. While he obeyed, she found a street plan of Reading in a big road map and he showed her where it was, though the actual road was not marked on the plan.

'Thanks,' he muttered. 'It's very good of you.'

'I'll write to you at the prison,' she told him. 'I can't come and see you. I'm sorry.'

'I wouldn't expect you to,' said Jim. 'It isn't very nice. But it would be best if I phoned you. It's allowed.'

She understood. His letters would be read.

'Try not to brood about it,' she advised. 'That's difficult to do, but it's sense.'

'Yes.' Jim fidgeted, then said, awkwardly, 'I'll miss coming here.'

Audrey was going to miss him, too, but she would not say so.

'What will you be doing next?' she asked.

'I don't know. Farm work, perhaps.'

She couldn't give him anything. If she were to give him cash and it was found on him, he'd be in trouble. He was just the sort of man to get caught if he attempted some trivial contravention of the rules and it might cost him part of his remission.

Back in his room at the prison, Jim thought about Maureen. Dreaming about his release, and his return to her and Nicola, had kept him going through the first part of his sentence. The few visits she had made were painful, and she didn't bring Nicola. A prison, she said, was no place for a child. How could you talk, sitting at a table watched by screws who had eyes in the backs of their heads as they looked this way and that, expecting to catch prisoners passing drugs across as they kissed, or touched hands under the table? You couldn't blame them, really. It was their job. Jim wouldn't have believed what went on right under their noses until he saw it for himself.

She had never been to Lockley, where his own life was undemanding and had become almost pleasant. He had privacy in his room, and he enjoyed working outside. He'd got to know other men and most of them were reasonable beings; even those who had a string of convictions behind them could be good company. One, Bob Waters, was dreading leaving the prison.

'I've got a nice room to myself, three meals a day, enough work to keep me busy,' he said. 'What have I to go out for? A high-rise flat with water dripping down the walls and piss on the stairs. Half the time the lift doesn't work and my old woman has to lug the shopping up eleven flights. That's no life. It's better here.'

Jim believed him, and he had seen the wife, too: a tough-looking woman with orange hair and purple lips, and an angry face. Perhaps Bob had taken to petty thieving to escape.

He and Bob had become quite friendly. They played cards together and had both worked in the carpenter's shop. Jim had tried various classes but he wasn't in for long enough to complete an open university course. He had settled for French, and had been getting on quite well until he started to worry about Maureen and Nicola.

When he came out, they would have to start all over again. He'd have no job, though he was determined to find one. In the past he had tried to give Maureen everything she wanted, and it was buying her goodwill, combined with her extravagance, that had led him into

44

crime. In a fundamental way he knew that really she craved something other than the material goods she had bought on credit. She had an emotional need that he did not understand, although she must know that he had never looked at another woman and thought the sun rose and set with her. Without her and Nicola, there was nothing to live for.

He looked at their photographs, both out of date. Nicola was five now, not a toddler as she had been when he was sentenced. You'd think Maureen would send him some new ones. From thinking about his own daughter, he progressed to wondering about Mrs Bannerman's. He had seen her photograph on Mrs Bannerman's desk. She was a pretty girl with dark curly hair and a lovely smile. When asked, Mrs Bannerman had agreed that this was her daughter but had added no information about her, and some instinct stopped Jim from asking.

Where was she now? Married, with a family?

On Mondays Charles was always eager to go back to work. In theory he unwound at weekends, but in practice he worried about problems at the office, and he consciously missed his daughters. That seemed to get no better with time; it was a constant dull ache, and when he looked at Yvonne's small, dark-haired Emily, he wished she would turn into his blonde Celia.

Philip and Emily were nice children and Charles liked them, but he became impatient when Philip was late for meals because he had been out in the garden studying beetles and lost all sense of time. At the moment he thought he might become an entomologist, and he kept collections of various creatures in boxes in his room.

'Just as long as they stay there and don't escape,' Charles had said. So far, they had.

They were both good with Robin, and Emily, in particular enjoyed playing with him. He supposed she had a built-in maternal streak.

While Charles was eating his muesli and two slices of toast, he was planning the day ahead at the office. Meetings and consultations must be arranged. Much could be predicted, but unexpected developments would require him to show the initiative which the board had already commended more than once. Egos would be on parade and hobby horses would be ridden; surprise tactics would be used by some, including Charles, to influence thinking and move decisions in certain directions. There might be complaints from customers to be dealt with, or from personnel, but usually something similar would have happened before and there would be a precedent to follow. Secretaries sometimes left, and that could be devastating, but Charles had had the same one now for three years and she looked like staying, though nothing in this world was certain.

He liked the early drive through the lanes to the motorway, then the fast trip to the works. It was very different from the mornings in Shepherds Bush, when he had left home an hour later and still missed the rush-hour traffic. The seasons meant nothing, then; now, he was aware of the trees, their leaves lingering unusually late in this wet autumn, the colours varied, yellow and umber and russet, and the mixed greens of the grassland. Once he had decided what he would do after he had dealt with his mail at the office, he listened to tapes and at the moment was busy with Dickens. There were large gaps in his knowledge which Charles sought to fill, and this was a way of using time well. Yvonne read very little, but she liked music and could play the flute. Later on she might have time to take it up again and join an amateur orchestra. Leckerton was large enough to have something like that. He wanted her to use her talents and yet her independence, which seemed to grow daily, alarmed him. What if she no longer needed him?

When they met, Yvonne was feeling very low, her self-esteem at zero. She had had some minor romance between her husband disappearing and their meeting, but the man, unable to handle a ready-made family, had ended their relationship. What put him off fired Charles with its challenge. He was drawn, at first, by her lost look, her somewhat forlorn air. She scraped along on a meagre income; he did not see how she managed to feed herself and the children on what she earned from her work. The house though, was hers: lawyers had managed to get her husband to pay off the mortgage and make it over to her and she was planning to move. She could get more for it than she would have to pay for a cottage somewhere in the country.

Meeting Charles had changed that. He found her company restful after squalls at home when Olivia threw tantrums. Yvonne seemed, by contrast, blessedly calm. Soon Charles convinced himself that she needed him and that he had a major role to play in her life. The physical attraction between them was strong, and a new joy for Yvonne. After Charles came to live with them, there was no more talk of moving until after Robin was born. Even then, it took years to happen, and meanwhile Yvonne had changed. Now she rarely asked his advice about anything, making decisions about her own children without consulting him, though she did refer to him before entering Robin for the playgroup. She was becoming forceful, and Charles saw himself being written out of the role he had thought was his. Work had always absorbed him; he had plenty of energy and enjoyed manipulating people. Often, these days, he stayed late at the works where it was quiet and peaceful, with only the cleaners moving around the offices; they left his till last.

If he were to be appointed to the board, financially things would be transformed and Robin would benefit. Yvonne had given him this wonderful stake in the future and nothing would be too good for his son, but he longed for his daughters' visits. When they were due, he collected them after work on the Friday, leaving earlier than usual, and he returned them to their mother on Sunday evening, driving back to his former home where Olivia now lived with Hugh. She had remained in their old social circle, and their friends frowned on him because he had walked out of the marriage.

Charles did not mind that. He had colleagues at work and Yvonne at home; he had no time for anyone else.

It was only a few days now until the weekend when the girls were coming. This happy thought deflected Charles's attention from *Bleak House* as he wondered what they would like to do on Saturday. It was difficult to find things that were suitable for all of them, from Rosalind down to Robin. He would go to the video shop and pick up some film for the older ones to watch, and perhaps they might all visit the Severn Wildfowl Trust if the weather was good.

With this thought he reached the works gates and there was his reserved parking slot. In the office, his secretary would bring him a cup of strong black coffee when she arrived, some time after him. A well-organized man, Charles complacently pitied those now enmeshed in traffic snarls on the road behind him as the rush hour got under way. Like a juggler, he had to maintain a number of balls in simultaneous motion, but he managed to keep an eye on them all. He was in control.

Audrey was annoyed with herself for offering to look into Jim Sawyer's problems. They were no concern of hers. Still, having volunteered, she must see it through, and without delay.

First, she attended to various things. She had booked a holiday in Florence for the following spring. Rupert had never wanted to travel, and since they had parted she was gradually visiting all the places she had once longed to see. Planning her trips gave her something to fix on in the future, and she read widely before each expedition. She was often the best-informed member of the exclusive tours she joined and tried to be helpful to the courier. She liked to think she was useful as she helped inexperienced tourists when they needed advice about traveller's cheques and where to meet the coach, though few seemed grateful and no one ever asked for her address at the end of the holiday.

She had finished her current piece of knitting, a soft sweater in shades of blue and purple. She wrapped it in tissue paper, then in a polythene bag, and put it away in a drawer upstairs. Next, she would make something in yellow; maybe a dress. Jenny would have grown out of the last one by now. She would get the wool and the pattern tomorrow; there was a good wool shop in Leckerton, new since her day, of course, but then Leckerton was totally changed. Once, it had been a busy market town, but in the sixties the centre had been razed and a vast shopping complex built. New factories and houses had sprung up on the outskirts and people had moved in from other areas, attracted by its possibilities. The town had lost its former community spirit and was now an agglomerate of different groups and areas, still expanding, with petty crime on the increase and even serious incidents now common. Drunken brawls in the old market square were a usual weekend occurrence, and in the last year two policemen had been attacked and badly hurt. To Audrey, everyone looked so young: youths in jeans strode about or loitered outside the fish and chip shops. Very young women pushed babies in stroller prams, the children always facing away from their mothers into the wind and the weather, and deprived of communication with their attendant.

Audrey had pushed Hesther in a big, deep pram, bought secondhand because such things were scarce after the war. There had been a large hood to protect her from the rain, and a mackintosh apron to hook over the blanket. When she was old enough to sit up, Hesther had

49

peeped out across the bib of the apron which stretched across the lower part of the hood, attached by elastic loops. Inside, she was warm and snug and she could talk to her mother, and have things of interest pointed out. They would look at cows and sometimes go to the railway line to wave at the engine drivers who usually waved back. Later, Hesther had graduated from this fine carriage to a small folding one with an end that let down so that she could step in and out. She still faced her mother and they could talk. Modern children were swept along in an isolated capsule behind thick plastic sheeting, or else exposed to the tempest, their little faces blue. What must it be like to be propelled towards an advancing forest of knees? No wonder juvenile aggression was a current problem.

Audrey took out the street map of Reading and studied it again, then the route to the town. Once on the motorway, it wasn't far. She would be there in just an hour, say an hour and a half to be on the safe side.

Perhaps she would get the wool in Reading. It would make a change. In that case, she could go tomorrow.

6

Jim had given Audrey directions for finding his house but when she reached the outskirts of Reading she misread a sign, entered the wrong traffic stream and therefore missed a vital turning. Without intending to, she went through the centre of the town and became thoroughly confused by one-way systems, sunken roads and a heavy flow of traffic. She almost despaired of ever discovering the right area, but at last she found herself in a residential district where the traffic was less dense, able to ask advice, and in the end she reached the street.

It was part of a private estate of identical houses set in rows radiating from a main road. Doors were painted different colours; gardens varied; windows displayed pot plants or china figures, or were unadorned; others had net curtains stretched across. Number 15 looked in good order, its paintwork smart, a large pot of leafy plants standing on the window sill of the front room. Audrey could not identify them; she did not like foliage that reminded her of aquaria, preferring blooms. She sat in the car and checked her own appearance in her compact mirror, dabbing more powder on her long thin nose. Then she got out of the car and walked up to the front door.

A few people were about, mostly women pushing children in the strollers she abhorred, some with toddlers walking beside them. She rang the bell.

There was no response, and Audrey rang it again, pressing it for longer. Then she remembered that Jim had said his wife was working. How stupid to have forgotten that. Of course, she would be out until the child came back from school. She turned away, but as she did so heard the sound of movement from the house, and the door was opened.

A burly man stood there. He was about twenty-eight, with a chin shadowed with stubble and dark untidy hair falling over his face. He wore a singlet and slacks, and Audrey formed the distinct impression that he had just got out of bed. Was he the reason for Maureen's silence?

'Good morning,' she said briskly. 'I've come to see Mrs Sawyer and Nicola.'

'Oh!' The man smothered a yawn and rubbed his eyes. 'They're out. I'm sorry. Can I help? You must be from the welfare.' They'd been before, checking on how Maureen was coping.

Audrey did not correct him.

'Mrs Sawyer's at work, I suppose,' she said. 'And Nicola's at school?'

'That's right,' agreed the man. 'Would you like to come in?'

Audrey decided that if she did, she could form an impression of how things were and also of this man. It would be a pity if Maureen had replaced Jim with an out-of-work slob. She stepped into the hall, which had a polished wood-laid floor covered with a good rug. The living room into which he led her was clean and bright, with gold and white striped wallpaper and a sofa covered in gold Dralon, with two matching chairs. A large rubber plant stood in a corner, and there was a television set with a video recorder underneath. A child's doll lay on the floor and some picture books were scattered about.

'I'm afraid you've caught me,' the young man said. 'I'm on nights.'

'You're not a lodger,' Audrey stated.

'No. And Maureen's not getting supplementary benefit. There's no fiddle,' said the man. 'I moved in a while ago – nearly three months, it must be now. Me and Maureen are thinking of getting married, as soon as she

52

can sort things out with her husband.' He laughed. 'It's funny, really. I'm a policeman.'

'Oh!' That startled Audrey. 'He doesn't know about you,' she said.

'Well, how do you tell a guy that sort of thing when he's inside?' asked the man. 'It needs working out. How to do it, I mean. He's not a bad guy, Jim. Just a bit user-friendly with other people's money. Would you like some coffee? I can do with some.'

'That would be very nice,' said Audrey.

'Take a seat,' he said, and she sat down on the sofa while he went off to the kitchen.

Exactly what she suspected was what had happened. Well, it was better for Jim to know the truth than struggle on in doubt. He'd have time to face up to things and plan some sort of future before his release.

Her host returned, carrying a tray with two cups and saucers of steaming coffee and a plate of custard cream biscuits. He had slicked down his hair and washed his face, and she saw now that he was a good-looking man, if a trifle overweight. She was very ready for the coffee, and she ate a biscuit.

'I should have come in the evening,' she remarked.

'Yes – well, you've got other folk to see. More urgent cases,' said the man. She was older than the usual social worker. He rasped his hand across his chin. 'Sorry I haven't shaved,' he said.

Audrey waved a hand.

'I've disturbed your rest,' she said.

'Maureen had better write to Jim,' said the man. 'We've let things drift.' He drank some coffee. 'The marriage was on the rocks anyway, before he got nicked. He kept buying things for Maureen because he thought they'd keep her happy. Nice things for the house – smart clothes – jewellery. Everything she has is the best.'

'I can see that,' said Audrey. This wasn't quite Jim's

53

version of events. He had implied that Maureen had run up debts.

'He was great at do-it-yourself,' said the man. 'Laid the floor in the hall himself.'

'There's no hope then,' Audrey said. 'Of a reconciliation, I mean.'

'Not a one. Of course, he'll see Nicola when he comes out, if he keeps his nose clean. I suppose he may do that. He's not a hardened villain, after all.'

'What about Maureen's job?' asked Audrey. 'She likes it?'

'Oh yes. She's been promoted. She's in the sales office now.'

'Ah. So she does a full day?'

'Stops at four. The next-door neighbour takes care of Nicola after school until she gets back.'

'I see. Well, that seems satisfactory for the moment,' Audrey said, and stood up. 'I must be going now, Mr – Er –?'

'Trevor Black,' said the man. 'Traffic division.'

He watched her go down the short path to the road. She walked a little stiffly. She'd got terrible feet; he'd noticed them as she sat with them planted side by side on Maureen's yellow carpet. He saw her get into a small black Fiat parked outside. He did not wait to watch her drive away.

She would have to see Maureen. Audrey knew that she could not go home able only to tell Jim that he had been supplanted by a personable policeman; unshaven and half dressed though he had been, Trevor Black was in another category altogether than poor balding Jim.

She should see the child, too.

Audrey looked at her watch. It was nearly noon. She would go into the town as she had planned, and buy her wool and pattern, then return. The route might be a little easier tackled for a second time. She'd come back at four.

54

By three thirty she had parked the car across the road from Number 15. In the back was her package of wool and a new pair of shoes she had bought after seeing wide fittings displayed in a window. Her mother had had narrow, neat feet, and could not accept that Audrey had inherited her father's broad frame. Regularly, her feet had been crammed into shoes much too tight, and Audrey had continued to buy shoes too narrow for years until a trained fitter had given her better advice, but by then it was too late and her feet had been badly damaged. However, they were rarely painful if she wore loose, easy shoes; they were a fact of life, like requiring spectacles and the two teeth on a plate which she had had to accept as necessary. Audrey's mother had never become socially confident and had indoctrinated Audrey with the importance of maintaining appearances. She had clung to this training during her marriage, aware that to Rupert they mattered too, but in a different way. He and his sisters, and Felicity, now his wife, had known automatically what was appropriate and when it was acceptable to wear what looked like rags.

These things didn't matter so much nowadays. People were no longer docketed and labelled according to clothes and voice. In Coxton, Audrey had once had an assured position because she had lived in the big house. Her marriage to Rupert repeated the pattern, and she had thought by returning to Coxton, even after so many years, she would slot into her former place. It no longer existed. The village had grown and was full of hard-working couples with two cars and two salaries, living in new houses ten times more comfortable than Ford House had ever been, or was now. There were a few retired couples, and several widows. Audrey had not joined in any of the charitable activities they undertook in the village, and even the vicar had shown only fragmentary interest in hearing that her father had bought Ford House just before the war. He had risen from obscurity in the Midlands to run a factory making metal components and had made a great deal of money. He had moved to Ford House to become a country gentleman, but he did not hunt or shoot and had no wish to learn. He had married his secretary, who had always been shy and soon became physically frail. They had done the accepted things for Audrey: sent her away to school to acquire the right accent, and later to a gentle institution where she learned some cooking, how to arrange flowers, and a little shorthand and typing. It was here that she met Felicity Morton, who invited her home for a weekend. It was the first time she had ever stayed as a guest in a private house.

Rupert Bannerman's family lived nearby in a small manor house where they farmed several hundred acres. Mortons and Bannermans had always been friends, and when Audrey met Rupert he was on leave after being a prisoner of war for nearly four years. He had had a bad time in the weeks before the German surrender, being moved from camp to camp and threatened with death. Audrey asked him about his experiences in a forthright way, which he found refreshing after the velvet-glove approach of everyone else, and he found himself telling her the truth about his fears, his guilt at having survived when others died, his nightmares.

Later, he came down to the school and took the two girls out for the day in his battered MG. They took turns to sit in the tiny cramped rear space. Later still, Audrey was invited to stay at the Mortons to go to a charity ball. They went with a group of young people, but Rupert monopolized Audrey, who had expected to be a wallflower, which was her usual experience at the few such events she had attended.

Soon after the ball he came to Coxton to see her, arriving unexpectedly, his MG scattering the gravel as he turned with a flourish outside the front door. Her mother was put into quite a flutter but the house was always clean and tidy, the flowers just so, and in the kitchen Mrs Truman was able to stretch lunch to include him. Excited and flattered, Audrey supposed this was love.

When he proposed, she instantly accepted, for her whole upbringing had been geared to this future. She had no need to make her way in the world; she had been trained for marriage, the aim of most upper- and middle-class girls at that time when only a few of them went to university.

Six months after her wedding her father had a stroke and died, and her mother, with no further reason for continuing her frail existence, faded away and followed him within a month.

That was long ago, and now Audrey was outside the home of a woman whose husband was serving a well-deserved prison sentence. Why was she meddling in their affairs? He had broken the law and merited no pity. Still, his wife should have kept in touch, written about the child and then, if she felt they could never be reconciled, have had the courage to tell him the truth.

As she watched, a woman propelling a small child in a pushchair came into view. Two small girls skipped along in front of them, one with tight red curls and the other with dark hair drawn into two bunches. The quartet turned into Number 14, the red-haired girl opening and closing the gate for them all. Half an hour later, during which several other people passed, a woman in a pink raincoat and high-heeled leather boots came hurrying along. Her hair was fashionably styled like the tangled mane of a lion and it bounced as she walked up to the door of Number 14, which opened at once. The long-haired little girl appeared and reached up to be kissed by her mother, then kissed the second woman, who now stood behind her. You did not have to be a trained social worker to conclude that there was nothing much wrong here.

Audrey got out of her car. She wondered if Trevor Black was still in the other house as she waylaid Maureen Sawyer beside her own gate.

'Mrs Sawyer,' she began.

'Yes?' Maureen, who was in a hurry to get home, paused and looked questioningly at the trim elderly woman in her tweed hat and expensive fawn quilted jacket.

This was no time for finesse, even if Audrey had been capable of it.

'You haven't written to Jim for months, and you've gone ex-directory,' she accused.

Maureen paled. It was as if someone had pulled a plug and drained all her blood away. She almost staggered on her spindly high heels.

'I've met your friend Mr Black,' Audrey pressed her. 'Don't you think Jim has a right to know the position?'

'What business is it of yours?' Maureen retorted.

'I'm concerned with his welfare,' said Audrey, taking her cue from Trevor Black's earlier assumption.

'Mum, I want to go home,' Nicola said, swinging on her mother's arm.

'Shush, Nicola. We won't be long. The lady has something to say to Mummy,' said Maureen giving the child a little push. 'You run ahead.'

'I've seen Jim recently,' Audrey told her as Nicola obeyed. 'He's worried and I promised to speak to you.'

Maureen had recovered her poise.

'Yes, well, I'm afraid you're wasting your time,' she said. 'How can he think – after what he did –' Her voice trailed off. 'I've got a good future now,' she said in a defiant tone. 'I'm happy.'

'Are you?' asked Audrey, who wondered if anyone ever was, for long.

'Certainly. I just want Jim to leave me alone and keep out of my life,' said Maureen.

'What about Nicola?' Audrey asked.

The child was by now standing on her own doorstep, vigorously pushing the bell. Since no one had opened the door, Trevor Black must be out.

'Her too,' Maureen said. 'I've been so ashamed.'

'He did it for you. You must know that,' said Audrey.

'Look, bits of jewellery and new clothes don't make up for other things – not getting along, not having what it takes,' said Maureen.

'What does it take?'

'Oh, surely I don't have to spell it out?' exclaimed the younger woman, exasperated now. 'Excuse me. I must get Nicola her tea.'

Audrey pictured the young policeman. She meant sex.

'I see,' she said slowly. The money was only a symptom.

'It's over. Finished,' said Maureen. 'If you want to help Jim, you'll get him to see that. Please make him understand.'

'You should do it yourself. You should visit and tell him.'

'I can't,' said Maureen.

'Well, write, then.'

'I've tried. I can't find the words,' said Maureen. 'I just don't want to have anything more to do with him and I've Trevor to think of now.'

No doubt the wife of a convict was not the most desirable companion for an ambitious constable. Audrey walked back to her car, defeated. If it hadn't been this man, it would have been someone else, some man met at work, perhaps. Sex would have been the alchemy that precipitated events.

Had that been what drew Rupert and Felicity together? They should have married when they were young. Rupert's pursuit of her had been some absurd quixotic post-war folly, and when he realized his mistake he had stayed with her from convention or duty. Besides, Felicity had married a year after their wedding. Her husband was a naval officer, at that time stationed in Malta. They had three children, two boys and a girl, and Felicity now was a grandmother. Rupert and Felicity had been clandestinely meeting for years before the death of Felicity's husband, who by then was long retired and farming in Hampshire.

Such thoughts were painful. Driving home, Audrey sternly banished them. She would concentrate on something pleasant, like her next visit to Ford House. It was kind of Yvonne to have asked her. Perhaps the girl would like to make her some curtains. The blue velvet ones in the dining room, which she had bought with the house, were quite shabby and she had always intended to replace them, but had somehow never mustered enough interest and energy. A commission on the doorstep might help Yvonne.

She must take the children something when she went to tea. What would they like? A toy car, perhaps, for the small boy, but the bigger one would be more difficult to please, and there was the little girl, too.

She would go into Leckerton where there was a large toyshop and seek a helpful assistant, if such a person existed in a world where it had become difficult to pay for one's wants in such places as Boots with tills only sparsely distributed throughout the store. It would be quite a treat to think about something so far removed from today's expedition.

7

Denis was happy. He had money in his pocket, his personal Walkman and a place to live.

He was sleeping in Alan's van. Tracy had found him a sleeping bag and a blanket, and she gave him a thermos of cocoa to take out there each evening.

Alan wasn't too happy about the arrangement and stressed that it was temporary. He had a feeling that the law wouldn't like it, if a copper looked in the van one night. It had to be left in the street: the one parking space outside the house was used by Mrs Dove from the first floor, where she had a real flat, not a bedsitter. However, Alan was sympathetic, for hadn't he rescued Tracy from the very situation which Denis had left? She, though, was older and had a job at the check-out in one of Leckerton's supermarkets.

'You ought to go back to school, Denis,' he said.

'What for? It's boring,' said Denis. He wasn't going to admit that there were things he had enjoyed, like woodwork and football. 'Anyway, I'll be sixteen next month.'

He'd soon have the money from Len. Denis could even provide wheels for the job, if Len had none; they'd need a getaway car and he was king of Alan's blue van. Meanwhile, to keep in funds, he bought a brown plastic pail and a large rubber sponge and went round the better areas of Leckerton looking for cars to wash. He charged two pounds, the middle price at the automatic car-wash in Market Street, and it was surprising how many people were willing to pay for his services. He made a good job of what he did, getting satisfaction from seeing the paintwork come up and the chrome shine.

Denis could manage on very little money. He gave

some to Tracy, who included him in the evening meal, and he helped wash up. He could tell that Alan wished he wasn't there but didn't know how to get rid of him. Denis cleared off as soon as they had eaten and wandered round the town until he was too tired or bored to stay out any longer. There was little enough to do in the evenings, as he already knew. The youth club was all right if you liked playing snooker, and sometimes it ran a disco, but Denis felt silly prancing about under the strobe lights, though he was happy gyrating alone to the sound of his Walkman. He didn't go for girls, except Tracy, who was different. Most girls were silly and giggly and all they wanted to do was get married and have kids and expect to be kept for life, or that's what his father had said. Often enough, Denis had heard his father calling his mother names and saying she'd caught him, whatever that meant. He'd hit her, which made Denis feel sick. After that there would be scuffling and noises and it would all end upstairs in a lot of animal sounds which Denis found frightening. He'd gone in once, when he was about seven, thinking his father was still beating his mother, but they'd both yelled to him to go out and get lost and after that his father had given him a belting. It was a few years before he understood what had been going on and he didn't like the discovery.

Sometimes his mother was nice. She would buy him a new shirt or sweater and ask if he'd like to have another boy round to play, but how could Denis let that happen when he never knew what would be going on at home? How could he foretell if his mother would be in a good mood when the day came? It was better to keep to himself, and when he was able to get into the house after school he stayed in his room as quiet as a mouse, with his transistor, which he'd saved up for. Sometimes his mother gave him money to keep out of the way. He'd go down the town and spend it on something to eat or on tapes, and occasionally on comics. He liked the ones with pictures of scary monsters and spacemen; they were different from what really went on all around.

School began to go wrong when he grew big and started to make wise-cracking answers in class when he didn't know what else to say. The other pupils laughed, but it didn't go down well with the staff and he was often kept in and given extra work to do. Gradually he began staying away, at first missing the lessons he found difficult and avoiding the teachers ┕ ... ┑ht picked on him, then more frequently as he got older. Once he wrote a note making out that it came from his mother and saying he was ill. Another time he wrote in her name, alleging that she was ill herself and that he was looking after her. After these breaks, which ended when he ran out of things to do in town and couldn't think of how to pass the time, he'd give school another brief trial, maybe staying as long as a week, but it never lasted.

Unknown to Denis, staff had come round from the school to see his parents but had never found anyone in. Something must be done, people said, if this went on, and each time that decision was reached, Denis would thwart it by a new appearance in class.

The best time was when he had a key to the house, but that was two years ago. One Saturday, he took his mother's from her bag and had one cut in town. He returned hers without it being missed. He'd had one cut for Tracy, too. Though she was already working, she hadn't been allowed to have her own key. It was good after that. He could watch television and make himself things to eat after school. He always went out before they got home, and he cleaned up after himself, too. But one day he forgot the time and was watching television when his mother caught him. She found his key, took it away and had the lock changed in case he'd been sly enough to have another one hidden somewhere.

Tracy had given him a key to the bedsit. She was a good girl and he didn't want to make things hard for her and Alan. To him, they seemed rich, with Alan earning good money on the building site, and Tracy getting her regular wages from the supermarket, but they had to pay out forty pounds a week for just this one room with the use of the bathroom. All they'd got to cook on was a couple of gas rings.

He gave them a toaster, that took four slices of bread all at once. They both thought he'd bought it with his earnings, but he hadn't. He'd lifted it from a big electrical store and it was quite a challenge. It was a bit large to hide under his loose jacket and he'd taken a chance, sliding it in under his arm and clamping it to his side while looking at something else. He'd already bought a plug so as to seem like a genuine customer. He'd fitted the plug. As a gift, it was a huge success. They all enjoyed toast for breakfast.

He had to go out on Saturday because Tracy had the day off and Alan, who worked most Saturdays, had decided to skip this one although overtime was welcome. Denis had handed over his Ford House pay the previous day and he needed more money, but he couldn't go car-washing today for it was raining. No one would pay him to wash their cars in a downpour.

He hitched out to the prison, getting a lift in a lorry for most of the way and walking the last part along the lane to the former military camp which was now used to house several hundred men. He went up to the gate as bold as brass, and asked for Len.

'Which Len?' asked the gate officer.

'Well – er – he was working in Coxton,' Denis said.

'You want to keep away from here, son. You might find yourself on the wrong side of the fence,' warned the officer. 'The proper procedure for visiting is to apply – '

'Ta,' interrupted Denis, and was about to walk off when the man called him back.

'Len White worked in Coxton. He's out now,' he said. 'Left last week.'

He'd be getting in touch any day, then, thought Denis. Len knew that Denis worked at Ford House on Tuesdays and Fridays. He'd make contact there, or with a note under the stone they'd used before.

He walked away briskly, his Walkman in place.

Having committed herself to Audrey's visit, Yvonne wanted to make it a success. She must ensure that her guest felt really welcome. Audrey probably wouldn't stay long.

She arrived promptly at four and the small girl, Emily, appeared round the side of the house to lead her inside. It seemed that they never used the front door.

Emily was friendly. She showed Audrey a Plasticine model she had made at school.

'Very nice,' said Audrey. 'And how did you think of making a mouse?'

'It's not a mouse, it's a hedgehog,' said Emily. 'Can't you see the prickles?' And indeed, along the body of the creature were etched faint, spiky lines.

'Of course it's a hedgehog. I see that now,' said Audrey.

'They get run over,' said Emily.

'Yes.'

'It's sad.'

Audrey agreed.

Yvonne appeared then, coming to greet them still dressed in jeans and loose sweater, a bright smile in position.

Hesther had worn jeans and loose sweaters, too, but Hesther had bitten her nails to the quick and often her hair and her clothes were dirty. Sometimes, she even smelled.

Audrey pushed the image away. She gave the children the toys she had bought for them, a toy car to push for Robin, a vintage model for Philip to make, and a colouring book for Emily, with a huge box of crayons. All were received with evident approval and Audrey was flustered by their gratitude. She gave few gifts, these days.

She was unused to children, too, but she managed to sustain a conversation with these three until tea, set out on the kitchen table, was ready. There was an orange sponge cake, iced, and a plate of chocolate biscuits. The children all walked about as they ate and returned to the table merely to drink or pick up something else to eat. Emily had begun her colouring, her book spread out on the floor, and Philip was eager to start on his model. Robin had parked the car under the table and joined it there, in its garage, as he said. Audrey pursed her lips as she witnessed this conduct. Hesther had been made to sit at table with washed hands and face, and she had to eat a slice of bread and butter before she might have any cake.

Yes, and now she was dead.

The bleak recognition of what had happened chilled Audrey again, as it did every day of her life.

'I wondered if you'd make me some curtains,' she said abruptly. 'For the dining room. And perhaps some cushions as well.'

'Oh! Yes, I'd be glad to,' said Yvonne, surprised. 'Not at once, I'm afraid.' She had a new commission for bedspreads and curtains and would be pressed to finish it by the decreed date.

'Oh, there's no hurry,' said Audrey. 'Perhaps you could come and have a look when you're collecting the children one day.' She must repay this hospitality by inviting them round, although the children would be bored. She had a button box, though: a tin full of various buttons which Hesther, when she was small, had loved arranging on the floor.

'Yes, of course,' said Yvonne.

After tea she showed Audrey the rest of the house. She and Charles occupied the bedroom where Audrey's parents had slept. It was odd seeing the big, sagging double bed in the room where twin beds had stood, with a gap between, against a different wall. The carpet was worn and faded but there were fresh apricot curtains patterned with white which matched the duvet cover. Audrey felt that she was having a revelation of intimacy thrust upon her.

'We need a new carpet,' said Yvonne. 'This one came with the house and it's pretty grotty.'

Audrey could see that.

'The carpets were left in my house, too,' she said. She had changed them at once. 'I had mushroom broadloom fitted throughout,' she added. 'It goes with anything.'

'Very wise,' said Yvonne.

'I had it in my flat, too,' Audrey said, waxing loquacious. 'I had a flat in Sussex for several years before I decided to come back here.'

'Oh, did you? Are you glad you moved?' Yvonne paused with her hands on the doorknob of what had been Robin's room and was now ready for Rosalind.

'I think so,' she answered.

Yvonne had opened the bedroom door.

'Robin used to be in here, but he had nightmares,' said Yvonne. 'So I've moved him. This is for my elder stepdaughter.'

'Lucky girl,' said Audrey. 'It's delightful.'

'I hope she won't have bad dreams too,' said Yvonne.

'Why should she?'

'Well, there was a murder here, wasn't there? Long ago,' said Yvonne. She laughed nervously. 'I'm afraid the house may be haunted.'

'What nonsense,' said Audrey. 'There aren't any ghosts except those we make ourselves. And who's been talking about a murder?'

'Oh, just someone. A child was murdered, he said.'

'Well, I've never heard of it,' said Audrey robustly.

'It's an old house and must have seen births and deaths in its time.' She was about to say that her parents had died here, but decided against it; the girl seemed rather morbid. 'It all happens in the course of natural life.'

'Are you certain there was no murder?'

'Positive,' said Audrey.

'What was this room in your day?'

'A spare bedroom,' Audrey replied. 'I had the one at the end of the corridor.'

'That's Philip's,' said Yvonne. She showed Audrey the room, where Philip's precious possessions were arranged. There were several small labelled boxes on shelves. 'He collects beetles,' said Yvonne. 'Nasty!' She smiled.

'It's a good interest,' Audrey said. 'Children need interests.'

'What about your daughter?' asked Yvonne. 'What did she like doing.'

'Riding, when she was young. Then she went to university. I was proud.' Audrey picked up a beetle box, looked inside at a defunct earwig and closed it again.

'What happened?' asked Yvonne.

'I'll tell you,' Audrey said.

To her own amazement, she found herself talking freely, telling Yvonne about Hesther's gradual distancing of herself from her home and her parents, her baffling loss of self-esteem.

'She'd had a good home, we thought,' Audrey said. 'Everything she could want. An allowance, too, and a good job. Why did she need to steal?' She stared at Yvonne as she said that, hardly noticing the younger woman's startled expression. 'Oh yes, she stole,' Audrey said. 'She went to prison, but she was ill. It was hospital that she needed, not locking up.' She shuddered. 'It was dreadful. Body searches. Filth. She was sedated to keep her quiet. When she came out she went to a clinic as a voluntary patient but she ran away. She jumped in front of an Underground train in the rush hour one Wednesday evening.'

8

Charles was angry. At six o'clock, as arranged, he had arrived to collect his daughters for the weekend and found only Celia ready. Rosalind had been invited to a party that evening and did not want to miss it. The party was not due to end until eleven o'clock.

'How's she proposing to get home?' Charles asked, standing in the front hall of Olivia's house, which for so long had also been his home.

'I shall fetch her,' said Hugh, looming large and bearded behind Olivia. 'Come and have a drink, Charles.'

'Not when I'm driving,' said Charles.

'How prissy you've got,' Olivia mocked. 'There was a time –'

She was right, but he preferred to forget the early years of their marriage when they had both drunk enough to make them foolish and amorous. He looked at her now, this woman with her corn-coloured ringlets who had shared with him moments of rapture and moments of misery. She must remember them too, and this knowledge fuelled his wrath.

'The arrangement is – ' he began.

'But Daddy, I want to go to this party. It's important,' said Rosalind. 'I can see you another time.'

'Or you can fetch her tomorrow,' Olivia offered. She was not going to suggest that she or Hugh would drive Rosalind over to Coxton; that would be making things much too easy.

She seemed very calm, not like the woman who had flung things at Charles and made scenes.

It was pointless to antagonize Rosalind.

'I'll come back for you in the morning,' Charles told her. 'Come along, Celia.'

Celia was happy to go off alone with her father. She couldn't remember when it had last happened. It wouldn't be for long, because when they reached Ford House the other children would be there. She quite liked them, especially Robin who was a sweet little boy, small and cuddly; she enjoyed reading to him, curled up together in a big armchair, one of those which she remembered from her own babyhood and which Mummy hadn't wanted to keep when she married Hugh. Mummy's cuddles were all with Hugh now. Celia hadn't got used to seeing him tucked up in bed with Mummy; she didn't like going into their bedroom when he was there. She had never gone into the room Daddy shared with Yvonne. Of course, she understood all about it. People got tired of one another and preferred someone else, and Daddy had tired of Mummy. They'd had awful rows; she remembered that. Mum was better now, with Hugh, but it was sad, all the same. She would never get married in case it happened to her.

Philip and Emily were all right and they let her play with their toys and games, but they lived all the time with Daddy and it made her feel left out of things. Why should they go swimming with Daddy? He'd been teaching Philip to dive. They weren't his children. Celia was not proud of these feelings; they made her feel mean; but nevertheless, they were strong.

So now she sat in the back of the car as her father drove off and hugged to herself her moment of joy. She looked with love at the back of his head, the crisp, dark hair that curled at the nape of his neck, his ears, rather pink, slightly pointed. He looked much nicer than Hugh, who was a bit like a bear, though a kind one.

They hadn't gone far before he picked up the telephone to talk to Yvonne. Celia thought the car phone was brilliant and Daddy had said it was useful to let Yvonne know when he would be home and if he had got held up in the traffic. Now, he put on the special voice he used to talk to her, the one he had used when Mum was in a rage and he'd tried to calm her down, sort of deep and coaxing. Calling her 'darling' with every other word, as it seemed to Celia, he was explaining about Rosalind and saying that he'd be collecting her the next day. Celia could imagine Yvonne's response. She'd speak quietly, in that clipped way she had, not letting you see if she really minded. Of course, she'd really be glad, though she'd have to pretend to Dad. She didn't want Celia and Rosalind there. She had to put up with them, just as they had to put up with Philip and Emily. She was always nice to them, and gave them lovely meals. She was a much better cook than Mummy, but Celia would never say so aloud; it would be too disloyal to Mummy. In a way it would be easier if she wasn't so kind, if she was mean and nasty and fed them on gruel and pinched them when Dad wasn't looking. Then Celia wouldn't feel so bad about everything.

They came to Coxton and drove slowly through the village, past the telephone box and the shop, and the school where Philip and Emily went, then along the lane that led to Ford House.

It was a lovely house. In spite of herself, Celia's spirits rose when the headlights picked out the trees that dotted the long grass at one side of the drive and then lit up the building. It was a good place for biking, and Dad had got them cycles which were kept here, although they had others at home. She liked the big front door with its heavy knocker and funny chain bellpull. The outside light was on, and there were lights showing at some of the upper windows. Yvonne, the perfect Yvonne who cooked and sewed and never got into rages, hadn't yet made curtains for the landing and stairs windows.

Celia ran into the house, willing and eager to say hullo to Philip and Emily. Robin had been allowed to stay up till they arrived and he welcomed her with flattering delight. She managed to dodge kissing Yvonne.

It was lasagne for supper, her favourite. Celia accepted a glass of Coca-Cola as a treat and began to eat her supper. Then she laid down her fork and stared at her plate. It would be hard to do it, but she would manage.

'I'm not hungry,' she said. 'I don't want any supper.'

She allowed herself to be coaxed and cajoled into eating the runner beans that Yvonne had cooked to go with the lasagne, and to toy with some apple crumble, and her self-martyrdom was worth enduring when Yvonne went all quiet and her nose turned pinched at the end. She'd got the message.

In the morning there was a discussion about what Charles called the logistics of fetching Rosalind. Who should go with him? Celia, obviously, because she would not want to forego two hours of his company.

'Can I come?' asked Philip, who liked going out in the BMW.

If he said no, the boy and his mother would be hurt. If he said yes, he would not have his girls to himself.

'I thought we might go swimming,' said Yvonne.

'But Rosalind will miss out. Couldn't we go this afternoon?' said Charles.

'I can't. I promised to go to a bring-and-buy sale in the village,' said Yvonne.

'Whatever made you let yourself in for that?' asked Charles.

'I was asked to go.' In fact, Audrey Bannerman had said that she meant to be there and suggested Yvonne should come too, as a way of meeting some people. Yvonne had seen it as a means of leaving Charles alone with his children, for she would take hers, and Robin, with her. 'I think we ought to take part in a few village

73

events,' she said. 'I'm not helping. It just means putting in an appearance, and I might pick up a few useful things.' There would be a jumble stall and over the years she had found bargains for both herself and the children at such events, but it was better for Charles not to know that.

Charles would not take all four older children swimming without her; the morning expedition would stand, Yvonne knew, as she waited for Celia to decide what she meant to do.

Must she go with Daddy all the way back to Mum's again, or could she go swimming with the others? Celia thought Dad might be hurt if she chose that.

She did, and he was.

You managed to solve one set of problems only to find you had acquired others which were as difficult to handle. Charles acknowledged this as he drove to fetch Rosalind. He faced no dramatic scenes now, no storms of tears if he were late home. Olivia used to create a situation implying that she had seen herself as a widow if he were delayed, even though he always telephoned a warning. There would be high emotion over every decision, from whether Celia should learn the piano to the location of the holiday. All that had ended, replaced by regular demands for increasing sums to support the girls which Charles did his best to meet; why should they lose out?

If Yvonne had not owned her house and sold it well, so that she had been able to help buy Ford House, the move would have been more difficult. So much was down to money: what you ought to afford, what you could afford. The girls needed tennis rackets, and Rosalind wanted to go on a school trip to France. What about when Robin began to cost more? Philip and Emily would move on to Leckerton Comprehensive when they left the village school, but Charles wanted his son to go to his old public school. There was no end to it.

There would be more weekends like this one, when Rosalind's wishes conflicted with what had been arranged by her elders. Naturally she wanted the best of both worlds, and Celia too.

She was ready when he arrived, which was something, and came running out of the house with her belongings in a Laura Ashley carrier bag. She wore a pink padded jacket over a dark sweater and jeans, and had on shabby trainers. It was a relief to see her thus; Charles felt afraid when she was dressed up and looking older than her age; he was too aware of the threats that would soon surround her. Today, she had put on some eye make-up, or possibly, like the pink streak in her hair, it was left over from the previous evening. Her face was white. Perhaps she was tired after a late night.

She was pleased to see him, kissed him warmly and jumped into the car beside him. She was old enough now to sit in front.

'Sorry about last night,' she said.

'Never mind,' said Charles. 'Was it a good party?'

'I suppose so,' said Rosalind.

'Well, did you enjoy it?'

'Yes and no. You dance and drink – all that – but it doesn't lead anywhere much.'

What did she mean? Where should it lead?

'What sort of drink?' Charles asked suspiciously.

'Oh, Coke and stuff,' said Rosalind, deeming it wiser not to mention that there had been wine and beer. 'You can't talk much, it's too noisy,' she added. 'Saves trouble, really.' She saw her father's expression and laughed. 'Don't worry, Daddy. Nothing wild happened.'

'I hope not. You're only thirteen,' he reminded her. 'And Hugh brought you home?' He needed to hear it confirmed.

'Mm.'

But it was he, Charles, who should be collecting her from her hazardous social engagements, not this other man whom he scarcely knew. Charles put his foot down hard and drove the car on through the cold, damp morning. The road glistened and water was sprayed up by the wheels of other traffic. He wanted to talk to Rosalind, find out how she was coping with adolescence and the problems of her divided life, but he was afraid of the answers.

'Yvonne's changed your room,' he said. 'She's moved you to the one that was Robin's. I hope you won't mind.'

How weak of him to lay the blame on Yvonne, when he had been party to the decision.

'Oh, that's all right,' said Rosalind sunnily. 'I like his room. It's got a terrific view.'

'It's a bit smaller,' said Charles.

'I'm not there very often, am I?' Rosalind said carelessly. 'I expect Robin will have trains and stuff before long, all spread out on the floor.'

She thought Robin quite cute, though she didn't go overboard for him the way Celia did.

'The others have all gone swimming,' Charles said, as he turned in at the gate, driving carefully between the potholes on the neglected drive. The whole thing needed resurfacing but that was impossible. He'd get some ballast and fill up the worst of the holes before he injured the car by hitting a bump.

'Oh, why couldn't they wait for me?' wailed Rosalind.

'Yvonne has to go to some do in the village later,' said Charles, and could not resist adding, 'If you'd come last night, you'd have been able to go too.'

This time she let him off.

'Never mind,' she said. 'I've got you all to myself for a bit instead.'

Charles hugged the moment. It could be a long time before it happened again.

*

76

The mail had arrived after he left that morning.

Charles saw that there were three bills and some junk circulars. He took everything, unopened, into his study and clasped them together with a big clip marked PENDING and laid the bundle on top of the walnut desk that had belonged to his father.

Rosalind had dumped her carrier bag on the floor in the hall and run out to the kitchen to make some coffee.

'Like some, Daddy?' she called.

'Yes, please.'

Charles followed her along the passage.

'You had no breakfast, I suppose,' he said.

She shrugged.

'No time,' she answered, lifting the Aga lid and moving the kettle across. 'What a slow old thing this is,' she added. 'You should have one of those plastic jugs without a flex. Mum's got one.'

'Bully for her,' said Charles.

'Will Yvonne mind if I take some cake?' Rosalind asked.

'Of course not,' said Charles. 'It'll be in the larder.'

Rosalind found a tin and cut a big slice from the new cake destined for tea that afternoon. She came back into the kitchen holding it, and as she took a bite a shower of crumbs fell to the floor. Charles gazed fondly at his pretty daughter and took down two mugs from the dresser. He made the coffee while Rosalind strolled about eating her cake. Then he tidied everything neatly away.

'You're so fussy, Daddy. I'd have done that,' she said.

'Would you, Ros? You might have forgotten,' said Charles mildly.

'Hugh isn't fussy,' Rosalind remarked. 'But he can usually find things for Mum when she loses them.'

Olivia was very untidy. She left a trail of scarves shed, bracelets removed, even her rings, wherever she went.

At first Charles had been amused by this careless habit but later it wearied him. Luckily Yvonne was orderly in most respects, although she allowed the children to leave their toys about more than he thought they should.

He suddenly felt a desperate urge to hear details of Olivia's life with Hugh. Did they really get on? Did they argue and make it up in bed? Was Hugh generous with money? Did he succeed where Charles had failed? But he must not turn Rosalind into an informer.

'Things are all right, then?' he said.

'What's all right?' she asked. 'I suppose so. You know Mum.'

He did, and, after eleven years of marriage, probably better than Hugh, but she would be different with him, as Charles was with Yvonne.

Rosalind had got up to put her mug in the dishwasher. She glanced out of the window.

'Who's that?' she asked.

'Where?'

Charles came behind her and looked out. He saw a youth in jeans and a combat jacket dancing across the yard towards the back door.

'I've no idea,' he said, and went to discover.

Denis, leaving the prison, had decided to take a look at the target. He'd think of some excuse for his visit when the need arose. Yvonne's car was out, but he saw the BMW and supposed it belonged to Charles, whom he had never met.

'Hi,' he said, when the man came to the back door. He had pushed his earphones up but Charles could hear the tinny sound of his Walkman.

'Yes?' Charles frowned down at him, his eyebrows, which would be thick and bushy when he was old, raised above his grey eyes.

'I was just passing and remembered Mrs Davies had said the yard needed sweeping,' Denis invented. 'I told her I didn't mind.'

Light dawned. Yvonne had mentioned that the young gardener was addicted to his Walkman.

'You're Denis?'

'Who else?'

'Hmph.' Yvonne had said nothing about expecting him today, but it was true that the yard was a mess. Damp leaves had blown into the corners and were slimy after the rain.

'She'll be pleased to see it done,' Denis declared. 'I could clean out the garage, too. Maybe wash the cars now it's stopped raining.' There was no end to his willingness to help. 'Where's she gone, then?' he added, curious.

'She's taken the children swimming,' said Charles. 'Very well. You know where everything is, I suppose. The stiff broom – all that?'

'Too right,' said Denis, in Oz style. 'I'll need a bag for the rubbish.'

'Put it on the bonfire,' said Charles. 'I'll light it later, if the rain holds off.'

Denis set to work, aware that Charles might watch him start. He began industriously scraping leaves and sludge from under a water butt, and was sweeping them into a heap when Rosalind sauntered across, her hands in her pockets.

'Hullo,' she said. 'What are you listening to?'

Denis never knew what to say to girls. Sometimes he made defensively lewd remarks but that wouldn't do here.

'Michael Jackson,' he mumbled.

'I don't go for him,' said Rosalind. 'I like Madonna.'

'What? And you a girl?' Denis crowed with laughter. Such a comment was too silly to answer.

'Do you work every Saturday?' she asked.

'No. Just thought I'd offer today, seeing your mum wanted the place done,' said Denis.

'She's not my mum,' said Rosalind coldly. 'She's my stepmother.'

'Well, she's all right, is Mrs Davies,' Denis pronounced, turning his back on the two thin, denim-clad legs which composed the only section of her he was able to look at without extreme discomfort. That hair with the funny pink streak and the bright eyes made him feel very uneasy.

There was no amusement to be had here. Rosalind turned back to the house wondering what to do now. Her father had gone off to his study. He'd be opening his mail. He had said he wanted her here but they soon ran out of things to talk about. This was called access: his to her, or hers to him? It was meant to be two-way, wasn't it? She sighed, weighed down by the problems that lay in a future peppered with these weekends when she didn't really know where she wanted to be .

Still, the house was great. It was a pity none of her friends could be brought round to see it; they'd be impressed. Rosalind went upstairs to her new bedroom and unpacked her belongings. She hadn't brought much.

Dad couldn't really be as hard up as he made out if he could buy this place. When Mum said she wanted to get a bit more out of him, Hugh told her he'd done it all on the bank, whatever that meant. A mortgage, she supposed. Hugh told Mum not to be greedy. Dad was pretty good; he paid up for extras and anything else they needed. She supposed he had to, really, or he'd feel very bad as he was the one who had walked out on the marriage. And he'd walked out on her and Celia, too. That was what hurt. He liked Yvonne best.

She was glad when the others returned from swimming and she successfully pretended she hadn't minded not going.

Yvonne was surprised to find Denis busy washing the BMW. She supposed Charles intended to pay him and would not leave it to her. He was allowing Robin to help him, giving the small boy a fragment of sponge and telling him to do the wheels, which Denis himself had already scrubbed. That endeared him to Yvonne. She'd find him some lunch, later on; there was quite enough for them all. His grandmother probably found coping with his large appetite demanding.

Yvonne never discovered that Denis had let Charles think she had asked him to come round.

Full of shepherd's pie and treacle tart, which he had eaten in the kitchen with all the family, and the richer by five pounds, Denis set off for Ivy Lodge. He had decided to offer his services to the old bat he had met at Ford House. He felt refreshed and benign. Those kids didn't know they were born, living in a great place like that with food better even than his gran's had been. Denis often thought wistfully of those long-ago visits when he and Tracy were fed on lamb with fresh vegetables out of the garden, and helped pick the fruit that was made into puddings and jam.

The old girl came to the door when he rang. She was blinking and rubbing her eyes. Getting past it, thought Denis, who had woken Audrey after her own humble meal of soup and a wholemeal roll. She often slept badly at night and would drop off in her chair after lunch if there was nothing she had to do.

'Can I do any jobs for you, Missis?' he asked.

Audrey frowned at him, trying to remember who he was. She had certainly seen him before.

'Mrs Davies thought you might need some help,' he declared. 'I've been up there this morning.'

'I see.' Now Audrey remembered him.

She pondered. A young person eager to work should, if possible, be encouraged.

'I could wash the car,' he suggested.

She'd had it done by the machine in Leckerton only

the other day, but in this weather it didn't stay clean for long.

'Very well,' she said. 'I'll just get it out of the garage for you.'

'I'll do that,' Denis volunteered.

'It's not insured for anyone else to drive,' said Audrey firmly.

He watched while she backed it out and pointed to the hose and pail which he had noticed before.

'The tap's on the side of the house,' she explained. 'Come and tell me when you've finished.'

He did it well, leathering the car off with a chamois he found hanging in the garage behind the door. He didn't mind this sort of work. One day he'd have someone doing it for him, when he had a big house like Mrs Davies, not that he'd want an old place full of draughts, oh no. Give him a nice pad on the Costa Brava: that would be a bit more like it, with a flash car and a speedboat. Oh, and a big pool. He liked swimming.

Mrs Bannerman gave him a cup of tea and a chocolate digestive biscuit, and three pounds, a pound more than she would have paid at the car-wash, because he had done it so well.

He got a lift back to Leckerton quite easily and took himself off to McDonald's for something to eat, beans and sausage and chips. The waitress was cheeky, asking him if he could pay before she served him. He knew her: she'd been at the same school. Afterwards, he went to the cinema, but on the way there he rang the emergency services and said there was a fire at McDonald's. He heard the fire engine coming as he went on his way. They'd lose trade while the place was emptied. That would show them.

Tracy had put his flask of cocoa in the van. After his busy day, and with his stomach full, Denis curled up in his sleeping bag, quite content. He'd still got some money and soon he'd have more, when Len got in touch.

9

The best way to break bad news was firmly, without equivocation, and when Jim telephoned Mrs Bannerman she told him bluntly that a man was living in the house with Maureen and there was no chance of a reconciliation. He heard her words but he couldn't accept their message and he decided that he must go home to sort things out, face to face. It must all be some dreadful mistake and if he could just kiss Maureen's soft lips and soothe her, she would change her mind. Besides, there was Nicola.

Jim had scarcely slept since he heard what Mrs Bannerman had to say. When he thought of Maureen in bed with that unknown man, rage overcame his despair and he was filled with jealous hatred of his usurper. What had happened to the promises he and Maureen had exchanged at their wedding, a church one with her in white satin and tulle and Jim in a hired morning coat? He had known himself to be the luckiest man in the world on that memorable day. He was ten years older than Maureen but he had been able to cut out younger rivals. She had wanted security and he could provide it, but she had expected too much from marriage. Maybe most people did. You were only two imperfect humans, after all.

He'd make up to her for the shame of his prison sentence if she backed him up now. Somehow he would find a job when he came out, even if it was nothing special, and in time things would improve. There was no other future for he could not face life without her.

Jim's desire to see Maureen became an obsession. Now he had something to plan for, though he would lose remission if he broke out. It might not be much if he gave himself up or came back as soon as he had got some sort of assurance about the future from Maureen. If he failed, what happened to him didn't matter. Tossing and turning in his prison bed, he rehearsed what he would say to her. He'd surprise her if he let himself into the house while she was out. He had no key but he had learned how to open windows. He'd make sure the man wasn't there, of course. Mrs Bannerman said he was on nights but his shift might have changed. She hadn't said what he did, and Jim had been too upset to ask.

It might be better not to catch her unawares. She'd be scared if she came home and found someone there; it might take her a minute to realize that it was him and she had nothing to fear.

With a head full of dreams, Jim never went back to the prison on Wednesday after leaving the farm where he had been working for the past week. Instead he cycled off in the other direction.

He wouldn't be missed at once, and when he was, there wouldn't be much of a fuss at first because he had no record of violence and offered no threat to the public. It was not unknown for men to stay out for a night or two and then return. Others absconded and were soon retrieved. Most didn't mind coming back after a taste of freedom, a booze-up somewhere, maybe a meet with a woman.

A drizzling rain was falling. Autumn this year was unusually wet but it was also extremely mild. Jim pedalled along unfamiliar lanes. He had never worked in this area and would have to travel in a wide arc to get round to the motorway, but he could not go all the way to Reading on his cycle. They were not allowed on motorways and anyway it was much too far.

The rain was cold on his face. He felt very conscious of his prison overalls but, in his navy donkey jacket, anyone noticing him would think he was some sort of labourer going home. His striped shirt would be more of a give-away, and that was well covered.

Most of the traffic was coming towards him; people returning from work, he supposed. He found the head-lights dazzling and was quite surprised when he saw that he was coming into a village. It was only a hamlet, a few dwellings strung out along a narrow road, too small and remote to have attracted the property developers.

There was no street lighting.

Jim soon saw several cars parked by the wide grass verge.

He knew that people were careless. He had heard often enough, inside, that it was easy to find unlocked cars with their keys in position. There was no need for clever stuff with wires. He dismounted and pushed his cycle towards a small Citroën.

It was locked, but the third vehicle he tried, a Honda pick-up, was unlocked and the key was there.

Jim put his bike in the back before driving away.

The pick-up was not missed until the next morning.

The Honda had enough petrol to get Jim to Reading and back. He settled down behind the wheel. Clothes were next. He needed some nondescript sort of coat instead of his jacket.

Suppose he went into a pub? Would anyone notice him, a stranger, in the general bustle? Maybe not, if the place was crowded, as pubs sometimes were soon after opening time. He had enough money to buy a half of mild, and maybe someone would have slung a coat over a chair or somewhere in such a way that he could snatch it without being seen.

At the next village he turned down a side road and soon came to the Coach and Horses. It had a big parking area at the back, and Jim stopped. He tried all the cars but though some were unlocked, he found no coat. He couldn't be that lucky twice.

But he was.

He walked up to the door and went in. To his left was the snug, to his right, the saloon, and on hooks in the lobby ahead hung several coats. There was a buzz of noise from the main bar and the publican was busy with orders. Most of his customers were regulars calling in on their way home. Men liked to unwind after leaving the office before going home to their wives, and women, too, often sought a break between work and home. He did not see Jim swiftly take down the nearest coat, a bulky beige anorak, rather worn, and scuttle out. No one else noticed, either. No outraged owner rushed in pursuit.

Some men in prison said all you needed was nerve. It seemed they were right.

Hopes high, he returned to the pick-up. Things were going his way. Such a good beginning was an omen for the success of his enterprise, and he resumed his journey weaving a scenario in which Maureen and her boyfriend would have quarrelled, and she would be overjoyed to see him. After a rapturous reunion, a further short separation would seem like no sentence at all.

Len had never liked the country. Some of the blokes in the nick thought it was wonderful, all that open space and air, but he liked to see buildings around him and to have a bit of noise about, people on the move, traffic passing, something happening. The only time he liked it quiet and peaceful was when he was on a job. In the country, you were always aware of the weather; the rain was wetter there than in the town, or so it seemed, and the wind blew harder. In town, one season was much like another and you had to go to the park to notice the difference because a few flowers might be out, or the trees in leaf.

He'd had a good welcome after his release. Bet had been working as a barmaid at the Grapes, and it hadn't been easy for her on her own, especially when Fingers, who'd done that job with him, failed to come up with the money she should have received. Len would have to settle that with him, one day. But he had nothing either, only the small sum they gave you on your release, and what he got from social security. She'd soon start to moan if he didn't bring in a bit more.

He liked working in daylight. He was expert at walking along a residential street sussing out which houses were empty, sliding round to the back to discover a vulnerable window or door. It was best to go prepared in case you'd made a mistake and someone surprised you, and Len always had a neat little cosh tucked up his sleeve when he went to work. It was just a slim stick, but it had an effectively loaded head. He had used it only once when he'd done that warehouse job, joining up with Fingers Smith whom he'd met in the Scrubs. The nightwatchman had caught them while Fingers was fiddling the safe, and Len had given him one. He'd caught the wrong spot, it seemed, as the bloke, instead of just being out for the count, had died in hospital. Len's brief had made out he'd had a bad heart and all that, and he'd got away with manslaughter. After being sent down for seven years, he'd served less than three because of parole and the time he had spent on remand. Fingers had a shorter sentence and had promised to look after Bet, but his old woman had got hold of the money and taken off with some young bloke.

It proved he was better working alone. Forcing safes wasn't his line; his best field was the domestic scene.

He'd got that key, the one made from the soap mould the kid had provided. That house would have plenty worth taking. There would be a television, for sure, maybe two, and other things he and the family might enjoy using besides what he could sell. The kid said there was a fancy sewing machine upstairs, and there'd be one or two cars in the garage, probably something flashy like a Porsche or a Mercedes. He knew where to pass on a car.

It made sense to work away from his usual area: it would put the fuzz off; they wouldn't connect it with him. Anyway, he never left prints. He and Fingers had been caught through a car; a bright copper had stopped them in one they had lifted two days before.

Nothing like that would go wrong if he worked quietly on his own, like before. He might go down to Coxton and have a quick look around.

That afternoon, Yvonne's Mini had refused to start when it was time to collect Philip and Emily from school. It gave a few moans and then seemed to expire.

It took less than five minutes to nip down in the car but nearer fifteen to walk, even wheeling Robin in the pushchair, which would have to be used to save time.

She had better ring the headmaster and explain.

Yvonne had been cutting it fine, anyway, finishing a seam on a bedspread before setting off. She unfastened Robin's seat belt and tugged him out of the car, leaving him to follow her as she ran in through the fine rain to call the headmaster.

He accepted her explanation and said he would keep the children until she arrived. Yvonne hurriedly put on her wellingtons and picked up an umbrella. Robin's plastic cover-up had long since been discarded since the pushchair was so seldom used, and she set off with the umbrella held more over him than herself. They would all get horribly wet walking home.

Audrey, returning from Leckerton, saw the quartet trudging back towards Ford House. The pushchair was being propelled head-on into the rain, and the other two children, in wellington boots, were walking doggedly along, heads down, lunch boxes in their hands. In fact they were looking for puddles to jump in but to Audrey they seemed a desolate group. She stopped her car and offered to drive them home.

'Oh, you angel,' cried Yvonne. 'Thank you. My car's packed up.'

Gratefully, she bundled the three damp children into the back of the Fiat and folded the pushchair, stowing it in beside them. Then she got into the seat beside Audrey.

'Those pushchairs are terrible things,' said Audrey. 'They don't protect the child at all.'

'No, well, we hardly ever use it now, but this was an emergency,' said Yvonne.

'Are the fields flooded yet?' Audrey asked. 'They used to come out whenever it rained for more than a day or two.'

'I don't know,' Yvonne confessed. 'I've been sewing all day and I haven't looked out.'

'There's a ford across,' Audrey said. 'Near the house. That's where it got its name.'

'Oh, of course. I never thought. How stupid of me,' said Yvonne. 'You must show us where it is when the weather's better.'

'There's a swimming place, too,' said Audrey. 'I expect the village children still go there.'

Yvonne invited her in for tea but Audrey refused. She was very tired and wanted to go home.

'Telephone if the car won't start in the morning,' she said. 'I'll gladly run the children to school. I'm always up early.'

'Oh, thanks,' Yvonne said. 'I haven't got anything worked out with the other mothers, but no one else lives in this direction.'

Philip thought someone did: children came to the school from several villages around. He said so.

'Well, we'd better get together, then,' Yvonne said. 'You must point out the mothers.'

Audrey drove home. Her passengers had made the car very wet inside; small pools had dripped on the mat at the back. She put it away and went into the house.

That afternoon, she had gone to a charity shop in

Leckerton and offered her services. She knew she was leading too reclusive a life and thought it would be a way of changing things.

'I don't mind giving you a day or two each week,' was how she had phrased her offer.

Looking at her pale, unsmiling face, her severe hair under the tweed hat, her expensive padded coat, the woman in charge had felt instant antipathy.

'Thank you, but we're fully staffed at present,' she had replied austerely.

It wasn't true, but such a haughty recruit would not fit in with the other helpers. Audrey, snubbed, had inwardly shrivelled. She still felt battered by the rejection.

She took out her knitting. The yellow dress was coming on well. It would be perfect for Jenny.

Perhaps she should have accepted Yvonne's invitation after all. She never had tea herself until half past four; the day had to be divided into orderly sections with regular things at regular times, otherwise existence became chaotic.

She sat knitting, thinking about other charitable work she might undertake. There must be something needed. She could visit old people, perhaps, but the trouble was that she didn't enjoy their company. In fact, she had to admit, she was not much good with anyone.

Her mind flitted, as so often, to Rupert. He'd be at home by the fire now. She still thought of it as home; she had lived there for nearly thirty years. He might be reading *The Field*, or perhaps *The Times* if he hadn't done that earlier, and Felicity would be sitting in what had been her chair, or perhaps she would be in the kitchen preparing dinner.

Rupert had been a regular soldier and after their wedding he and Audrey went to Germany, where he was stationed. She did her best to fit in with the other wives, accepting the general pecking order and the duties that went with it. After all, it was not unlike school, with privileges allied to seniority. But at functions she was silent, looking bored when in fact she was paralytically shy. She took German lessons, which was thought eccentric, and went for long walks with a dog they had acquired. The enclosed society in which they were obliged to live, not mingling with the local population, irritated her, though she did her best to come to terms with it. When she became pregnant, however, everything changed. Now her life held purpose.

After the baby was born in the military hospital, Audrey was quite ill for a time. Then Rupert, who had lost seniority while a prisoner, being outpaced by his contemporaries, was posted to the War Office and the couple, with their baby daughter, lived in a rented house in Purley, from where he travelled up by train each day.

He hated working in London, especially being confined in the train and then in the office. The war had given him a legacy of mild claustrophobia. As he had little hope of reaching field rank, he sent in his papers. There was plenty for him to do at home, helping his father run the farm and put the estate in order. He went to an agricultural college while Audrey and Hesther lived in a cottage on the estate, and after that he lived a life of apparently busy contentment. By the time his father died, he was on the local council, and later he became a magistrate, thus fulfilling some of the traditional roles of a landowner.

Audrey and he had drifted apart, but not acrimoniously. Her gaucheness, which at first had attracted him, grew no less, and after a time began to irritate him. It hampered her socially, and the people on the estate interpreted it as conceit. Both of them, though, adored their daughter, Hesther Isabel, named after each of their mothers.

When she died, there was nothing to hold them together. A so-called friend told Audrey about Rupert's affair with Felicity. The fact that it had been common knowledge, or so it seemed to Audrey, for years, was humiliating.

She had her own income, left to her by her father in trust for her lifetime, and could be independent, so she packed her bags, told Rupert she was leaving, and went to stay in a Sussex hotel while she decided what to do next. Sussex was a long way from home.

Rupert had found her there. There had been a talk during which he showed extreme distress and she remained icily calm.

'You must try to be happy,' she said. 'You and Felicity. Let that, at least, be saved.'

He had stared at her, unable to reply. She could remember it all as if it was yesterday.

Audrey put down her knitting, made her tea, and laced it with a generous slug of whisky.

10

Len took the train to Leckerton. He'd find a car there to get him to Coxton. If he dumped it after the job and took one from the house, the police would think it was a local job.

It was raining, and the town looked bleak, everyone hurrying past with raincoats on and umbrellas up. He decided to find somewhere warm and dry while he thought things through. The job couldn't be done until after dark, and if it was still raining, he might have to put it off or look for some casual pickings.

He went into a café just off the market square and ordered tea and a cheese sandwich.

He couldn't believe it when the kid appeared. There he was, standing in the doorway in his combat jacket, jeans and trainers, his short hair on end, his eyes alert. Len had never expected to meet him again.

Denis had recognized him instantly. He came lumbering over, a grin of astonished delight on his rosy face, and sat down facing Len.

'You going to do it, then?' he asked. 'Is that why you're here?'

A great warm glow had flooded his body. Len hadn't forgotten that they were mates, and he'd come to look for him. Denis forgot that Len didn't know he lived in Leckerton.

'Shut your gob,' said Len, looking round in case anyone could overhear.

'You'll need help,' Denis said. 'I know where there's a van you could use.'

'We can't take it until they're asleep,' said Denis.

He had explained to Len about how he was sleeping in Alan's van.

'Can you drive it?' asked Len.

'Course I can,' boasted Denis. 'Only I haven't got a licence so it might be best if you took it out.'

'Hm.'

The idea of the van was tempting. It wouldn't be missed and the kid could bring it back after the job, when Len had got away in the car from the house. He could be paid off with something from the house – a radio, something he would find easy to sell if he didn't want to use it. Len was not very handy with cars, and although he knew how to start one without a key he had never done it. Stealing cars wasn't really his line, apart from taking a ride in one with the key already there. Whenever he'd done that, he'd kept the keys and he had quite a little collection which was a help when he needed a ride. Sometimes he'd find one that was a perfect fit.

'Could you get the van keys?' he asked.

'Easy,' said Denis confidently.

He blessed Tracy for giving him keys to the house and to their room. She had wanted him not to feel shut out and abandoned, as he had done at home.

'You've to go into their room?'

'Yeah.'

'Will you be able to do it without waking them?'

With his practice at burglary, Len might succeed in creeping more quietly into the place, but if he happened to wake them, there'd be an uproar, whereas if it was only the kid, they wouldn't be alarmed. Len, himself, could scarper and go it alone, and let the kid talk himself out of the mess he'd be in.

'Course,' said Denis confidently. 'Mind, we'll have to put the van back by morning.'

'We'll do that,' said Len. If the kid got into trouble driving home on his own, the whole thing could be put down to joy-riding.

Len told Denis that he must see where the van would be parked. Then they would split up until after

94

midnight. He didn't query Denis's domestic arrangements. Plenty of kids left home; he'd done so himself. Denis was lucky to have a sister to turn to. He, Len, had slept rough before now, most recently just before he was nicked when Bet had locked him out because she said she was fed up with his life style, as she called it. Still, she was happy enough whenever he made a good haul. Once, they'd gone to Tenerife, to a self-catering apartment with a pool and shops nearby and she'd toasted herself golden brown and been very warm and loving. It would be nice to do that again.

After parting from Denis, Len wandered the streets of Leckerton. The rain had stopped and people were coming home from work as the shops shut. It wasn't a good time for a casual break-in: he must bide his time until later.

He went to a pub and made two halves last him all night while he read the paper and planned how to spend what he'd get from tonight's operation.

He liked padding about in a quiet house, knowing that those upstairs in bed were unaware of his presence. He preferred not to go into bedrooms unless it was a daytime job in an empty house. You could find quite a lot downstairs, like cheque books, and often women's handbags. Televisions and radios were downstairs, too, and drink. And silver, in the places that had it.

There'd be some at Ford House, for sure.

Denis lay in the van in his sleeping bag listening to his stereo, twitching his limbs and pounding his fists together in the darkness. Tomorrow he'd be in the money and could do anything he liked.

He dozed off by mistake and woke with a start, wondering what the time was. He had a torch, and shone it on his digital watch which his mother, in a rare moment of affection, had given him for his fourteenth birthday. It was only ten o'clock. He set the alarm for twelve, in case he fell asleep again.

After parting from Len, he had run into a boy from school who had told him questions were being asked about his absence. Masters had wanted to know if other boys had seen him.

'I've been ill,' said Denis. 'There were letters.' He'd sent another one last week.

'Yeah – wrote them yourself, didn't you?' guessed his informant.

What if they set the police or the social services on to searching for him? Would anyone come round to Tracy's? His parents didn't know he was there. Tracy had promised not to tell them, if she ran into their mother.

He decided to forget it. After tonight, he could run. They'd never find him in London.

The small piping notes of the alarm woke him, piercing the heavy sleep that had suddenly claimed him.

Now he had to get the keys.

Denis opened the door into the communal hall of the house and stood listening. The ground-floor front room was occupied by a man who worked in a Leckerton factory. He kept late hours, but Denis had seen his motor-bicycle in the tiny front garden, where he left it out of the way of Mrs Dove's car. So he was in, but he might not be asleep though there was no light in his room. At the back was old Mrs Crow, who seldom went out and had few visitors. Denis thought it was cruel, her living like that on her own, and that she should be put in a home, but Tracy admired her independence and said why shouldn't she keep her own place? She wasn't ill, only old. She had the use of an outside lavatory beyond her kitchenette. Alan's room was at the back, upstairs, and Mrs Dove had the rest of the space, quite a nice flat with her own bathroom. Tracy and Alan shared the other bathroom with Steve Fox from downstairs, and Mrs Crow when she felt bold enough to climb the stairs.

Denis could hear nothing. He had brought a torch, to avoid putting on the main light, which worked from a time switch. Softly, in his trainers, he went up the stairs. One creaked and he froze, but there was no other sound. He reached the door to Alan and Tracy's room, slipped the key in and turned it carefully. It made a small click and he paused again, but all was silent. He crept into the room, his hand over his torch, his fingers glowing red, and almost stumbled over one of Tracy's slippers which she had left carelessly in the middle of the floor. Where would Alan have put his keys?

Denis felt his way over to the chest of drawers where hairbrushes and cosmetics were jumbled together. Were they there? He couldn't see them.

A sigh came from the bed and he doused his light, freezing again, holding his own breath until he thought he would explode. If they woke, he would say he had a headache and was looking for an aspirin.

To the right of the bed was a sagging armchair and a small table. Alan had been living here for a year before Tracy moved in, and since then they had exchanged his single bed for a double divan. Apart from that, there was a beanbag to sit on, and Denis bumped into it now as he moved to the chair looking for Alan's jacket. The keys might be in his pocket.

The jacket wasn't on the chair. He shone his shrouded torch round again. If he failed to find them, the whole deal would be off, and he'd lose face with Len.

Then he caught sight of something on the back of the door. Of course! There were several hooks there, put up by Tracy in an effort to win more space. Alan's jacket hung on one and the keys were in the pocket.

Denis almost whooped for joy but he controlled himself, going quietly from the room and closing the door behind him. Again, it clicked as the lock engaged, but he was outside now and it wouldn't matter if they woke.

He hurried downstairs and out to the road. They would see nothing from their room. Only Mrs Dove or Steve Fox would be able to watch the van move off, if by chance they heard it start and were curious enough to look out.

As he reached the van, Len emerged from the shadows behind it. Denis's pounding heart seemed to fill his whole chest. He had never felt so excited in his life.

'I got them!' he said, waving them.

'Ssh,' said Len. 'Hand them over and get in.'

Denis obeyed. Len slid into the driver's seat and ran his eye over the controls. It was some time since he had driven a motor vehicle but he did not want Denis to realize this.

'Choke's there, and that's where the indicators are,' said Denis helpfully. 'You don't want to blow the horn by mistake,' he added.

Len silently agreed. He pulled out the choke and turned the key. The van fired at once, loudly and a little roughly, but soon settling down. Len did not adjust the throttle. He pulled out from the kerb and set off along the road in the yellow glow from the street lamps.

Denis leaned over and switched on the lights. This was the life! He might never see Leckerton again. He began to sing tunelessly as they went along, until Len told him to shut up.

'I can't concentrate with you making that row,' he said.

Denis sat back. His Walkman was in the rear with his sleeping bag and few belongings. Now he'd forgotten his plan to return the van for Alan to use the next day. He'd got all he needed for life in London. He and Len might stop for a meal at one of those big service stations on the motorway. It would be great. He'd been to London several times on school trips to museums, which he found boring, and once with two other boys. They'd ridden on the Underground for hours and only surfaced when they were hungry. It was a weird place, people playing guitars or violins with hats or bags on the ground for money and crowds on the pavements. Denis did not remember how glad he had been to get back to Leckerton, where if you were really determined you could walk from one side of the town to the other in a couple of hours, not that he'd ever done it.

'Which way?' asked Len at the roundabout outside Leckerton.

'Left. Then it's straight on for a bit,' said Denis. He was hungry again. He'd eaten his supper very quickly, hurrying out to the van as usual to leave Tracy and Alan alone, and it seemed a long time ago. Never mind. There would be plenty of food at Ford House. He and Len could have some of Mrs Davies's cake, even cook a meal on that old-fashioned range of hers.

As he reached this comforting reflection, they came to the turning for Coxton. Len's driving was rough when he had to change gear, but the van was in good order and once it had warmed up, ran well. He hadn't liked it when the kid leaned over to push in the choke. Interfering, that was.

'Give over,' Len had said.

Denis didn't mind. He knew Len saw himself as the boss but he, Denis, was the one with the local knowledge.

Len, however, also knew Coxton, although he had not approached it from the Leckerton side before. The first houses on the edge of the village came into sight, dark windows glinting in the headlights. He slowed down. There were a few street lights set widely apart along the narrow, twisting road. They passed the pub and the shop, and the lane that led down to the church and a small close of bungalows which Len had looked at with a professional eye during his stints in the graveyard. One often had a window open and the car gone from the garage; it had been hard to pass by without trying his luck. The van swerved as he glanced down the lane and Denis shrieked at him to mind where he was going.

Nearly a mile past the last building, a renovated Victorian chapel now occupied by an accountant and his wife, who was a nurse, they reached the entrance to Ford House. Len knew that further on a small humped bridge crossed the narrow river and the road eventually led to the prison. This was the way he had cycled so many times. He pulled the van on to the grass verge and turned off the lights.

'We'll go the rest of the way on foot,' he said. 'Is it a long drive?'

'Depends what you mean by long,' said Denis, still unnerved by Len's steering lapse. He'd thought they were going to hit a lamp post. 'Couple of hundred metres, maybe,' he added as they got out of the van.

Denis stepped forth boldly and led the way up the drive, trotting along in his trainers and carrying the torch he kept in the van. The heavy clouds which had brought the rain earlier in the day had parted, and a thin moon showed as the two padded along. Len stumbled once and cursed.

'Drive's full of holes,' Denis said cheerfully. 'I've offered to fill them in for the guy and he's thinking about it. Costs money to buy the ballast they'd need.' As he spoke, Denis really believed he had had this conversation.

Len was not interested. He was peering ahead to the dark shape of the house. A light showed at an upper uncurtained window and they both halted.

'It'll be for the kids, in case they wake,' said Denis.

'You never said there was kids,' said Len.

'You didn't ask,' answered Denis. 'There's three. One of them's pretty young, three or four.'

Len had imagined a prosperous middle-aged couple

living here in comfort, with their children off their hands and away from home.

'Where're the cars kept?' he muttered.

'Round the back.' Denis turned on his torch and brandished its beam in the direction of the yard.

'Turn that thing out,' hissed Len. He took the key from his pocket and went up to the front door, where he had to ask Denis to supply some light as he fitted it into the lock. He turned it and tried the latch, but the door held fast.

'Must be bolted,' said Denis, hiding his dismay. He had imagined them walking straight in through the front hall and helping themselves at their leisure.

Len was cursing.

'Not got a burglar alarm, have they?' he asked. He'd seen no sign, but then he hadn't really looked for one.

The idea had never occurred to Denis.

'Don't think so,' he said. 'We might get in at the back,' he added.

The pair went round to the yard and Len tried the back door. Naturally enough, it was locked. So much for making an easy entry: he was tempted to give Denis a piece of his mind but checked himself. That would have to wait.

'We'll try a window,' he said. He wouldn't give up now.

He moved towards the kitchen window and took out a knife. Just as he did so, they heard the sound of a car.

'Quick, hide somewhere,' Len snarled. What had he got himself into with this stupid kid?

Denis had already melted away into the space between the oil tank and the rear wall of the house. Len squeezed in beside him as a car turned the corner into the yard, its lights picking up the open doors of one of the garages. Charles Davies had been to a business function and had only now come home.

Len and Denis crouched where they were while he got

out of the car, locked it, then closed the garage. He walked right past them to the back door and Denis, who could see him clearly, watched him take a key from beneath a water butt and let himself in. He prayed that Len, crouched behind him, had not noticed.

Now lights began coming on in the house.

'We stay here till he's gone upstairs,' said Len, pulling Denis back as he started to move. The man had only to look out of the window to see them.

They waited for over half an hour, during which time they heard water gurgling down a nearby drainpipe and the sound of a lavatory flushing.

'There's a way out through the garden,' Denis said. 'We needn't go near the drive.'

It was implicit that the job was off. Both were impatient to escape undetected.

They got very wet about the feet on their journey down a rough grass path and across a patch of lawn. Len uttered some obscenities and he called Denis unflattering names for not finding out about the man Davies's movements.

'I didn't know you were coming today, did I?' Denis retorted. 'You didn't tell me.'

He marched on in silence and decided not to warn Len about two steps ahead of them in the darkness, with the result that Len lost his balance and fell, twisting his ankle painfully.

They got back into the van and after rubbing his ankle and swearing for several minutes, Len started the engine.

'We'll try somewhere else,' he said. He couldn't go home empty-handed after all this effort. 'There'll be another place hereabouts worth a try.'

'There's Ivy Lodge,' said Denis, ever helpful, mentioning the only other house in the village of which he had any knowledge. 'Belongs to a rich old lady. She's got lots of silver and stuff.' He wasn't sure about that, but he'd seen that it was full of that shiny dark old furniture people were so mad about. 'It's back in the village.'

Len turned the van round and they returned the way they had come, headlights dipped. Denis pointed out Ivy Lodge.

'But it's no size,' said Len, who had expected another mansion.

'Doesn't matter. She's got plenty,' said Denis. 'And a car, and money.' She'd had a wad of notes in her wallet when she paid him the other day. 'Course I haven't got a key.'

'No. Well, it wouldn't fit if you had, would it?' said Len nastily. His ankle was easing a little, still aching but he could operate the clutch with less effort. He parked beyond Ivy Lodge, two wheels up on the verge, leaving the driveway clear. Then the pair went through the gate.

'I can get in if she's asleep,' Len said. 'But you wait outside. Keep watch. I don't want you getting in my way.'

Denis followed him round as he looked at the windows, testing each in turn. All seemed to be held with security locks and were also double-glazed; then, round at the back, he saw one on the latch upstairs. Audrey always slept with her bedroom window open unless the weather was too bad.

Silently, Len pointed.

'It's upstairs,' Denis objected.

'What's wrong with that?' Len replied. It wasn't what he would have chosen but it proved his theory that you could get into most places without too much grief. 'I wonder if there's a ladder?'

'There's one in the garage,' said Denis.

Len made short work of undoing the padlock which fastened Audrey's garage doors together. He allowed Denis to help him carry the ladder to the rear of the house.

'What if she wakes up?' Denis asked, as Len tested the ladder, wincing a little as his ankle gave him a twinge.

'I'll deal with her,' Len said, and he let Denis see the cosh as he slid it down his sleeve and into his gloved hand.

11

Audrey had been dreaming about Hesther. In her
dream, she was walking through the fields with a small
girl in a print dress, holding a doll. Suddenly the dream
changed and she was in a cold, stark room with barred
windows, facing a haggard woman whom she scarcely
recognized, with huge pouches below her eyes and a
blank, sedated stare.

The nightmare made her start awake, and then she
heard a sound. She sat up in bed. A cool draught blew in
through the open window. The noise was probably the
branch of a tree creaking outside, or the old wood of the
house stretching. She lay down again, pulling the covers
round her, closing her eyes, trying to think of something
soothing, but it was useless. Her mind was full of the
image of Hesther as she had been during those months in
Holloway. Rupert had been stricken by Hesther's
deterioration, and her failure to respond to subsequent
medical treatment had been heartbreaking for them
both. For the umpteenth time, Audrey embarked on the
mental circle of self-examination and recrimination:
what could she have done that would have made a
difference? How could Hesther have been saved?

Certainly not by being sentenced to prison for minor
theft.

'To teach you a lesson,' the judge had said. 'And to act
as a warning to others.' No proper assessment of her
mental state was ever made, though she had been held
on remand for psychiatric investigation. There was a
doctor who showed concern for her, but was powerless to
get her proper treatment and she had seen him only
twice.

Audrey knew she would not sleep now. She pulled on

her green woollen dressing gown and tied the sash round her thin waist. Often at night she would fall asleep easily, her eyes closing as she read some undemanding book, and then an hour or so later she would start awake after a troubled dream and find her mind churning out of control. Sometimes making a cup of tea and reading again, or listening to the BBC World Service, would settle her down eventually.

She crossed to the door and found it ajar. That was odd. She always shut it when she went to bed, and it fitted properly, never coming open once it was closed. Then she saw the window was wide open, not latched as she always left it. Audrey barely took these facts in as she switched on the landing light and descended the stairs; she certainly did not suspect that there was an intruder in the house.

Len heard her coming. He was in the sitting room, going through her desk looking for a cheque book and anything else of use. He had decided to leave the bedroom, where there would be jewellery and maybe furs, until last, in case he disturbed her.

Audrey put on the hall light on her way to the kitchen. She opened the door and stretched out her hand to turn on that light, too. It was then that Len struck her from behind with his cosh.

Denis, bored outside the house with no active role to play in the burglary, had seen the bedroom light come on several minutes after Len had disappeared through the upstairs window.

What should he do? How could he warn Len?

He dithered about on the damp lawn. A blind was drawn across the dark kitchen window but it was not a perfect fit, and Denis peered anxiously through the gap at one side. He was in time to see, illuminated by the hall light from behind her, a figure in a green dressing gown, her grey hair in disorder, and the sudden O of her mouth

106

as Len delivered his blow. Audrey crumpled forward and Denis heard a curious muffled sound, part moan, part scream. Paralysed with horror, he saw Len advance, bend over the woman who now lay on the floor, and raise his arm to strike her again.

It was Denis's turn to utter a strangled groan. He clamped his hand to his mouth and ran back to the front of the house, where he crouched on the new patio, shaking with fear.

He must get away. Len had done murder, and he, Denis, had seen it and would be blamed when it was discovered. The exciting adventure had gone horribly wrong. There had been no talk of violence when all this was set up. Helping yourself to this and that was one thing; mugging folk was another, and Denis thought he was going to be sick. Gasping into his hands, which he clasped over his mouth, he ran out into the lane.

There was the van. He could escape.

He was trembling as he hurried towards it. He flung open the driver's door to see if the keys were there.

They were.

Denis got in and started the engine. Now he would have to prove he could drive.

Len made sure that the woman was out for the count. He administered a third blow to her head before he was satisfied that she was no further danger.

Funny that she went to the kitchen and not to the telephone. Maybe she hadn't heard him. Still, that was her hard luck; if she'd stayed quietly in bed no harm would have come to her. He was safe now, and could take his time.

He had already seen bottles in the dining room: whisky and sherry. The old cow liked her drop and so did he. Len pushed her with his foot before going off for a restorative nip. He drank from the bottle of Haig, wiping the rim with his leather-gloved hand before setting it down. That was better! No need to panic. He'd be well away before she came round. The kid needn't know there'd been a bit of rough stuff. Still, it meant he couldn't be let into the house to help carry things out to the van, as Len had intended; he was stupid enough to want to go looking for food and might see her lying there.

He'd stick to easily portable things.

Len found Audrey's jewellery – a pearl necklace, two rings, some brooches, and, beside the bed, a gold watch. He took her clock radio and a small colour television set she had in her bedroom, and a gold carriage-clock which he found on the sitting room mantelpiece. Her brown leather handbag was upstairs. He opened it and took her wallet which contained a bank card and about sixty pounds in cash. Her car keys were there, too, and a cheque book. He'd need a holdall to carry the stuff away.

He found several cases in a cupboard set into the wall on the landing, the zipped Antler bags Audrey used for her holiday trips. He packed up his haul, added the video recorder from beneath the larger television downstairs, which he left with regret; it was too heavy to manage alone. Then he opened the front door. He'd get rid of the kid now, tell him they'd best split.

But where was he? There was no sign of him. Len left the door ajar as he went searching for Denis. In the end he thought of going into the lane and he saw that the van had gone.

Bloody kid! What made him take off? He couldn't have seen anything of what had happened in the house. He'd just got bored, or was car crazy and wanted to get his hands on the van. What if there had been no car here for Len to use?

He'd got the keys, and the Fiat started at once. Len backed it out of the garage and loaded it up. He turned off the lights in the house and shut the door. Then he closed the garage and drove through the gates, turning away from Leckerton.

There wasn't a cat's eye in sight in the dark lane and the trees seemed to bend towards the twin beams of his headlights as he steered his way past Ford House again and over the bridge. It began to rain and he struggled to find the switch for the wipers. The damn kid would have known at once where it was.

He must get to a town. Not home: he didn't want to take the Fiat anywhere familiar, where he could be recognized by some nosy copper who knew his face, but in some other town, with people about, street lights, traffic, Len would feel safe, and he could lose himself and the car in the bustle. There were times when it seemed to Len that he was treading on top of the world, and this was one of them: he'd carried off a successful job, avoided being caught, and got quite a respectable haul. The cheque book and bank card would mean he could count on some money. He must simply decide where to go.

The lanes seemed to last for ever. He took an occasional turn one way or another; then he saw a sign indicating Swindon. That was a big place. He could go there.

He headed west.

Denis's departure from Coxton was shaky. He crashed the gears and scraped the side of the van against a wall as he turned into the village street. Still, there was no traffic about to get in his way and he moved jerkily onwards towards the Leckerton road. After a while he felt calmer and began to think about what he was doing. He had studied Alan and other drivers; he knew the procedure. His progress became steadier but then a car came towards him, its lights dazzling him, making him want to veer towards it. Concentrating hard, he managed to hold his course. It seemed easiest when he went slowly, but you shouldn't grind along in low gear. Now he realized that he had gained nothing at all from the night's expedition, not even as much as a pound coin, only the chance to drive the van.

Could he get it safely back so that Alan would never know he had borrowed it?

Approaching Leckerton, more cars came towards him and there was one on his tail, its lights reflected in the mirror on the door distracting him. Denis set his mind to keeping in to the kerb, and when the driver behind saw his chance, he passed. Denis went faster then, briefly reckless. He was getting the feel of it now. It wasn't so difficult.

The street lights in Leckerton made things easier. He drove slowly along, not impeded by other traffic as he made the various turns, but when he tried to put the van back in the space it had occupied outside the house he met trouble. Luckily Alan had left it next to the driveway, which had to be kept clear for Mrs Dove, so he had some room to manoeuvre, but as he went back and forth in first gear and reverse, he thought the noise would waken the whole of Birch Street. He stalled the engine twice and, lacking the skill to inch forwards, hit the car in front of him. He sat trembling, forcing himself to reverse away. When he finally stopped and turned off the engine he was shaking all over, crouching there in the driving seat, wet through with perspiration and weak with shock.

But he had done it.

Lights off, he sat gratefully in the darkness. Now he had somehow to return the key to Alan's jacket.

When he had calmed down, Denis got out of the van and looked at the car in front to see if he had done much damage. There were several dents and scrapes on the paintwork, and the bumper was bent. He couldn't have done all that. The car was an old Austin Maxi, long past its prime and regularly parked in the road. Even if some of the marks were new, the owner wouldn't be able to prove it. Denis looked at the van. It had a good strong front, and there was no obviously raw scratch. He glanced at the wing which he had scraped leaving Coxton. There was a slight scar. With luck Alan might not notice it for a few days and then he might blame a passing motorist for damaging it when it was parked.

It was getting on for four o'clock in the morning. Denis let himself into the house again and crept upstairs. He opened Alan and Tracy's door. This time he did not need to enter the room. A small moan came from within as he felt for the jacket on its hook, and dropped the key in the pocket.

He'd done it! He'd got away with it!

Denis went back downstairs as fast as he could, the tensions slackening. Suddenly, now, his bladder was bursting. He urinated into the bushes in the front garden, sighing with relief, then got into the back of the van. Climbing into his sleeping bag, zipping it up, fitting his earphones over his head to blot out the silence, Denis felt safe. Only then did he spare a thought for Mrs Bannerman, brutally struck down. She might not be dead after all. She could have come round by now and have called the police.

In the ground-floor room at the back of the house, old Mrs Crow awoke. She got up to make herself some tea. Steve Fox, in his room, slept until six when his alarm went and the radio began to play. Tracy and Alan woke up to make love before it was time to start their working day. Only Mrs Dove had heard the noise in the night as Denis struggled to park the van, and she pulled the duvet over her head to muffle the sound as she buried herself in sleep.

Next morning, Alan expected to find the keys in the right hand pocket of his jacket and was mildly surprised that they were in the left, but he gave that no special thought as he departed in his usual early morning rush. Nor did he notice that the van was not parked as tight against the kerb as usual.

12

By the time Jim reached the outskirts of Reading people
had settled down to their evening's occupation, whatever that might be, but though it would be some time
before the pubs and cinemas emptied, there was enough
traffic to worry him; he had not driven since his arrest.
He kept well below the speed limit; Jim had always been
a cautious motorist.

As he approached his own house a tight feeling came
into his throat and his heart beat hard under his stolen
anorak. It seemed to thunder in his chest as he stopped
the car and looked at the chinks of light showing between
the curtains. Maureen was in there, with their child.

What was he going to say to her? How could he win
her round? What if he rang the bell and the man
answered?

Jim's resolution faltered, now that fantasy must be
replaced by fact. He sat staring at the house for over half
an hour before he decided that he must wait till
morning. Perhaps he could catch Maureen when she left
for work, or to take Nicola to school. How did she
organize her routine? He knew not the slightest thing
about her present daily life.

To postpone action was a big relief, but he must avoid
being picked up before he had accomplished his
purpose. Surely Maureen would be moved by the fact
that winning her back meant so much to him that he had
absconded?

He had better dump the pick-up. It would be stupid to
get caught with that and by now the police might be
searching for it. He left it, with his prison jacket inside it,
in the station car park where, at this hour, there was
ample space. He shoved the key into the pocket of his

anorak and his fingers met some objects – a few coins, a twist of paper. He pulled it out and saw that it was a five-pound note. What luck! Now he could get something to eat, but he did not dare risk the station buffet. Was it even open at this hour? He'd be conspicuous if he went to see.

Wearily, he lifted his bicycle out of the pick-up and rode away from the city centre, by now almost incapable of rational thought. So much positive action had exhausted him. He was unused to that sort of effort; rearranging figures to appropriate money was merely mental exercise, a cleaner crime than stealing something tangible. He felt no guilt about taking the pick-up or the anorak, or his intention of spending the five pounds if he found a suitable café.

Riding on, he reached a district of large houses, few of them now occupied. Most were offices and empty until work began next day. Jim felt cold and afraid. He was too tired to ride on any further, and making sure that no passing car could see him, he turned into the entrance of the next large house with unlit, uncurtained windows, and thrust his bicycle into the shelter of some shrubs in the front garden. Then he went round to the back of the building, where he might find shelter in a garden shed or summer house, or even in a porch. He would not try to break into the house itself as it was sure to be wired up to an alarm.

He stumbled around in the darkness. Without a torch, he could distinguish very little, but at the rear there was a row of outbuildings which had once been the coal shed and store space. Jim tried the doors. One was loosely secured by a padlock on a hasped hook and it would be very easy to unfasten. Surely this wouldn't be connected to the alarm? If it was, he'd soon hear it and could be away on his bike before the police arrived.

He took the key of the pick-up from his pocket and used it to prise off the loop through which the padlock was attached, pausing as he worked, ready for the wail to start, but all was silent. He opened the door and slipped inside, sensing a solid mass ahead of him, and his outstretched hand met metal, but it was cool. He had found the boiler room.

Jim sank down on the floor, drawing his knees up, shuddering with fatigue and fright. Now he was safe for a while. It was dry in his retreat, and after a time his shudders eased and he laid his head on his knees. He was too stressed to sleep properly, and his shelter grew cold for the boiler did not operate at night, but eventually he lapsed into a fitful doze.

He woke early in the morning, and soon his refuge got warmer as the boiler came on and the pipes leading from it to the house heated up. It made a great roaring noise, but it was comforting and he enjoyed it for a while. He must not linger, though, for cleaners might soon arrive, or a handyman whose job it was to maintain this monster.

Jim left his shelter. He could not refasten the lock and it would be obvious that someone had entered the place. His bicycle was still under the bush; he retrieved it and pedalled off into the early morning traffic. Now it would be safe to go to the station. He parked his cycle outside and went into the washroom. Without a razor, there were limits to what he could do about his appearance but he felt better after a wash. He hurried, keeping his anorak on, fearful of someone identifying his prison shirt and overalls. By now the call would have gone out for him all over the country.

After two cups of coffee and some sandwiches in the buffet, Jim felt better. Now for Maureen.

His cycle had gone.

He had had no padlock for it. He hadn't needed one, working from the prison. You'd think it would be safe for half an hour. What a world it was.

With a feeling of fatalism, he caught a bus out to the suburb where he had lived for the span of his marriage. He tendered a pound coin. But for the money in the stolen jacket, he couldn't have eaten or taken this ride.

The bus dropped him at the end of the road. This time there must be no turning back, and Jim's feet seemed made of lead as he walked past the neat houses with their white wood trim and bright tiled roofs towards his own. He supposed it was still his.

In daylight, he saw that the front door, formerly green, had been painted blue. It gave him a shock and made the place seem strangely alien. He looked up at the windows and imagined Maureen moving about inside, perhaps in her housecoat, preparing breakfast. Was that man sitting at the table in the kitchen, Nicola beside him, eating cornflakes from the bowls they'd bought at Habitat?

Jim walked straight up the path and pressed the bell. As the chimes echoed inside the house he realized that he had brought nothing for Nicola, no toy, not even any sweets; he could have bought something at the station but it was too late now.

The door opened and Maureen stood there. Her hair was done a new way which altered her appearance, but she was still beautiful.

Jim saw her expression change from puzzlement to a look of horror as she recognized the gaunt man with the grey-stubbled chin who stood before her. Shock stopped her from banging the door in his face, and before she could recover enough to do so, Jim had thrust his foot in the way. He elbowed past her into the hall.

'What do you want?' she ground out. 'What are you doing here? You haven't been let out.' It was a statement, not a question.

'I had to see you,' Jim replied. 'Is he here? Your – that man you're living with?'

Maureen shook her head.

'How do you know about him?' she asked, her voice faint.

'Never mind.' Jim felt a surge of adrenaline giving him energy. He had the initiative and was safe for the moment. 'You never write. You've had the telephone number changed. You don't visit. Why?' he accused.

Maureen was beginning to recover.

'I don't want anything more to do with you,' she said. 'I told that woman the other day. What do you mean by bursting in here?'

She had looked at him with scorn, even contempt, before; she had not, however, displayed the disgust and loathing he saw now on her face.

'I had to see you,' Jim repeated.

He moved towards her, his arms outstretched. Somehow he must wipe that look off her face.

'Don't touch me!' she cried, backing away.

'Can't we talk? Can't we plan for the future?' he begged her. 'And where's Nicola? I want to see her.'

'I won't let you. Do you know what you look like? You're dirty – dirty – dirty – dirty.' She almost sobbed, then took a breath and hissed at him. 'Get out of here.'

'Mummy, is that a bad man?' came a voice. 'It's a stranger,' and suddenly Nicola was there, in her pyjamas, clinging to Maureen's skirt and staring at him with an expression that mirrored her mother's.

Jim saw that the child he thought about daily was terrified of him. Moreover, she did not recognize her own father.

'It's all right, Nicky. I'm not a stranger,' Jim said, bending down. 'Don't you know me?' I'm your – '

'Don't worry, Nicola. He isn't going to hurt us and he's just going. Go upstairs and get dressed,' said Maureen.

She glared at Jim as she spoke, and he stood up slowly. She was lovely and desirable, and she hated him.

'Mummy?' Nicola's voice was questioning.

'It's all right, Nicola. Run along,' said Maureen.

Casting a backward glance, Nicola obeyed. They heard her plodding steps ascending.

'She's my daughter,' Jim said. 'I've got rights.'

'Not now, you haven't,' said Maureen. 'You gave those up when you did what you did.' She sensed the short battle was won and moved away from the wall that had been her support. 'I've got a chance of a future now, for her and for me, and if you care anything at all about either of us, you'll not mess that up. We've both had enough shame and disgrace.'

'You should have told me,' Jim said. 'You should have written.'

To her dismay, Maureen saw tears start in his red-rimmed eyes. He looked terrible, and years older.

'Well, what could I say?' she answered, truculently, because she knew she was in the wrong. Still, she'd see it through now. 'I'm getting a divorce,' she went on. 'It's been more than two years. It'll be easy.' And if he tried to oppose it, there was always unreasonable conduct: going to gaol was surely that.

'What about Nicola?' he asked.

'If you want what's best for her, you'll stay out of her life,' said Maureen. 'How's she going to like having a convict for a father, when she's old enough to under-stand? It's much better if she thinks you're dead.' She went on, in a gentler tone. 'She loves Trevor. He's wonderful with her.'

So that was his name: Trevor. Jim felt like spitting.

'And that's supposed to make me feel better?'

'Yes.'

She would have left him anyway. She was a proud and fiery woman, and he bored her. Some man would have lured her away, whatever happened; it was simply this Trevor who had come along. He sank down on the floor, drawing his knees to his chin and, bowing his head, he began to weep.

118

Maureen felt a kind of awkward pity. Now she could afford to be generous.

'They'll come looking for you here,' she said. 'That's certain. I won't say you've been. It'll give you time to get away.'

'Thank you.' Jim's voice was muffled.

'It's not for your sake. It's for ours,' said Maureen. 'I don't want any more trouble. I'll give you some money. The best thing you can do is give yourself up, and don't mention that you've been here.'

As he heard her footsteps move away, he raised his head and looked slowly round the small hall, with its gleaming floor, his handiwork. He stayed there, motionless, until Maureen came back.

'Get up. Go away,' she ordered.

Jim gazed up at her. She was standing above him, holding out two ten-pound notes. Slowly he got to his feet and took the money.

'Is that all?' he said.

She misunderstood.

'It's all I can spare,' she snapped. Then she opened the door. 'Now go.'

Moving like an automaton, Jim obeyed. He had not touched her, not even the hem of her garment.

There was no cover nearby from which he could watch her leave later, with Nicola. Jim could not stand outside the house until they emerged. He stumbled off down the road, not caring where he was going, occasionally taking a turning one way or the other. If a policeman had come along then, he might have surrendered, but some thread of sanity made him aware that if he was picked up so near the house, Maureen would not avoid involvement. Perhaps he could get himself all the way back to Lockley and make out that he had hidden locally, just for the hell of it. He could send her back her twenty pounds.

But why should he? She'd accepted what he gave her over the years, hadn't she? Her Habitat curtains and china, her pretty furniture, her holidays abroad. He'd spend her money and enjoy it. At least he'd have a good meal, and perhaps a shave. Not here though. He'd have to put miles between them.

Jim had been gone less than a quarter of an hour when Maureen's bell rang again.

This time it was a uniformed policewoman who stood outside. Because Trevor Black was in the traffic division, she knew nothing of him or of his connection with Maureen.

'I'd better come in, love,' she said, when Maureen opened the door, and added, 'You're going to have a bit of a shock when I tell you why I'm here.'

Oddly, Maureen was glad that she already knew the reason. She steeled herself to react with surprise when told that her husband, Jim Sawyer, had absconded.

'He's most likely holed up in the area near the prison,' said the policewoman. 'But sometimes they run because they want to come home.'

'I'll let you know if he turns up,' said Maureen calmly, hoping that Nicola, who was now eating her breakfast, would not suddenly appear and mention their earlier visitor. 'There's no place for him here now,' she added.

The policewoman thought that she looked somewhat strained but that was hardly surprising, and no doubt the news was a shock.

'Are you coping all right?' she asked.

'Oh yes. I've got a good job,' said Maureen. 'And I'm going to get a divorce and get married again.' She'd get on with it now and make Trevor come up to scratch. He'd be a protection when finally Jim was released. Who better than a policeman? 'My boyfriend's a copper,' she added.

'Is that right?' The officer grinned. 'Well, good for you.'

120

If Jim was picked up along the road, Maureen hoped he would keep his head and not mention that he had been to the house. In a weird way, she did not want him to be taken, though his recapture was inevitable. Sometimes men managed to escape and vanish, but he wouldn't; he wasn't a crook in that sense, with a network of crooked friends to help him, though he might have acquired some in prison.

She'd tell Trevor that Jim had broken out; that was all he needed to know.

13

Yvonne had heard Charles come home very late after his dinner, but she had pretended to be asleep and he crept quietly about, undressing in the bathroom and getting into bed carefully so as not to waken her. There had been a time when she would have been eager to greet him, no matter how late he was. In a way he was glad not to have to make any effort now; there was always Saturday night.

In the morning, when she asked how the evening had gone, he was non-committal. Still tired and mildly hung over, he did not want the bother of describing what had happened.

Yvonne remembered the many nights when, very late, he had left her to return to Olivia. What had he told Olivia then? Had he really been to a business dinner this time? What he had done once, he could repeat.

He left home so early that, now the mornings were dark, she had given up coming down to have coffee with him before he went. Instead, she snatched at the chance of an extra half hour in bed, often with Robin tucked up beside her. Today he had appeared while Charles was in the bathroom shaving. He had wandered about in his pyjamas with Thomas the Tank Engine displayed across his chest and Charles had ordered him quite crossly to go back to his own bed. Robin had uttered a few shrieks of protest for form's sake before obeying, but as soon as his father had gone downstairs he had reappeared, singing cheerfully.

After a while, Yvonne took a grip on herself, put on her dressing gown and went down to the kitchen where Charles was standing warming his back at the Aga and drinking his instant coffee, a report in his hand. His briefcase was open on the table. Perhaps it really had been a business dinner.

Yvonne wished she had stayed upstairs as he glanced up impatiently and then made an effort to smile.

'My car wouldn't start yesterday,' she said. 'I had to walk down to the school. It was tipping with rain. Mrs Bannerman brought us back.'

'I haven't time to look at it now,' said Charles. 'You'll have to cope.'

'I didn't mean you to,' said Yvonne.

'It's the damp, I expect,' said Charles. 'If you run a hair dryer on the plugs, it might do the trick.'

After offering her this counsel, he left.

He'd got jump leads. He could have started the car with those. It wouldn't have taken ten minutes. Yvonne sighed. A year ago, he'd have done it. But a year ago he was living near his work.

While the children were having their breakfast, she went out to try to start the car. There wasn't a sign of life in it, and the rain was pouring down.

Audrey Bannerman had offered to run the children to school. Faced with another wet walk with the three of them, Yvonne decided to take her at her word. She and Robin could stay at home so that she need not make a double trip. Audrey had said she always woke early. At eight fifteen Yvonne dialled her number.

There was no answer.

Fifteen minutes later, she tried again, then five minutes after that. Still no reply, and now they must leave or they would be late.

In boots and raincoats, with Robin strapped into his pushchair and holding an umbrella over his head, they set off. Philip and Emily had wanted to go alone, but Yvonne would not give Philip the responsibility of getting his small sister safely there.

Once they were outside it didn't seem so bad, and all

123

of them had glowing cheeks by the time they reached the school.

Passing Ivy Lodge on the way back, Yvonne paused. It was odd that Audrey hadn't answered the telephone. Perhaps it was out of order. Sometimes, when that happened, it sounded to the caller as though the number was ringing. But she might be ill. She was getting on, though she seemed quite fit; hard to tell how old she was, really. Yvonne hesitated at the gate, then saw that the curtains were drawn at every window facing the front. Audrey must have overslept. But wouldn't the telephone have woken her? Not if she had no extension in her bedroom.

Yvonne pushed Robin through the gates and up the short drive. There was a milk bottle on the step and a newspaper was thrust through the letter box. Lucky Audrey to have one delivered: the boys would not go as far as Ford House and Yvonne saw no paper except *The Times* when Charles brought it back. She never bothered to read it. She'd no time for a paper, really, but she sometimes thought it would be nice to see one occasionally.

She glanced at the garage. The doors were closed.

It was after nine o'clock. Yvonne rang the bell. It echoed through the house and after a pause she rang it again. Nothing happened.

Yvonne parked Robin in the front porch, took away the umbrella before he used it to damage himself or Audrey's property, put the brake on the pushchair and walked round to the back of the house.

She saw the ladder at once, and above it, the open window.

Yvonne tried the back door before she climbed the ladder, but it was securely bolted. The blind was down, and she tried to peer round it but could see very little.

She went back to Robin, who was now getting

impatient, demanding to be released. She wheeled him round to the back of the house and told him to watch her climb the ladder.

'I'll come too,' he offered.

'No, you won't,' she said. 'Be good and I'll let you out in a minute.'

At least she could see him while she made her ascent. Intending at first only to look through the window, Yvonne climbed up. She saw Audrey's empty, disturbed bed, and the dressing-table drawers left open. Audrey's handbag lay on the bed, her compact and comb beside it.

Yvonne, in her jeans and waxed jacket, climbed over the window sill and made her way through the dim house. She pulled back the landing curtain to let in some light and looked in every room, calling Audrey's name as she went.

Then she found her.

There was blood on the floor of the kitchen, and Yvonne thought that Audrey was dead. But although her face, which was turned to one side, felt chilled, it was not icy and she seemed to be faintly breathing.

Yvonne rushed to the telephone in the hall and dialled the emergency services. Then she ran upstairs and pulled blankets from Audrey's bed and brought them down to cover her. She heard Robin begin to wail in the garden and went out to bring him indoors after she had put the kettle on, closing the kitchen door so that he could not see Audrey's still, huddled shape. She put him in the sitting room and turned on the television, telling him to stay there. Then she hunted upstairs for a hot-water bottle, in vain until she thought of looking in Audrey's bed, where she found a blue one in a hand-knitted cover which she filled and laid against the unconscious woman's stomach. There was nothing else she could do.

Robin was thrilled when the ambulance and the police arrived, and he enjoyed being driven home with his mother in the police car, but that didn't happen for quite some time.

'What relatives has she?'

The uniformed constable who had arrived first at Ivy Lodge, just after the ambulance had rushed through the village with its siren wailing, turned to Yvonne as they stood together in the garden.

The rain had stopped but the air was heavy with damp which clung to every vestige of leaf and blade of grass. A few late chrysanthemums bowed sodden heads in a bed to the right of the house. Dead leaves lay on the grass under an apple tree, and it seemed to Yvonne that the whole place was shrouded in a miasma of mourning.

PC Lucking had explained that they must not add their own finger and footprints to those already in the house because the CID would be coming along to investigate. But of necessity, Yvonne's entrance and attempts at first aid, and the arrival of the ambulance men, had overlaid any clues there might have been. Robin was kicking about among the leaves. He said he was hunting hedgehogs.

'She's divorced,' Yvonne said. 'She had a daughter, who died. I haven't heard her mention anybody. Someone else might know – a neighbour – the vicar –' Her voice trailed off.

'We'll inquire,' said the constable. 'But she lived alone, and you know of no one who should be sent for at once?'

'No,' said Yvonne, shaking her head. It seemed so inexpressibly sad. 'Who could have done this? Some casual thief?'

'Probably,' said the constable. 'She must have heard something and surprised him.'

At this moment, the ambulance men came out of the house with their burden. One of them shook his head at the constable.

'Is she dead? She wasn't,' Yvonne said.

The constable went over to ask while Yvonne prevented Robin from going to inspect the patient. Audrey would want nightdresses, her washing things, she thought: but perhaps there was no urgency about any of that. She might not need them.

Lucking returned.

'She's not too good, but she's still alive,' he told Yvonne. 'A man escaped from Lockley Prison last night,' he added. 'He may have done this.' All patrols had been instructed to look out for Jim Sawyer.

'Some prisoners have been working in the village,' said Yvonne. 'They were tidying up the graveyard. I don't think there was any trouble, but I was a bit surprised at the freedom they had to move around.' Then she remembered. 'One of them worked for Mrs Bannerman. He did some painting and gardening, I think.'

'I wonder if that could have been Sawyer,' said Lucking.

Detective Inspector Wright wondered the same thing when he arrived later. It wouldn't take long to find out.

Len had decided that Swindon was too near Leckerton to start using the stolen card and cheque book, and to dump the car which now he dared not risk trying to sell. Besides, it was not yet morning when he got there.

He went on to Bristol, a city strange to him, but it was large and there would be anonymous areas where he could move unnoticed. He was still elated. When he had loaded up with more loot, he'd go home to a fine welcome from Bet and the kids.

He'd hit the woman hard, but if she'd stayed in her bed she'd have been unharmed, or so he told himself now. As for the kid, Denis, it was as well that he had scarpered. He hadn't the stomach for seeing a job through, that was obvious. Still, the van had been useful.

Len felt a moment's unease lest the kid shop him, but decided he'd be too keen on preserving his own skin. Besides, he didn't know what had happened in the kitchen. If he got picked up driving the van he'd be intent on saving himself and it was better to be charged with a driving offence than breaking and entering, not to mention assault. No, he was safe enough.

He whistled, spinning along in the Fiat. There was a big service area outside Bristol and he stopped there for breakfast, enjoying an excellent meal among representatives and businessmen on their way to work. Traffic was piling into the city when he entered it. He drove towards the centre, and when he saw a multi-storey car park, he turned into it. The car would be safe from observation there, if an alert was out for it, and he would merge with the ordinary folk on the street.

Before he got out of the car he did a little job on Audrey's bank card, rubbing her signature down with a fine piece of glass paper. He signed A. Bannerman over the top, in bold writing. It would stand up to a cursory examination; only someone inspecting it closely would notice what he had done. How lucky that her name was not printed in full on the card, showing that it belonged to a woman.

He did a great deal of shopping, charging things and signing the flimsy forms A. Bannerman, spending under fifty pounds in each shop so that no one would ring up for sanction. He bought spirits, radios, a telephone, and when he could carry no more, he took them back to the Fiat and stashed them away. They were all highly saleable and would bring in easy money.

Then he decided to cash some cheques and had such success at three different branches of Audrey's bank that he made up his mind to hire a car.

He paid cash, using his own driving licence, and acquired a handsome Sierra which he drove to the park where he had left the Fiat. He had to wait for a while before a space near the smaller car became vacant, but at last one was free, two slots away from the Fiat. How lucky could you be?

Len transferred his haul from one car to the other, both of them backed against the wall. Nobody passing took any notice.

Minutes later, he was driving the Sierra down the ramp and heading for home. The Fiat might not be found for days.

After his nocturnal adventures, Denis had decided to spend the next day safely at school.

He had been certain that Alan would notice the van was not parked as he had left it, even if he did not at first see the scrape it had received, but he didn't. He got straight in, started it up and drove off, with Tracy beside him. He took her to the bus stop every morning.

Denis went up to their room for his breakfast. Tracy always left the bread out, and a packet of cereal, and after the first few days he had begun to tidy up, washing his own mug and plate and anything she had left by the basin which did double duty as sink. This morning he felt hungry and after eating a large bowl of cornflakes, helped himself to two slices of toast and margarine thickly spread with jam. He didn't think about the old woman at first, but as he was drinking his tea he started to wonder what had happened after he left Ivy Lodge. If she had come round quite quickly and phoned the police, Len might have been caught already.

Had she got a good look at him? He'd hit her from behind, Denis had seen that, but she might have glimpsed his face. One thing was certain, and that was that she hadn't seen Denis.

If the police hadn't arrested Len, they'd be all over the place today, harassing everyone in sight. He'd better not hang about in town in case they fancied roughing him up. Denis couldn't risk questions about being a truant. It should all have ended by now. He should have had money and been on his way to join a gang in the smoke.

The brave would-be gangster washed his face, found his school trousers and a once-white shirt, and knotted his tie round his neck. He passed Tracy's brush through his hair which was getting too long for his taste and set off for school, where his appearance was greeted with surprise and a good deal of sarcasm. He would have earned a reproof for his grubby appearance if the school had not formed the opinion that his home conditions were far from ideal. The various notes that had excused his absence were regarded as suspect, and only the fact that his birthday was so near and he was academically such an unpromising pupil had prevented a proper inquiry into the true position.

Now, when asked how he was, he remembered that allegedly he had been ill.

'Not too wonderful,' he said, putting on a brave look.

Various boys who had seen him about the town tittered, and made muffled comments. However, beneath his naturally ruddy complexion, he was pale, and there were dark smudges under his eyes. He bent earnestly over the text the rest of the class had studied during his absence but his boredom threshold had not altered, and soon he began to sigh and gaze out of the window.

Unable to concentrate, Denis left after the dinner break.

The cinema would soon be open, and he could spend the afternoon safely there, in the dark.

Later, he'd decide what to do next.

Jim had to see Nicola properly, just once. He had to wipe out the image of her frightened little face as she asked if he was a bad man. Children were warned against strangers.

He turned into a side road. Further on was a cluster of

shops which served the estate, and beyond them was the school.

If he waited nearby, he would see her arrive. Did Maureen bring her, or some friend? He had no notion of the child's routine.

It was really no wonder that Nicola had not recognized him, since clearly her mother was hoping he would soon be forgotten. There'd be no photographs around, no affectionate talk about him. He'd seen other cons receive warm greetings from their children, although visiting was always a strange, unnatural time. But he had been gone for over two years. How could a child her age remember?

He plodded on, an unremarkable man in his stolen anorak and dark trousers. The streets were busy now, with the rush hour under way. Children going to school walked past, older ones in groups together, smaller ones with mothers. Jim fell in behind a mother with a small boy beside her and two toddlers in a double pushchair. Soon they came to the school, a modern building with big windows and an asphalt playground.

A crossing patrol warden in her overall and cap held up the traffic to allow the children to cross the road by the school. Jim walked past and stood on the opposite corner. He'd see Maureen if she came along. If someone else brought Nicola, he might have trouble identifying his own child. She'd grown so much! In that fleeting moment he had seen such a change in her. You'd think Maureen could at least have sent him some photos. How cruel she was! He had never realized what a core of steel she possessed.

Then he saw them both, Maureen in her pink raincoat, her blonde curls standing out round her head, holding an umbrella in one hand and Nicola by the other. The little girl wore a green duffle coat; white socks twinkled below. There was another little girl with them, with red hair. Jim watched the trio cross the road under

131

the benevolent gaze of the lollipop lady and disappear into the yard. So Maureen was careful; she took the child right into the building. He was glad of that. You never knew who was hanging about these days.

Nicola had been chatting eagerly to her mother as they came along the road. Neither of them had glanced his way.

Jim moved off before Maureen emerged from the school yard. If she saw him again, she might change her mind about turning him in.

14

Felicity Bannerman saw the police car coming up the drive.

She had been down the garden to pick parsley and dill to decorate the salmon mousse she had made for tonight's dinner party. She and Rupert occasionally entertained other couples of similar ages and tastes, most of whom they had known for years although Felicity had been absent from the area during her first marriage.

She had been happy then. She had enjoyed stations in Malta and Gibraltar, where Harry had had shore jobs, and she had settled easily into the house near Fareham which they later bought as a base and where she had spent long spells with the children while he was at sea. Harry was charming and handsome, and he had swept her off her feet when they met at a dance just after the war. Now, she understood that he had been ready to marry then and was looking for a suitable wife, programmed, as she was, to fall in love. It had worked out well enough; with three children born in quick succession, she had been too busy to question her own contentment, though she was often lonely. Their reunions had always been romantic, and Harry had always gone again before either could feel any strain. She became efficient at coping with things on her own and made friends with other wives similarly placed. Sometimes his return was almost a nuisance, interrupting the routine she had evolved.

When she met Rupert again, their easy friendship, long established in youth, was soon re-established, and when she learned about Hesther's problems Felicity felt infinite pity for the girl and her parents. Only gradually did Rupert reveal that he and Audrey lived like amiable strangers.

'She can't face what's happened to Hesther,' he had told her when the trouble began. 'She has such rigid ideas – high standards, if you like – that she can't understand how Hesther fell into such a way of life. She won't talk about it.'

'You should make her,' said Felicity.

'I can't. I can't bear quarrels,' said Rupert.

'Must a discussion become a quarrel?'

'It can if the least comment is interpreted as criticism, which is what happens with Audrey. But you see, I understand her. She's so insecure, and I've never been able to make her feel otherwise. It's my failure,' said Rupert.

'She was an odd, touchy girl,' said Felicity. 'I liked her because she was so straightforward – there was no guile in her – and I was sorry for her because she was socially inept. She got a lot of teasing and she never lost her temper, just went quiet, and then would come out with some hopelessly inappropriate remark in an attempt to put things right. She had a genius for putting her foot in – asking about someone's mother, for instance, when everyone else knew she was terribly ill and likely to die.'

'But she asked,' Rupert said. 'She wanted to do the right thing.'

'Yes, but she couldn't find the proper response – the sympathetic touch that comes naturally to some people. I thought she'd learn in time, and that being friends with me would help.'

'It did, to some extent,' said Rupert.

'It brought her you,' said Felicity.

'Mm.' He had felt protective towards her, and that was a sort of love, Rupert supposed.

'If she'd had brothers and sisters, she'd have lost some of her prickles,' said Felicity. 'But she was the one ewe lamb of that elderly couple – the hardheaded businessman who'd come up from the bottom, and that sweet, timid wife. If they'd lived in some comfortable house in a town among other wealthy industrialists, it might have been easier for Audrey to learn to mix, but there she was, isolated in that huge place in the middle of nowhere, with no friends.'

'Ford House wasn't all that large,' Rupert demurred. 'Not as big as Tettlebury.'

'No, and you thought she'd slot easily from one to the other. In some ways, I suppose she did.'

'She slid from one form of isolation to another,' said Rupert. 'I can't bridge it.'

Their affair had been almost inevitable, but they had been discreet. Felicity did not want to hurt Harry, and she was sometimes astounded at her own duplicity, but like other lovers since time immemorial, she had decided that as long as he never found out, no harm would be done, and Rupert felt the same about Audrey.

He found it easier to be patient with Audrey and her brusque ways when he knew that he would soon be alone with Felicity. Even after years of marriage, Audrey would ask someone met at a party why she had chosen to wear that particular shade of yellow, implying that she thought the colour unbecoming, when all she had intended was to show interest in an unusual choice. As a dinner guest, she would refuse some dish she disliked, unable to toy with even a token fragment.

'Why should I?' she would retort, if Rupert suggested a little dissembling. 'It's so wasteful, leaving food on your plate.'

She would never compromise.

Hesther could dissemble only too well, as they discovered. She had her father's charm but no great self-confidence. By the time Audrey understood that the girl was more like her than her father though less resilient than either, it was too late to prevent her headlong descent into self-destruction.

Though Felicity often thought of Audrey, and with guilty remorse even now, she was not in Felicity's mind as she crossed the garden to greet the police officer getting out of his white Ford Escort. She saw that he was not the constable who lived in the village, and who, although he was attached to headquarters in Swalton, knew most of what happened in Tettlebury.

'Good morning,' Felicity said in a questioning tone as she approached the man.

'Mrs Bannerman?' he asked.

'Yes.'

'Is Mr Bannerman at home? Mr Rupert Bannerman?'

'He's over at the farm office with the VAT man,' said Felicity. 'Can I help?'

'Well, I don't know about that,' said PC Wilson. 'It's more a question of breaking some news to him.'

'News? What sort of news?'

Policemen didn't break good news. One had come in the night to tell Felicity that her son had had a car accident, fortunately not very serious, and Rupert had told her how another had woken him and Audrey one night to tell them that Hesther was dead.

'It's about Mrs Audrey Bannerman,' said Wilson.

'Audrey?'

'She's a relative? Mrs Bannerman of Coxton?'

'My husband's first wife,' said Felicity. 'What's happened? Is she ill?'

'You could say so,' said Wilson cautiously. He wetted his lips with his tongue. This was a tricky one.

'Well, either she is or she isn't,' said Felicity with a tartness worthy of Audrey herself.

'I'm sorry to say she's met with an accident,' said Wilson unhappily. 'She's in a critical condition in intensive care in Leckerton Hospital, and there seems to be no next of kin. Except possibly Mr Bannerman, that is. The local officers found his name and address at her house.

'Oh, poor Audrey! How dreadful,' Felicity exclaimed. 'I suppose it was a car accident. It's not likely to have been her fault. She's a very good driver.' Audrey was, in fact, efficient in a great many ways and intolerant of lesser capabilities in others.

'No. I'm afraid she was mugged,' said Wilson. 'Someone broke into her house during the night and she was attacked.'

'Oh no! That's awful!' Felicity was appalled. 'Come in while I ring through to my husband.'

She led the way into the mellow old house built of Cotswold stone, and she knew as she stepped over the threshold that she would never forget this moment. Life could be changed – even lost – all in seconds, and Rupert was going to experience terrible guilt.

Wires and tubes ran from Audrey's body to various pieces of equipment. A heart monitor ticked.

Rupert stood gazing down at her, and as a nurse moved the covering over her legs, he had a brief sight of her ugly, distorted feet. The glimpse made her real to him, for the deeply unconscious, grey-faced woman, her head bandaged, looked like no one he knew. Her hand lay exposed, the knuckles large, the metacarpal bones standing out against the pale transparent skin. They were capable hands; she was a good gardener, a good cook, and a skilful knitter.

A policewoman sat nearby in case she came round and could give a description of her attacker.

Rupert had seen a doctor who had said that her skull had been fractured. They had operated to relieve pressure but at this stage it was difficult to prognosticate. Her heart was not very good, he added.

To Rupert she looked as if she was dead already. Was she being kept alive solely by all this machinery? What could he do to help her? He put his hand over the thin little shell of bones that was hers. She felt cold. A sense of failure oppressed him as he turned to the policewoman, who told him that routine inquiries were under way and that it was thought the attacker might be an escaped convict who had once done some work for Audrey.

So she was still mixed up with prisons. Before she moved to Coxton, while she was living in that impersonal flat in Sussex to which she had gone after they parted, she had been involved with some form of after care. What had happened to Hesther had shown them both that terrible things could be done in the name of justice, and Audrey, aware that it was too late to help her own child, had tried to do something for others.

He never quite knew what had made her give up and move back to Coxton. Perhaps she had known that her heart had begun to fail and had sought comfort in familiar surroundings.

He went straight from the hospital to the local police headquarters to find out what was being done and why a dangerous man had been allowed to work for an elderly woman.

'Jim Sawyer was convicted for fraud. He wasn't a dangerous man,' said Detective Superintendent Hawkes.

'But under altered circumstances, he might become violent,' Rupert suggested. 'If she told him to give himself up, for instance.'

'Anything's possible,' said the superintendent.

'That's what she'd have done,' said Rupert. 'She wouldn't meekly hand over her cash and wave him goodbye.' He could imagine her rounding on the man, ticking him off severely.

'She was struck several blows on the back of the head,' said the superintendent.

'She might have turned away to pick up the telephone,' said Rupert. Audrey, he knew, would show no fear; indeed, she might have felt none.

Hawkes knew there was no telephone in the kitchen at Ivy Lodge.

'It wasn't quite like that,' he said. 'She must have heard a noise and come down to investigate. He heard her, hid, and surprised her. I doubt if she even saw him.'

'He didn't – there was no other sort of attack?'

'No,' Hawkes reassured him. 'Nothing like that.'

'Thank God.' Monstrous assaults on elderly women seemed to be part of a great many robberies these days. 'Well, at least you know who to look for,' said Rupert. 'You'll find him in time, I suppose.'

'Oh, we'll do that all right,' said Hawkes. 'And he'll be facing a very serious charge.'

If she died, it would be murder.

Jim walked away from the school, more than twenty pounds in his pocket and without a plan but reluctant, now, to go back to prison before he had spent it.

Soon he came to a bus stop, and almost at once a bus came along. It was going to Oxford. He climbed aboard and paid to travel the whole way. He was used to being told what to do and where to go, and it was restful to sit there being borne onwards, regardless. Soon he began to relax, and after a while the long, wakeful hours of the night caught up with him, and he slept.

He woke to find himself wedged into his seat by a large woman with bulging thighs and two big shopping bags on her lap. She smiled when she saw him looking at her.

'You were dead to the world,' she said.

'I was,' Jim agreed.

That night, when his photograph appeared on television news programmes because he was wanted in connection with the attack on Audrey Bannerman, she was supremely confident that he was the man on the bus. She achieved instant local fame and was considered by her neighbours to have had a lucky escape herself.

'He seemed quite normal,' she said. 'But he needed a

shave. He was asleep when I got on the bus.' She'd been on her way to visit her married daughter, and the man had taken such an interest in what she told him about her three grandchildren. He had a daughter himself, he had said.

She discovered that that was true.

Jim had been to Oxford before, but he did not know it well. He felt lost and alone, wandering the busy streets in his stolen coat. The pavements were crowded, and although the centre of the city seemed to be a precinct of sorts, taxis and buses came wandering through. He walked down a road and, realizing that a sombre fortress to his left was the prison, turned quickly back and went to the library, which he had seen at the top of the hill, where he sat quietly reading the paper for quite some time. He couldn't stay there all day and at last he went out into the street again and wandered into Marks and Spencer's where he bought a pair of socks. He would have liked to buy a shirt too, but he could not afford one.

He wandered along another street and, at the end of it, saw a cinema.

Like Denis, he found it a haven for the afternoon.

When he came out, Jim walked up the road towards some traffic lights. On the corner there was a news vendor selling the *Oxford Mail*, and on the billboard beside him Jim saw the words: WOMAN ATTACKED. MAN SOUGHT.

He bought the paper, but not because of that message. He tucked it under his arm and saw a bus pass, heading north. It stopped, and he got on.

'All the way,' he said, and was charged so little that he couldn't be going far.

As his bus travelled up St Giles and the Woodstock Road, Jim read in the newspaper that Audrey Bannerman had been attacked. Someone had broken into her house during the night, stolen various things, and taken her Fiat car. The police wanted to interview Jim Sawyer, thirty-eight, who had absconded from Lockley prison that evening.

Jim's heart thudded as he read the text. He was described, but the paper had gone to press before a photograph was available. Nevertheless, he felt as if every eye in the bus must be noticing his balding head, grey eyes and pale complexion.

The bus went relentlessly on. It had stopped once, but now bore inexorably up the wide street with large houses on either side towards a roundabout at the top, which it crossed. Then at some lights, it made a right turn. Jim had mounted the Park and Ride bus and was now delivered to the parking lot where people were encouraged to leave their cars before entering the city. Everyone hastened off, many with larger carrier bags labelled Selfridges or Marks and Spencer. It was too early for office workers to be going home.

Jim too got off the bus, throwing his ticket in the bin provided, and walked away towards the road, feeling sick and giddy.

He knew that his fingerprints, and probably traces from his clothing, would be found in Mrs Bannerman's house because he had painted her kitchen and sat in her armchair. He could not prove that he had been in the boiler room in Reading when she was attacked. The police would say he had fled there later, if they found evidence of his presence in the place. In any case, he doubted if he could find it again, and even if the broken lock had been reported, the police wouldn't go chasing that up just to get him off the hook. It would be child's play to fix the blame on him, unless Mrs Bannerman had seen her attacker and recovered enough to describe him.

Who had done such a thing? Who would mug a decent old lady like Mrs Bannerman? Some thug without any mercy, obviously.

There was no question of giving himself up now. He

was not going to face such a serious charge if, by lying low, he could avoid it and wait for her to recover.

Jim had turned right at the entrance to the car park. A big roundabout lay ahead, with massive roadworks in progress beyond it, and, nearby, a motel and service station. The mass of traffic was daunting. It was no place for pedestrians and no one would stop here to give him a lift.

He still had the keys to the pick-up.

Jim returned to the big car park where the bus had stopped. It had gone now, with a fresh load of passengers, but another pulled in as he walked towards the furthest row of parked vehicles, where his efforts to snatch a car would be remote from observation. People were returning to their vehicles from the new bus, and others who had just arrived hastened to board it. Soon it moved off again and things became quieter, though another car drove in as Jim began trying doors. He looked for a Honda, hoping the key he had might fit, but though he found one, it didn't. He discovered an unlocked Vauxhall but the key had gone. Then he remembered something he had heard a con say. As another bus drew in, he sat in the Vauxhall and felt under the dash: no spare key. When the bus had gone and once again there was no one near him, he began feeling under the wings and rears of cars parked some distance from the entrance where his activities might not be noticed. He found a spare key securely taped under the wing of a VW Polo. A few seconds later he drove off in it, hurrying, lest its driver be on the next bus.

There were traffic lights outside the car park. Jim turned north towards the roundabout. He went three quarters of the way round it, heading for Bicester, then, at the next, bore left and found himself in Kidlington. He contemplated stopping to buy a razor and some hair dye, for he knew that he must disguise himself. Then he saw that he was passing the headquarters of the Thames Valley Police.

His heart raced as he accelerated onwards, but those inside had no presentiment of his passage and he went safely by, heading for Banbury.

He'd need more money, and he'd have to steal it.

15

Len parked the Sierra outside the high-rise block where Bet had her flat.

He'd moved in with Bet after her husband had disappeared leaving her alone with a small baby, and since then they'd had one of their own. Sharon was seven now, and Bruce five; Len had seen them regularly during his time in prison and hadn't lost touch. His relationship with Bet was stormy but self-renewing. He didn't believe she had lived like a nun while he was inside, that wouldn't be natural for someone like her, but she seemed pleased enough when he came out, and he'd seen no other bloke hanging about. If he went on a drinking bender, she was ready to join in, and if he occasionally cuffed her, she hit back. Her mother lived nearby, and when he was inside she stayed with the children while Bet worked at the Grapes. Len wouldn't like it at all if Bet slung him out, and he'd done last night's job to keep her happy.

She knew very well that he hadn't come honestly by the car, though he told her truthfully that he had hired it. He set to work fitting up the small television set and the video.

'I don't want to know where you got those,' Bet remarked. 'Then if someone comes asking, I won't give any wrong answers.'

'I had a win on the dogs,' said Len, grinning.

He was exciting, she had to grant that. Now that he was back, her life had taken on an extra dimension. They'd had good times in the past and they would again. Bruce was happy to have his dad home; she just hoped he'd keep out of trouble, by which she meant that she hoped he wouldn't get caught.

He'd disposed of some of the liquor on the way home, and he had cash in his pocket. It was a pity Bet had to go down to the Grapes that night. He'd get in a Chinese meal to enjoy when she returned, and on Saturday they'd take the kids out somewhere.

He had a few drinks while he waited for closing time. Bet's mum was quite glad to be freed from babysitting; she didn't like leaving her old man on his own. Quite like Darby and Joan, they were, those two; Bet's dad was a postman and her mum worked part time in a corner shop selling papers and sweets. They'd been married for over thirty years.

The Chinese meal had been delivered and was ready to heat up again. Pity that old cow down at Coxton hadn't had a microwave oven; one would be useful for Bet. He'd get one as soon as he could. It would mean calling at several banks, picking up fifty pounds at each one. The card and the cheque book might see them through for quite a while.

Bet was a good sort. Len sighed uxoriously, anticipating the night ahead. He'd missed it, inside. He turned on the television.

The news bulletin included a short clip about a robbery in Coxton during the previous night, when an elderly woman had been attacked and seriously injured. Pastoral shots of Coxton were shown, the twisting main street with its shop and the houses around, then Ivy Lodge, white tapes at the gate. A drab photograph of Audrey Bannerman, taken from her passport, appeared on the screen, followed by a mug shot of Jim Sawyer who was wanted by the police for questioning in connection with the assault.

'Phew!' whistled Len, who had watched the short sequence intently. He remembered Jim Sawyer at Lockley, a quiet, grey bloke who never said much. Now that he thought about it, Jim had worked somewhere in

Coxton but not at the churchyard. What a break! And fancy Jim blowing! Well, he was for it now.

There was no need for Len to worry. No one was going to think of questioning him.

Not unless the kid mentioned that Jim hadn't been there at all, and why should he do that?

By the time Jim reached Banbury he had calmed down enough to resume his normal careful driving style. It would be stupid to get stopped for speeding now. He looked about for a permitted parking slot while he went shopping, but when he left the Polo in a space between two other cars he did not realize it was a pay-and-display area and he went off towards the shops without buying a ticket.

He found a large chemist's shop and bought a toothbrush, razor, soap, shaving cream and some hair dye which you washed in – he read the instructions carefully – in a colour called Honeyglow. His beard was so grey that he would have to remain clean-shaven or look very odd, but he would let his moustache grow. Now he must find somewhere with a washbasin where he could carry out his transformation.

When he returned to the car, there was a parking ticket under the wiper. He threw it away.

The shops were closing now, and the traffic was heavy as Jim drove on northwards, skirting the Cross. He had never been here before. He came to some traffic lights, then, at the foot of a hill, some more, and as he was already in the left-hand stream, he turned that way. Crawling along, cars nose to tail, he saw to his right a large modern police station. Jim put up a hand to hide his face as he went past.

He needed money to rent a room where he could lie low until something happened to bring the true attacker of Mrs Bannerman to the notice of the police. Whoever it was might do something else, Jim reasoned, and be picked up for that.

Passing a filling station, he thought about trying to raid a till, but at this hour they were all much too busy. That was a crime for the dead hours. However, he might be able to deal with his hair at one; many had washrooms behind, and unlike public lavatories, they were small, often unisex, if he remembered correctly, and little used. There was still plenty of petrol in the car; he had no need to waste money buying more and he decided to park openly at the side of the forecourt, out of the way of other customers. and hurry round to the back of the place as if in some discomfort.

Jim stopped at the next one, tucking the car into a corner and slipping round behind the buildings to where there was a chilly little cubicle containing a basin and lavatory. He locked himself in and had a quick cold shave while the rinse was taking, not daring to wait for the recommended length of time, but no one came and rattled the door while he was inside; most customers were in a hurry to get home. He'd been lucky to find the place unlocked. He remembered Maureen having to ask for a key before now, when she and Nicola had wished to pay a visit.

No one questioned him. A damp honey blond, with a clean fresh chin, wearing new socks, Jim drove steadily on. He had shoved his old pair of socks into his pocket; he'd wash them when he got a chance. He hated wearing dirty socks.

He would have to dump the car. It would probably have been reported stolen by now and he could be stopped at any minute. Jim knew about the computer which verified registration numbers instantly.

He turned left at a junction, anxious to get away from the heaviest traffic. There was less chance of being stopped on a minor road, or so he hoped.

He had to concentrate, however: the road was twisty

and there were a lot of sharp bends. Some impatient people dashed past him when he thought it most unsafe to do so. Eventually he came to a very steep descent; he went down it behind a lorry, engaging low gear as advised by a notice beside the road. It was dark now, so Jim did not see spread before him the glorious plain beneath Edge Hill, site of a famous battle in the Civil War. He concentrated on keeping a safe distance from the lorry, which he passed later, and before long found himself entering Stratford-upon-Avon.

He had studied *Julius Caesar* at school and before his marriage had enjoyed the theatre but he had no time to think about Shakespeare now.

He decided to leave the car in a quiet road where it might not attract attention straight away. He turned off at a large roundabout, filtering into the traffic, then took a side turning which led him into a residential road. He parked the car there, between two others, and walked off with his carrier bag of toilet things and the two car keys. He might find them useful.

He knew he looked very different now from the man in the photograph. Colouring his hair had made him look younger, he had decided in the washroom. He would get something to eat – there would be plenty of places in such a popular tourist town – and they wouldn't all be expensive. He passed one big hotel before walking over Clopton Bridge and ahead was the mass of another. To his left, its lights glinting in the water of the river, was the theatre. A lot of traffic was crossing the bridge and there were a great many people on foot. Jim felt uncomfortable among them, but they offered protection, intent as they all were on going on their own way, some of them to the theatre. Jim did not know that there were now three in the town.

Very soon he saw several restaurants, and most displayed menus outside. Jim studied them and chose one that seemed among the least expensive. It was busy, and he thought he would not attract attention among so many other people. He ordered fish and chips, ate them as quickly as possible and then went back to the safety of the street. The food had done him good; he had eaten nothing since his meal at Reading station early that morning.

He walked past the Memorial Theatre and saw cars in the road beside some gardens. A few might be unlocked, but it was a busy, well-lit area and if he started trying doors looking for wallets or purses, he would soon be observed. He went on and turned right, passing an old timbered house, something to do with Shakespeare, he supposed. *Hall's Croft*, he read on a plaque.

He walked right through the town, which was easily done in quite a short time, and finally he went into an old, dark pub furnished with oak tables and benches, and, though his money had almost gone, he ordered a beer.

It gave him courage, and he got his chance as the place filled. One group of people left a corner by the fireplace under a low beam, and he took a vacant place on an oak settle. The woman who had already set her handbag down on the floor had no reason to suspect the quiet fair man in the anorak who sat beside her, staring into space. She talked animatedly with her three companions who faced away from Jim, and no one noticed him hook a foot round the bag and draw it towards him, then bend down and take out her purse. He manoeuvred the bag back to its original position before finishing his drink and leaving. She did not miss her purse until the next morning.

Once outside the pub, Jim walked rapidly up the road expecting to hear shouts of 'Stop, thief!' at any second, but there was no pursuit.

There was a lot of money in the purse, enough to pay for an overnight stay at a bed and breakfast place and have plenty over. There were credit cards, too. Jim was calmly proud: all he'd needed was nerve, and it had worked. He returned to a street where, earlier, he had noticed a number of houses displaying bed and breakfast signs and picked the most modest, putting on his best manner as he spoke to the landlady and quite impressing her by his pleasant approach. He looked vaguely familiar and she asked him if he had stayed there before, but he said no.

She had seen Jim's mug shot on the television news at six o'clock, but his blond hair dye had effectively changed his appearance, and she had other worries on her mind as she answered the door to this late caller.

In the morning, Jim thought of leaving without paying, but that would only arouse suspicion, and anyway the woman was entitled to her money. Instead, he enjoyed the excellent breakfast she provided, eggs and bacon, fried bread and sausage, and departed, bathed and with his singlet, socks and pants washed and dried over the heater in his room.

From the house, he walked straight to Marks and Spencer's, which he had seen the evening before. The purse he had taken contained a Marks and Spencer's charge card and Jim had studied it carefully. L. Wilson was the woman's name, and she had signed it Lesley. That was a unisex name, though men, he thought, spelled it with an *ie* at the end. He practised her signature on a corner of newspaper until he could do it easily; he was good at that sort of thing. He used the card to buy trousers, a shirt, a blue crew-neck sweater and a small holdall. No one challenged his signature and the card had not yet been reported lost.

He changed into his new clothes in a public lavatory, bundling up his prison garb into the carrier from the Banbury chemist and dumping it in a litter bin he saw in the street. Then he went to the railway station. He'd go to Birmingham, a huge city, where he might be able to survive.

150

There would be other chances to steal enough money to live on, or he might get a job and he could use Lesley Wilson's bank card to charge up small amounts.

On the way to the station, he bought a newspaper and looked in it for news of Mrs Bannerman. She had not made the front page of the national press, and he saw only a small paragraph inside, but there was a grainy photograph of him reproduced from the one taken when he was arrested. SAVAGE ATTACK. MAN WANTED, he read.

Jim had looked at himself in a plate-glass window as he walked along and was satisfied with his disguise. His moustache was meagre, but another couple of days would make a difference. He might get a jacket to match his new trousers, and then he would look like the white-collar worker he had been before his conviction.

By nightfall, he had acquired the jacket and had rented a room in a cheap lodging house in an area of dark rows of terraced houses some way from the centre of Birmingham. He went down the road to a pub for something to eat; it was noisy and crowded there, and he hid behind a newspaper, not wanting to talk. There was a television set in the bar, and he saw on the news that Audrey Bannerman had died that afternoon.

Jim was wanted for murder.

He fled from the pub before any of the drinkers present connected the well-dressed man with sparse blond hair and an infant moustache with the depressed image now flashed upon the screen.

Jim rushed back to his dingy room and locked himself in.

Now he was well and truly on the run.

16

After the police had driven her and Robin home, Yvonne found it hard to concentrate on any of the things she should be doing. They had taken a statement, which she had signed, and they had treated her with kindness, aware that she had undergone a shocking experience. Robin was the only one to have found the morning thoroughly satisfactory, with the comings and goings of the various vehicles and the final treat of the ride in the white car with its blue light on the roof, which the driver had operated for his entertainment as soon as they passed through the gates of Ford House.

She had just suggested that Robin should bring some toys upstairs to her workroom when she remembered that her car was still out of action.

If Charles had started it for her, she would have driven straight past Ivy Lodge without giving a thought to Audrey, who would still be lying on her kitchen floor. She could have lain there all day, even for several days, without being discovered. It was a terrible thought.

Yvonne telephoned a garage who sent out a man in a van. He was able to start her car and fitted a new battery.

'This'll last for years,' he told her. 'Modern ones do, but they run down if you leave the lights on and that sort of thing.'

'I know,' said Yvonne, who had not left the lights on but had never replaced the battery since she had had the Mini. This little incident was going to cost money and she would have to find it; why should Charles pay for her car?

That afternoon she rang up the hospital to ask about Audrey, wondering as she did so whether anyone else would bother to inquire. She learned that after an operation, Audrey was in a critical condition and in intensive care.

Charles arrived home at eight o'clock, earlier than usual. He had telephoned from the car to tell her when to expect him. Most evenings she got on with some work after Robin was tucked up. She had weakly lapsed into allowing the others to watch television if they had nothing else to do, though there had been a time when they played games or read together before bed. She comforted herself by reflecting that they were older now, and more independent, but she resolved that as the winter approached she would sit with them round the fire, even if she had to be sewing.

Over dinner, she told Charles about Audrey.

'I told you those convicts shouldn't be allowed out in the village,' he said.

'Charles, it was awful. She lay there on the kitchen floor with blood in her hair and I thought she was dead. She's very likely to die, in fact.'

'Poor darling, what a shock for you,' said Charles.

'Yes, it was,' Yvonne said. 'I climbed into the house through her bedroom window, the way the burglar went.'

'It might have been wiser to call the police and let them do the climbing,' Charles suggested.

'It would have taken longer. I'd got her covered up with blankets and a hot-water bottle by the time they arrived,' said Yvonne.

'Well done,' said Charles, spearing a piece of potato with his fork and hoovering it round his plate to absorb the sauce from the pork chops Yvonne had casseroled.

'Charles, this is Coxton, not some inner city. Audrey was mugged,' said Yvonne.

'Well, you were the one who wanted to live in the country,' said Charles.

Alan and Tracy had not heard about the crime in

Coxton. Alan's work that day had lain in the other direction, and the news had not been discussed in Tracy's supermarket. Unable to face them over the evening meal, Denis called on her at her check-out after the cinema to tell her that he would not be in to eat. He went to McDonald's and had a hamburger, then stood on a street corner talking to some boys from school. He told them he was leaving Leckerton and joining the Marines.

'Pull the other one,' said one boy.

'It's the truth,' Denis declared, and in that moment it became his intention.

'They won't take you,' jeered another boy.

'You'll see,' Denis told him.

Eventually the other boys drifted off to the snooker club and Denis decided to go back to the van. He would be safe there, in the darkness, curled up in his sleeping bag listening to his tapes. The old woman must be all right by now, and Len would have got clean away. He'd been wrong to hit her like that. She was only an old bag, true, but she'd done nothing to harm Len, and she'd let Denis wash her car and paid him a fair price. Len could have tied her up or something, stuffed a rag in her mouth to keep her quiet. Denis would have lent a hand with that. Or would he? Thinking about it, he wasn't sure. He wouldn't have liked touching her, feeling her flesh, knowing that she was a person, not a beetle to be treated like this.

He didn't like his uncomfortable thoughts and he turned his mind towards Ford House and the problem of whether or not he should go there the next day. Mrs Davies would be expecting him, and he'd quite like to complete turning over the vegetable bed. He'd quit when that was done, and he might help himself to a few things from the place before leaving, but then again, he might not. Mrs Davies was sharp and she'd miss even a quid from her purse. She'd know who had had the opportunity to lift it, and she wouldn't have any mercy.

If Len had got into Ford House the previous night, he might have mugged Mrs Davies.

That was a new and unwelcome thought, with those kids in the house and all. You couldn't just go about mugging anyone who got in your way. Lifting things was different, especially from a shop, when they didn't belong to anyone. Shops could afford it, even expected thieving, and a bloke had to look after himself. The main thing was not to get caught and that wasn't easy, with video cameras fitted all over the place and people disguised as ordinary shoppers who were really detectives.

Denis was up early on Friday morning and he told Tracy he would go to the launderette for her that afternoon, if she liked. She was grateful, and said she would leave out two bags of washing and some money.

She was worrying about having Denis there. The school authorities might catch up with him, and it was asking a lot of Alan to let him sleep in the van. Luckily Denis would always do as she said and he was a good kid in some ways, but it wasn't right for him to be hanging about with no proper work, though she knew he had washed a good few cars, and he had this gardening job over at Coxton. Alan had been amazed that he had stuck to it but Denis had always liked that sort of thing. Tracy could remember their visits to their grandparents years ago. They had lived in a village near the sea and Denis had liked helping their grandfather dig and feed the chickens and mend fences; he was good with his hands, and if he could take up some practical work he would be all right. She supposed he would have to survive in this hand-to-mouth way till his birthday but after that he would have to leave. He'd be able to sign on, if he couldn't find a job straight away, and he could get digs somewhere.

It was a pity their grandparents weren't still in that village; he could have gone to them. Their grandmother had died and their grandfather was in a home. Tracy meant to visit him, but it was a long way and she hadn't managed to do it yet.

Denis was really quite thoughtful. Many a kid wouldn't have bothered to mention that he wasn't coming in to eat, like he had the previous evening, and now he'd offered to do the washing. She was sure he'd remember: look how he kept giving her money for food. He was all right; once he got going in the adult world, he'd make out.

Denis was lucky in getting a lift to Coxton that morning but the motorist who stopped for him dropped him outside the village and he had to walk through it, past Ivy Lodge.

A policeman stood outside the house and part of the garden was marked off with white tapes. What did that mean? His scalp prickled as he continued on past the bus stop towards Ford House. He was nearly there when Mrs Davies stopped beside him, on her way back from dropping the children at school and playgroup.

'Hop in, Denis. Save yourself five minutes,' she said, as she leaned over to open the passenger door.

'Been keeping all right, then?' he asked brightly, getting in.

'Yes, thanks,' said Yvonne. 'You too, I hope. We're lucky not to be lying half dead in Leckerton Hospital.'

Denis blinked.

'Why?' he asked cautiously.

'Mrs Bannerman is. Haven't you heard?' said Yvonne. 'You've met her – she came to tea once when you were here. About two weeks ago it was, I think. She lives at Ivy Lodge. You must have seen the policeman outside.'

'Yeah. I wondered what was up,' said Denis.

'Someone broke into her house during Wednesday

156

night and attacked her. Left her for dead,' said Yvonne. 'But she wasn't, quite. I found her the next morning.'

'You did?' Denis stared at her in astonishment. 'How come?'

They had arrived outside the house now. Yvonne unfastened her seat belt and got out of the car, and Denis slowly did the same.

'I was passing and saw her curtains drawn and the milk on the step,' answered Yvonne. 'It was on the television news last night. Didn't you see it?'

'No. I don't see much telly,' said Denis.

'They think it was one of the men from the prison,' said Yvonne. 'Someone escaped that night and was on the run. A man called Sawyer. I think he was the man who did some work for Mrs Bannerman.'

'Never!' said Denis, truly amazed.

'That's what the police think,' Yvonne said. 'He took her car.'

'Bloody hell!' Denis could not believe it. Now the heat would be off and he could breathe freely. He beamed at her.

'It's nothing to grin about, Denis,' Yvonne rebuked him sharply. 'Mrs Bannerman may die.'

'Oh, I'm not laughing at that, Mrs Davies,' said Denis quickly, composing his features into a more solemn expression. 'I was just thinking it was smart to get on to the villains so fast.'

'Only one villain, Denis,' said Yvonne. 'As far as we know.'

Trevor was off nights now, and when he came back after his shift on Thursday, he already knew that Jim had escaped.

'I've got something to tell you, love,' he said to Maureen, just as she was about to utter the very same words.

'You first,' she said.

In the end, what he had to say made it easier for her.

'A policewoman came round this morning,' she said. 'She seemed to think he might come here.' How easy it was not to mention that that was exactly what had happened.

'There's a bit more to it now,' said Trevor. 'The WPC wouldn't have known, if she came so early.' Maureen had explained that the visit was before she went to work.

'Known what?' Had he been recaptured? Been hurt, perhaps, in some chase? Maureen wanted to think that it served him right, but she couldn't; it would be so typical of Jim to make a mess of things, even get in the way of a bullet.

'He's wanted for assaulting an elderly woman,' said Trevor. 'It seems he broke into a house in a village where he'd worked when he was out from the nick on one of those schemes. She was found there this morning, unconscious, and the place had been done over.'

'Oh no! Oh, I don't believe it!' Maureen stared at him. 'Jim wouldn't do a thing like that.'

'Wouldn't he? He'd need money, on the run. He took her car and everything of any use from her handbag.' Trevor, on patrol, had been looking out for the Fiat.

'But then – ' Maureen began. She had been about to say that Jim had been glad to have the twenty pounds she had given him. He wouldn't have needed that, if he'd robbed someone. 'That's not like Jim,' she said instead. 'He was never violent.' She pictured him crouched on the floor in the hall. That weeping man couldn't hurt a mouse, much less an old woman.

'Well, it seems that he did,' said Trevor. 'She's pretty bad. You must face it, love. The local lads have found his dabs eveywhere. There's quite enough evidence to get a conviction. If she dies he'll be down for murder, though a sharp brief might get a manslaughter verdict.'

'But he hasn't been caught?'

'Not yet. It's only a matter of time.'

'People seem to escape and not get caught,' Maureen pointed out.

'Hardly ever,' said Trevor. 'In the end they give themselves away. They need cash and food. They can't stay in hiding unless they've got pals to help them, and I doubt if Jim has those sort of friends. I suppose he went stir-crazy and just had to get out. It's easy enough at these open places.'

Someone might have seen him in this neighbourhood that morning. Well, she would deny that she had done so, whatever happened and however many times she was asked. She wanted no more trouble. All the same, it was hard to believe that Jim could have resorted to violence and she said so again.

'He just isn't like that,' she repeated.

'The woman probably disturbed him and he got scared,' said Trevor. 'That's how it happens. That's why he might get manslaughter.'

'Has anyone thought that somebody else could have done it?' Maureen demanded. 'Why are they so sure it was Jim?'

'Well, his prints were there and he broke out that night,' said Trevor. 'Who else could it have been?'

'You said he'd worked for the woman. That could explain the prints.'

'Sorry, love. It looks like an open and shut case,' said Trevor. 'He'll be running now.'

Maureen shivered and clasped her hands over her chest.

'I'm going to get a divorce, Trev,' she said. 'I'm not taking any more of this. I want out.'

'That's my girl,' said Trevor. They'd discussed it often enough. He'd have to face up to it now, taking her and the kiddie on properly, doing it right. Once the bloke was locked up for a good spell, it wouldn't be difficult; no chance of him suddenly turning up and making a scene.

'Don't let him in, if he comes here,' he warned. 'He might think you would help him.'

'No chance,' said Maureen. 'I'd turn him right in.'

17

After all the rain, the soil was heavy and clogged Denis's fork as he dug. He felt quite sorry that he would not see what grew here in the spring. He should finish his task today, which was just as well because the ground was almost too wet to work. There wasn't much to do in a garden in the winter, and he didn't think Mrs Davies would have other jobs lined up for him. It might be safer to stay away from Coxton for a while; he hadn't liked seeing that policeman outside Mrs Bannerman's house. Coppers were apt to ask you what you were doing when you were simply minding your own business, and they could soon fit you up with a charge when they wanted to score a few arrests.

'You'll not be needing me any more,' he told Yvonne after she had inspected his completed work.

'Well, you'll soon be starting your YTS programme, won't you?' she said.

'I'm going into the Marines instead,' Denis announced.

'Are you? What a good idea. You'll see the world,' said Yvonne. 'Your parents don't object, then?'

'Why should they?'

'Well, you said you live with your grandmother because you can't get along with them,' she reminded him.

'They'll be glad to get rid of me,' said Denis with conviction.

He didn't seem to feel sorry for himself; Yvonne studied his round face with its tough expression. He'd had rebuffs enough in his life, she thought.

'Where does your grandmother live?' she asked. 'In what part of Leckerton?'

'Why do you want to know?' Denis asked warily.

'I'd like to know where to find you, in case I have some odd jobs to be done before you go,' she replied. 'You'd think about doing some painting, wouldn't you?' She and Charles were going to take months to get through what had to be done.

'I might,' he allowed. 'It's Seven Birch Street, near the old asylum. But you'd better write, not call. My gran's a bit forgetful and she might not pass on the message if I was out.'

'Very well,' said Yvonne. 'What's your last name, Denis?'

He would not tell her the truth.

'Crow,' he said, at random, not consciously thinking of the old woman who lived at the back of the house.

'Right,' said Yvonne. 'I'll give you some lunch today, Denis, and run you back into town. I'm going to see Mrs Bannerman this afternoon.'

The thought that Audrey might lie there without any visitors had distressed her. What matter if she seemed to be in a coma? She might drift in and out of consciousness and be vaguely aware of a friendly presence. Yvonne had arranged to take Robin round to the vicarage, where Amy Parker would look after him for a couple of hours. It was the first time she had asked such a favour from anyone in the village. She must do it again and show herself willing to have other children round to play. They all needed a social circle.

Yvonne had asked whether the vicar was going to see how Audrey was, and learned he had been to the hospital the previous evening. At the moment there was nothing he could usefully do, he had said. Audrey was deeply unconscious. The hospital had its own chaplain who would see her on his regular rounds. The vicar would keep in touch and would pray for Audrey, but he had other claims on his time.

Fat lot of good that would do, thought Yvonne,

offended by such logic. Audrey should not be left to the total care of strangers.

She asked Denis to tidy up the garden shed while she went to fetch Robin from playgroup. Then the three of them sat round the kitchen table eating mashed potato with mince and carrots. The amount Yvonne had prepared would have fed her and Robin several times but there was none left after Denis had had two big helpings. They had stewed apples and custard for pudding.

'You'll get well fed in the Marines, Denis,' said Yvonne.

'I've not applied yet,' he said cautiously. 'I haven't found out how to do it.'

'The library would know,' said Yvonne. 'That's the place to go for that sort of information. I expect there's somewhere you can write to for forms and things.'

She made it sound simple, and she dropped him outside the library on her way to the hospital.

'Let me know how you get on, Denis,' she said.

He gave her a casual, embarrassed wave as he sauntered towards the swing doors of the library, his Walkman in place. That would have to go, for a start, she thought, if the Marines took him. Was he old enough to join? He was an odd, tiresome boy, and yet there was good in him, waiting to be drawn out. He worked hard and he'd been nice to Robin. The Marines could be the making of him.

Yvonne was told at the hospital that Audrey was too ill for visitors, except relatives, but when she explained that it was she who had found her, Yvonne was allowed to go into the ward.

An elderly man was sitting beside Audrey's bed. He had thick silver hair and, as he rose to his feet at Yvonne's approach, she saw that he had piercing blue eyes under strong, bushy brows.

Rupert Bannerman introduced himself.

163

How weird, thought Yvonne. Here was Audrey's ex-husband. What a marvellous looking old boy!

'I was afraid no one would come,' she said aloud.

'That's why I'm here,' he replied.

Yvonne couldn't imagine her ex-husband feeling the slightest pang if she ended up in such a state.

'Tell me how you came to find her,' said Rupert, who had heard only a bare account from Detective Superintendent Hawkes.

In a quiet voice Yvonne explained, glancing now and then at the unconscious woman as she spoke.

'I was too late, though,' she said. 'If she'd been found sooner –'

'I don't know,' said Rupert. 'Maybe. I doubt if anyone can tell. Her heart's none too good, it seems. She had a slight heart attack some time ago, but I didn't know that.'

'Fancy leaving her in that state, though. I mean, whoever did it – fancy going off,' said Yvonne.

'Well, whoever was responsible was hardly likely to ring for an ambulance before making his getaway,' said Rupert with a smile for this rather solemn young woman. Finding Audrey unconscious must have been a shocking experience. He said so.

'It was, and I so nearly didn't go in,' said Yvonne. 'Only the day before she'd given me and my children a lift because my car wouldn't start.'

'Did – do you know her well?'

'No. I don't think anyone did, in the village,' said Yvonne, unconsciously using the past tense.

Yvonne had heard the other play group mothers discussing the attack. Few had spoken to Audrey though most had seen her about the village and one had wondered why she didn't have a dog, as she seemed to like walking.

'She was very shy,' said Rupert. 'Most people manage to cope with that as they grow older, but she never did.'

He frowned. 'My fault, perhaps.' He smiled again, turning his sharp gaze towards Yvonne. 'So you live at Ford House. It's a nice old place. I think Audrey hoped to put the clock back in some way by returning to Coxton, looking for some sort of security she had in her childhood, but one can never do that.'

'It's changed,' said Yvonne, 'It's bigger. There are quite a few new houses, and it's deserted by day except for mothers with young children and a few retired couples. Everyone else goes to work. There are plenty of jobs in Leckerton.'

Rupert nodded. He had driven through the town's expanding industrial area.

'Does your husband work here?' he asked.

'No.' Yvonne explained about Charles's job.

'A lot of travelling,' was Rupert's comment.

'Yes, but it's worth it to live in the country.' To Rupert, Yvonne suddenly sounded defensive. 'I'll have to go,' she said. 'I've got to pick up my children from school.'

'Give me your telephone number,' said Rupert. 'I'll let you know if there's any news.'

'You're staying?'

He nodded.

'Someone must hold her hand if she's dying,' he said.

Yvonne had been home for only half an hour when he telephoned to tell her that Audrey had died.

In Detective Superintendent Hawkes's opinion, there was no mystery about how Audrey Bannerman had met her death. She was the victim of a savage assault made by Jim Sawyer after he absconded from Lockley Prison, and he had to be found and arrested without delay. There was plenty of evidence with which to convict him: his prints were in the house and especially in the kitchen, where she had been attacked, though he had left none on a glass from which he had drunk some whisky. It could not have been Audrey who used the glass or hers would have been found. There were other prints about, of course, some of them the dead woman's, and naturally she would have had visitors. There was no sign of the weapon, something thin but heavy, the surgeon who had operated on Audrey had said. A poker from the house had been inspected, but bore no traces of such misuse and Audrey's own fingerprints were on the handle.

House-to-house inquiries in Coxton had not been productive. Audrey's immediate neighbours, a young couple on one side and a middle-aged woman on the other, all said that they barely knew her. She seemed to want to keep herself to herself. The young couple had asked her round for coffee after dinner one evening but she had refused. The middle-aged woman, an accountant working in Leckerton, had exchanged a few words with her when they met in the road, but, she said, to be frank, Mrs Bannerman had not seemed very friendly and so she had not asked her round. Of course she regretted that now.

On the night in question, the middle-aged woman had been woken by the sound of a car starting up nearby, but she had gone straight back to sleep and had not noticed the time. The couple had heard nothing.

The detective constable who had visited these neighbours had noticed some tyre marks on the grass verge just past Ivy Lodge, but as the man they were seeking had taken Mrs Bannerman's car, they seemed irrelevant and he did not mention them in his report.

No one else in the village had noticed anything unusual. Percy Bates, who lived with his widowed mother near the church, had been coming home from Leckerton some time after three o'clock in the morning and had met a blue van which was wandering about all over the road, but as he had had a heavy night out himself, which had ended up in an illicit amorous adventure, he kept quiet, too. It was, anyway, nothing to do with what had happened; the police were not asking about sightings of vehicles other than Mrs Bannerman's Fiat.

Jim Sawyer had taken a prison cycle, and that hadn't been found. He must have abandoned it, as it would not have fitted into the Fiat. A search for it in the neighbourhood had so far been unsuccessful. Some boys might have found it and put it to use. It had to be traced.

In a village eight miles from Lockley Prison, and twelve miles from Coxton, a Honda pick-up had been stolen from outside a house. Some miles further on a man's anorak had disappeared from a pub. Had it not been for the crime in Coxton, these episodes might have been linked with the prison escape, but because of the attack, they were thought to be separate incidents. So far, the pick-up had not been found.

Hawkes looked at the other reports. A woman travelling by bus from Reading to Oxford had sat next to Jim Sawyer on Thursday morning. Well, he would have had plenty of time to get there after committing the crime, though he would surely realize that the police would look for him there. The Fiat might turn up in Reading, since clearly he had dumped it. A car had been stolen from a Park and Ride car park in Oxford later that day. That could have been Sawyer.

It seemed, for the moment, as if he had got clean away, but he'd show up soon. He would start passing Audrey's cheques or using her bank card.

The police had found her bank statements, neatly filed away in a drawer, and they had been able to put a stop on her account.

No one who lived in the quiet road where Jim had left his stolen car had thought of mentioning its arrival to the police. It was in no one's way, and for all anyone knew had been acquired by a resident.

18

Rupert told Felicity that the inquest would be opened on Monday so that funeral arrangements could be made for Audrey.

His face was grey. The last time Felicity had seen him looking like this was after Hesther had died.

'She was really being kept alive by technology,' he said. 'In the end her heart beat even that.'

'From what you've said, she can't have known a lot about what happened,' suggested Felicity.

'No, I don't suppose she did.' And she wouldn't have known that he was there at the end, not that such knowledge would have been any comfort to her.

'It's no good making yourself wretched by feeling responsible for what's happened,' said Felicity gently. 'It's like a road accident. She just got in the way of that man.'

'You're right, of course.' But if she had still been living at Tettlebury, she wouldn't have been in Coxton that night.

'You said there'd been no struggle.'

'No. She was knocked out cold from behind with some sort of heavy rod or bar,' said Rupert. 'I've spoken to her solicitor – a man in Sussex. She wants – wanted to be buried in Coxton near her parents. I've agreed to meet him at her house to discuss things. There isn't anyone else. I'm sorry, darling, but I'll have to do it.'

'Of course you must see to things, Rupert,' said Felicity. 'She's always been your responsibility.'

'Friday, we thought,' Rupert said. 'For the funeral I mean. The vicar's got to go to some meeting or other on Thursday and said that would be difficult. Wednesday seemed a bit soon after the inquest, somehow.'

'Friday seems a good choice,' said Felicity, thinking drat the vicar and his previous engagement, though it would make no difference to poor Audrey.

'We'll be in for a battering, I'm afraid,' said Rupert. 'The press will probably drag all that up about Hesther again. It's too much to hope that no one will remember and make the connection.'

If they missed it now, they wouldn't when the man Sawyer was caught and brought up for trial.

'It can't hurt her now, or her mother,' said Felicity. 'It can only hurt you, my dear, and by extension, me. It will pass,' she added. 'Things do.'

At the Bell in Coxton the talk was all of their local murder. Television and newspaper reporters flocked to the village seeking people to provide human interest stories about the dead woman, and they soon discovered that she had been found by someone who lived in Audrey Bannerman's former home. That could be turned into a real tear-jerker.

No one had much to say about the dead woman herself. She had never been into the Bell, though she walked about the village and used the shop. One woman said she often took the field path to the river, when it wasn't too wet. She had no dog, so there was no moping pet needing a home.

'A cat?' someone asked, but no: she had not had even a canary.

'A recluse,' one reporter suggested, and it seemed that to some extent she was, though it was known that she had been to France the summer before. She drove into Leckerton two or three times a week, presumably to shop. She did not employ a cleaning woman, though she had made inquiries about finding someone. Such help was difficult to get in the village; people preferred to work in Leckerton factories and several firms arranged transport for their employees.

Old Mrs Feathers, who always went into the snug for a stout at six o'clock sharp, remembered the family at Ford House before Audrey married. The father had been respected, even liked; he did all the right things, subscribing to village appeals and allowing the garden to be used for fêtes, though it was too far out to be much requested. The mother was frail, almost an invalid. Audrey had been a quiet girl and Mrs Feathers remembered nothing remarkable about her except her wedding in the church, an affair of white satin and tulle. She'd looked nice enough; most girls did on their wedding day, Mrs Feathers opined, but she was never a beauty. The family had not lived in the village through generations, as their predecessors at Ford House had done; they had made little impact.

The reporters departed to go to Ford House. They'd get some reactions from Mrs Davies.

As they left, Mrs Feathers spoke to the landlord.

'Ring Ford House, Albert,' she said. 'It's a shame what these people do and she's got those three kiddies to get to bed. Tell her to lock herself in and keep those reporters outside.'

The other regulars thought this was a good idea, and Albert managed to get through just in time. Yvonne was battened down, not responding, by the time the press came battering at her door. She rang the police and asked them to come and send the reporters away.

When Charles arrived back on Friday night he found a small group of them in the road. As the gates were closed he had to get out of the car to open them. The journalists converged round him like bees round their hive.

'How do you feel about your wife finding the body?' called one.

'How well did you know the dead woman?' asked another.

Until now, Charles had not known that Audrey had

170

died. Yvonne had not told him when he telephoned to announce his time of arrival. In silence, he pushed through the mob to get into the car again and edged forwards as if he were driving through a flock of sheep.

Grim-faced Charles Davies returns to fatal mansion, said one paper less than accurately the next morning, and showed a blurred photograph of a scowling Charles.

He was furious. The weekend would be ruined if the house were under siege from the press. If only Yvonne had minded her own business, they would not have been involved.

He knew he was being unreasonable. Her warm heart was one of her charms. He had bought her some flowers because he knew he had been short-tempered lately, but things seemed to be slipping from his control. Charles liked to feel that he was in charge.

'He can't go on living in the van,' said Alan.

'I know.'

Denis had taken the washing to the launderette, as he promised, and brought it back all nicely tumble-dried. Now Tracy was folding what could be worn unpressed, and making a pile of things to be ironed. She liked ironing.

'What's he going to do?' Alan asked. 'It'll be too cold out there soon.'

'He wants to join the Marines,' said Tracy. 'He went to the library today and found out how to apply. He's got an address to write to.'

'What a good idea!'

'Yes. If he gets in, they'll look after him – give him somewhere to live, and a training,' said Tracy. 'They'll take you at sixteen.'

'He'd see the world,' said Alan enthusiastically.

'Yes,' said Tracy. 'He's a funny one, sort of a loner. He's never been one to run with the other kids and he doesn't seem interested in girls.'

'Late developer,' Alan pronounced.

'Maybe. Anyway, it's his birthday soon and after that he'll be able to sign on and go to the Job Centre in the proper way, if the Marines don't take him straight off. I expect there are things you have to do first, like pass the doctor.'

'Well, he seems fit enough,' said Alan.

'Yes. He likes all that outdoor stuff. The Marines would suit him. Or the army. Anything like that,' Tracy said. 'You didn't know you were taking him on too, when you rescued me,' she added, getting out the iron and plugging it in.

'I needed a woman,' said Alan. 'Otherwise I'd got to do my own ironing, hadn't I?'

She threw a towel at him and he caught her wrists and pulled her down to him, both of them laughing, Tracy pretending reluctance to turn her face to his. She had to break free to unplug the iron and as she turned eagerly back to him, the fleeting question went through her head as to whether her parents had ever felt like this: had she been conceived in such a moment of joy? If so, how had things managed to go so terribly wrong?

She knew that her parents still came together, but it was in a fierce act of hate; never love.

Later, watching television, they learned for the first time of the attack in Coxton and that the victim had died. There were shots of the village and of Detective Superintendent Hawkes referring to 'this heartless assault on an elderly woman.'

'Poor old soul,' said Tracy. 'I wonder if Denis met her when he was working over there. I must ask him.'

But Denis did not come in for breakfast until they were leaving for work, and by then she had forgotten.

He spent most of Saturday washing cars, and as the recent weather had made them extremely dirty, he had plenty of customers. The rain held off, and on Sunday he was washing the van when Tracy and Alan surfaced. He had got water from Mrs Crow, who had let him use her Fairy Liquid, and he scrubbed away, wiping off what he could of the scrape he had caused and cleaning the wheels.

Tracy and Alan were going to spend the day in the country. He pretended that he had arranged to meet a friend, and when they had gone he locked himself in their room where he spent the day.

Len and his family had a lovely day out on Saturday. The rain held off and they went to Alton Towers, where the children had a high old time, or Len decided they did, ignoring Bruce's near hysteria on the roller-coaster.

Complacent because Jim Sawyer was being blamed for what he had done, Len had not given a thought to his victim, and he did not learn she had died until the next morning, when he went down to the corner shop to buy the paper. The attack was written up in sensational terms and Jim's photograph, enlarged and grainy, was published again. It did not look very like him, Len decided, squinting at it critically.

He had better return the hired car. It was a shame to give it up so soon, but when the police discovered that the stolen bank card had been used in Bristol, which they would soon enough, they'd be nosing about down there looking for more clues and they might find the Fiat. He'd better sever his connections with the place.

He told Bet he'd be gone for most of the day. She was quite upset; she'd made up her mind that they'd have another day out, maybe go to the coast.

'Sorry,' he said. 'Some other time.'

After he had gone, she pottered about doing a bit of dusting. It was nice having him at home and in funds. Her philosophy was to enjoy this good spell while she could. He'd get done again one day, that was certain, and in time she would have to find someone else; this was an insecure way of life but it was great while it lasted.

He'd given her quite a flash ring, rubies and diamonds. It was old-fashioned, not really her style, but it fitted and she'd worn it all day yesterday.

It might be worth a bit, if he went down again. She decided to hide it away so that he couldn't get hold of it and sell it himself, if the money ran out. The children were watching cartoons on television, not interested in what she was doing. Bet buried it in a bag of flour in the store cupboard.

After taking this precaution, she sat down at the kitchen table to have a smoke and a cup of coffee. She was still in her dressing gown, a pink quilted one she'd treated herself to before Len came out. She hadn't let herself go while he was inside; her looks and her bright manner had got her the job in the bar and these were assets she took care of, for they were all she had. You had only yourself to depend on, when it came to the crunch; the odd bit of luck on the way was just that: a bonus. Len would never be in the league who set up major heists and ended up living in Spain. Sooner or later he made a mistake, or got rough, or both.

He had left the paper behind. She turned the pages, reading the latest speculation about one royal marriage and a rumoured pregnancy in another. There had been a drugs scandal in the world of show business.

Her attention was drawn to the piece about the events in Coxton rather by chance, when her eye caught the name of Lockley Prison from which the wanted man had escaped. That was where Len had been for the last part of his sentence. She'd visited him with the kids, and each time Bruce had screamed fit to bust, though it was nice there compared with other places he'd been in. He'd worked outside, from Lockley; hadn't he mentioned Coxton?

Bet read the piece carefully. An elderly woman, Mrs Audrey Bannerman, had been attacked by an intruder

174

on Wednesday night and had not been found until Thursday morning.

Len had gone away on Wednesday and had not returned until late on Thursday, with the hired car and the loot. If the paper had not stated, in black and white, that the police wanted to question Jim Sawyer about the crime, she would be wondering where Len had been at the time. The job had just his touch. He took that small cosh whenever he went thieving and look what happened on that last warehouse job. It was a neat little weapon he'd picked up somewhere, a slim leaded club with a narrow, leather-bound handle. He'd shown her how easy it was to tuck it up his sleeve or into his sock.

Bruce had been quite tiny when his father went down for using it on the night watchman. Len was only on parole now, after serving just a third of his sentence; he'd go back fast enough if he offended again.

She would ask him about this Jim Sawyer when he came home from wherever he'd gone, and about Coxton. Or maybe she wouldn't. There were some things it was best not to know.

After seeing the television news on Friday night, Jim slept only fitfully. He kept waking up imagining that any moment he would be arrested and put into a cell. Outside in the street cars passed, and he heard the wail of a police siren which grew louder and louder. He held his breath until it faded away. Towards dawn he gave up and lay on his back with his hands clasped under his head, staring at the ceiling. The immense problem of evading capture was almost too much to contemplate at this chill, dead hour and he longed for his safe room at Lockley. That would be denied him now. There would be no more open prison if he went down for murder, or not for years, and no parole unless he were to admit the offence. He couldn't do that. He hadn't killed that woman.

However little she cared for him, surely Maureen would never believe him capable of such a terrible crime?

His room was damp and cold. There was a gas fire with a meter but he had no matches. He would have to go out and buy a few things to enable him to survive the weekend. If he stayed here for a few days the police would accept that the trail had grown cold and their search would become nationwide. Birmingham was a large city and unless, by ill luck, someone recognized him, he would be relatively safe. In cities there were plenty of people with things to hide and no curiosity about others. It wasn't as if he had a circle of criminal friends whom the police would watch.

Against the increasing traffic noise from the street, a radio suddenly blared in the room below. The fact that there were other people in the building was both a reassurance and disturbing. For so long Jim had been used to institutional life, where his days were ordered, that the effect of locking the door of this shabby room and closing himself in alien isolation had been eerie. All the self-congratulation that had sustained him earlier had evaporated.

The blankets on his bed were frayed and thin and the sheets were rough and scratchy. Lockley Prison seemed like the Ritz by comparison. He almost laughed at the thought. Then the knowledge that no one was looking for the real killer of Mrs Bannerman made him start shaking with fear. That man might be caught only if he attacked someone else, and even then, unless he confessed, who would link him with events in Coxton? For the first time, Jim began to wonder who had been responsible. Was it just chance? Had some passing villain simply had a go? Some lad from the area, perhaps, who knew she lived alone and thought he'd get easy pickings, then panicked when she came downstairs? Mrs Bannerman wouldn't be one to shrink from confronting an intruder; he could imagine her being foolhardy enough to challenge the man.

At last the appalling nature of what had happened to her penetrated through his absorption with his own fate and he felt reluctant anger on her behalf. The real killer must be found, not only to save his own neck but in the name of justice.

The house was stirring. Jim got up and went down to the bathroom on the floor below. It was occupied. He would not risk waiting outside but left his door ajar, hoping to hear when whoever was in there emerged, and as a youth in jeans went pattering down the bare stairs, Jim took his place and locked himself in. He did not want to meet any of the other residents.

He had breakfast at a snack bar among a row of shops some half a mile away. While he ate, he read the paper, which he had bought on the way. The crime was thoroughly reported. Much had been made of Mrs Bannerman's isolation. *Lonely recluse,* declared the tabloid paper he had chosen because the story was on the front page. Inside, there was his photograph again. Did he really look like that?

Jim had scrutinized himself that morning in the small mirror in the bathroom. The pale face that looked back at him as he shaved, carefully missing out his tiny moustache, had not seemed at all familiar, surmounted as it was by its honey hair, but the features were still his, the thin lips not yet shadowed by the growth above them, and the hunted eyes. Perhaps he should get some dark glasses, but wouldn't they draw attention to him?

He looked smart, though, in his suit, almost too smart for this run-down area. He must behave normally, not skulk about in places where the police would be looking for anyone acting suspiciously, not because they expected to find him but because that was their way.

Bracing himself, he left the snack bar and went shopping. He bought a cheap electric kettle, some packets of soup, a loaf of bread, cheese and half a dozen eggs, which he could boil in the kettle. He found some ham sealed in a package. That would do over the weekend. Finally he bought a small radio, because he must somehow survive the time he would spend in hiding.

He'd read a lot in prison. Passing a junk shop with a row of shabby paperbacks displayed outside, Jim picked up the fattest and looked at the first page. *I am born*, he read. He bought *David Copperfield* for twenty pence, and he also bought, for the same price, a bundle of steel cutlery which would provide a spoon, knife and fork, not that he could be fussy about how he ate. On the way back to his room, he thought about milk and instant coffee. Funny how you got out of the way of housekeeping: he'd always enjoyed going shopping with Maureen at weekends.

He had spent a fair bit of money and he would have to get hold of some more. Returning to the house, he saw some letters on a shelf in the hall. One was from the DHSS and he knew what it was, a cheque. He saw another letter addressed to the same name, and he took them both. One would provide proof of his identity when he cashed the cheque contained in the other.

You learned some useful tricks in prison.

19

A red Citroën drew up outside Ford House on Sunday morning.

The three children were in the garden riding their bicycles. Even Robin had a two-wheeler, though with stabilizers attached. He wore a policeman's helmet which had once belonged to Philip and was uttering shrill siren sounds. Emily was pretending to be on a pony and Philip was circling aloofly further afield, as befitted the eldest. He was on his way in a large jet to Australia, and had just reached Singapore. When he arrived in Sydney or Melbourne, or maybe in Perth, he hadn't decided which, his father would meet him and take him out to a farm with a thousand sheep.

When a police officer in uniform got out of the car, the children came towards him. He asked to see their mother, and Philip cycled round to the rear of the house calling out, 'Mum, a policeman wants to see you.'

It was Charles who came to the front door. He wore stained overalls and had a smudge of pale green emulsion on one cheek.

'Can I help you?' he said. 'I'm Charles Davies.'

'It's Mrs Davies I want to see, sir,' said the policeman. 'Constable Moody from the Coroner's office.'

'You'd better come in,' said Charles. 'Carry on playing,' he called to the children. 'And keep well away from the policeman's car. That means you, too, Robin.'

'Fine family you've got there, sir,' said the constable, following Charles into the house.

'Yes,' said Charles. 'The two older ones belong to my wife. The other one's ours.' Sometimes he felt obliged to make this distinction.

'I see, sir,' said Moody calmly.

'I suppose it's about Mrs Bannerman's death,' Charles said. 'I'm sure my wife's told you all she can.'

'I'm sure she has, sir, but she'll be needed at the inquest. That's why I'm here.' As Coroner's officer, PC Moody always tried to deal personally with witnesses.

'Oh, surely that won't be necessary? She only found the body,' said Charles.

'Mrs Bannerman wasn't dead then, Mr Davies,' said Moody. 'I'm afraid she will have to appear.'

Yvonne had been up in her workroom when Philip called. Receiving no answer, he had entered the house by the back door and rushed upstairs to tell her about the visitor. Now she appeared, descending the staircase into the hall, a pale young woman with her long dark hair tied into a pony tail. Moody thought she looked exhausted.

'I must insist that she be excused,' said Charles. 'The whole thing was a most unpleasant experience for her.'

'Charles, please let me speak for myself,' said Yvonne. 'Of course I must go if I'm needed.' She spoke from the half landing and continued on down the stairs, moving in what was almost a glide. She should be wearing a crinoline gown with some of her hair swept up on to the top of her head and ringlets round her ears, thought Moody fancifully. She would look the part of the chatelaine of this sort of house, dressed like that.

'It's only red tape,' said Charles.

'I found poor Audrey. I rang for the police and the ambulance. By climbing through the window I obscured evidence that might have helped the police,' Yvonne recited.

Charles stared at her. He was only trying to help her, have her spared further distress. Why oppose him?

'It's tomorrow at eleven, at the hospital, Mrs Davies,' said PC Moody. 'There's no coroner's court in Leckerton, so inquests have to be held wherever's most convenient and there's a room at the hospital we often

180

use. It's quite handy – no problem over parking and so on.'

'I'll be there,' said Yvonne.

'Can you get there? We can arrange transport, if not,' offered Moody.

'No, that's all right,' said Yvonne. 'I'll have to make some arrangements for Robin. The other children will be at school.'

'If you have to bring him, a police officer will look after him for however long it takes,' said Moody. 'It won't be a long business, it's just to identify the deceased and enable funeral arrangements to be made. It will be adjourned and re-opened at a later date when there's been time to go into all the circumstances.'

'But you know who did it, officer,' said Charles testily. 'This convict. He must have had his eye on the place after working there. They should never be let out to roam around among law-abiding citizens.'

'The man we want to interview was in for fraud, Mr Davies,' said Moody. 'He had no history of violence. And sooner or later most prisoners are returned to society. Best they get gradually acclimatized.' He smiled at Yvonne. 'Thank you, Mrs Davies. I'll see you tomorrow, then.'

'Yes.' She would ask Amy Parker to take Robin for an extra morning and keep him until she collected him.

'If you'd just left that to me, Yvonne, and not interrupted, the constable would soon have seen that your presence at the inquest isn't essential.' Charles spoke brusquely after PC Moody had gone.

'He wouldn't have, Charles. It's legal procedure,' said Yvonne. 'And it's no good you planning to tele-phone the Chief Constable or our MP to get me let off, because I intend to be there.' She turned away from him and stalked off upstairs.

How had she had known that he was thinking of

ringing the Chief Constable? What had got into her since they came to this house?

He went crossly away, unaware that Yvonne was crying in her workroom. She was afraid. She had pinned all her hopes on the move to this spacious house where they would no longer all be on top of one another but the result was a new isolation.

Charles returned to his painting, viciously daubing great swathes of pale green on the yellowed cream that had previously covered the drawing room walls. He worked thoroughly over the plastered expanse which he had previously washed and rubbed down. He cut no corners with this type of undertaking.

He had painted the house where Olivia and he had lived after their marriage, then he had papered the walls when she tired of their first choice. He had stuck a frieze of animals around Rosalind's room before she was born. He had fetched and carried, dried Olivia's hysterical tears when they fell, worked long hours at the office in order to advance his career and had gradually dropped his own former pursuits, his tennis and squash, his occasional round of golf. Olivia was uninterested in any sport and had begrudged him time thus spent. It wasn't enough, though. She had not been content and in time he had become less ready to placate her; then he had met Yvonne, who seemed to him to need help. Her brave insouciance had been appealing because he had read into it a longing to offload some of her cares. He had been wrong. She was self-reliant and he found that a threat.

He supposed you could live with someone for twenty years and still be surprised by something they said or did.

Playing father to another man's children was not easy; Charles was serious about his role and anxious to provide a strong male influence for Philip. Emily was a pretty little girl, and both children were polite and

182

biddable, but as time passed he began to wonder about their own father, to resent the years he had spent with Yvonne and to wonder what characteristics they had inherited.

You could only do your best, he supposed, and no one could say he had not done that. There were families like his all over the globe, reshuffled like packs of cards.

Now this business in the village – this murder – had come to upset things further. If only Yvonne had not got involved, had left the old woman to be found by somebody else, it need not have affected them and would have made no difference to Mrs Bannerman in the long run. Now they had reporters at their gate and had been obliged to leave the telephone off the hook, since they had had several calls asking for comment. Such notoriety was unfortunate, to say the least.

He painted on. At least the children were playing in the garden, and so far in peaceful concord. Emily was good at watching out for Robin, and Philip, though he sometimes distanced himself from the others, kept an eye on them. It was right for the older ones to have a care for younger children.

Things would improve. Yvonne was over-reacting to the tragedy in the village. He had only wanted to spare her more distress and she would recognize, in time, that he was right.

Jim spent Sunday in his room. It was quieter outside in the street than it had been the day before, and he felt it would be very risky to go out and buy a paper. Suppose his face stared back at him from the front page? It would stare back at every other reader, too.

He had a bath and rinsed his hair again, to make his blondness more secure. It was a pity it was sparse; his disguise would be more effective if he had a thicker crop. His moustache was becoming quite presentable, however; it was neat and dark, with, when you looked at it

183

more closely, some grey hairs among the brown. Perha[?]
he'd better dye it, too.

There was nothing else to do.

He had bread and cheese for his lunch, and boiled
eggs for supper, thinking wistfully of the substantial
meal his former companions would be eating in the
prison.

That night he slept badly again, missing the fresh air
and exercise to which he had become accustomed.
Images of Maureen curled up with her lover made him
writhe with jealousy, tormenting himself in the darkness. A quarrel broke out somewhere nearby and
disturbed the night. He heard insults hurled back and
forth between a man and a woman. That was marriage,
he thought.

He had spent some of the day listening to the radio,
and he had read a great deal of *David Copperfield*, who,
despite misfortune, seemed certain to win through. He'd
had friends. People didn't have time for friendship these
days; all they thought about was sex and money.

On Monday morning he packed up his few belongings, put on his suit and caught a bus into town. It would
be foolish to try to cash the DHSS cheque in an area
where the genuine recipient was known. He had a good
breakfast with eggs and bacon and felt better after that.
No one paid him any attention in the café, which was full
of men eating before they went to work. Did they all live
in lodgings?

He successfully cashed the cheque at a busy post office
and was not asked for any identification. Outside, he
dropped the second letter he had taken into the mail box.
It might as well go to its true destination now. After this,
he had gained enough courage to buy a newspaper. It
contained no reference to Audrey Bannerman. Perhaps
public interest was already dying down. It was the police
whom he must fear; his photograph would be displayed
in every police station in the country.

Made bold now, Jim booked a room at a four-star hotel in the name of Lesley Wilson. He said that he was in Birmingham on company business and would be staying for the week, mentioning the name of a well-known frozen food firm whom he said would pay the account. Wearing his sharp suit, his anorak over one arm, he was every inch the executive and was given a room with bath, television, tea-making equipment and a trouser press without demur.

This was better. He could stay here in comfort watching house movies on the video, and leave before the week was up and the bill presented. He might eat in the restaurant, if his nerve held, but otherwise there was always room service.

Yvonne sat at the back of the room where the inquest was to be held. PC Moody had greeted her when she arrived and, remembering that she had a small boy to park, had asked what she had done with him. Yvonne immediately felt calmer as she replied that he was being looked after in the village.

Moody cared deeply about his job. Sudden deaths needing investigation were often tragedies – road accidents, suicides, even murder. There were always shocked relatives and friends who, while grieving, still had to comply with bureaucratic demands. To each, their own disaster was the worst in the world; it was only to outsiders that some seemed more dreadful than others, but by any standards the death of Audrey Bannerman was appalling.

Moody left Yvonne to speak to some new arrivals and Yvonne recognized Rupert Bannerman. With him was a small, plump woman with smooth white hair. She wore a navy coat. Yvonne realized that this was Audrey's supplanter, as she was Olivia's: an uncomfortable thought. When they came across and Rupert introduced his wife, Yvonne saw that her fresh colour came from a threadwork of broken veins, apparently innocent of make-up, and she had a sudden fleeting vision of Audrey's careful matt complexion. A surge of loyalty towards the dead woman swept over her, and Felicity noticed her expression suddenly hardening. Not under-standing why, she supposed it was because Yvonne resented being dragged into a distressing experience which was not her affair.

'This won't take long, I believe,' she said.

'No.' Yvonne was curt. She turned to Rupert. 'Is there any more news? Have they found Sawyer yet?'

'No,' said Rupert. 'I don't think they've got the faintest notion where he is.'

The three sat together. Rupert gave evidence of identification and the coroner asked Yvonne to describe how she found the injured woman. He thanked her for her public spirit in acting as she had, gave permission for the funeral to go ahead, and arranged a date for re-opening proceedings two months hence.

'We're going out to Coxton now,' said Rupert as they filed from the room. 'Audrey's solicitor is meeting us at the house. There are things to see to, and we're going to talk to the vicar about the funeral.'

'I see,' said Yvonne.

'It's all a little unusual,' said Rupert. He sounded embarrassed. 'Audrey had no one else, you see.'

'I know.'

'Can we give you a lift home?'

'Thank you, no. I've got my car here,' Yvonne answered. Equipped with its new battery, it had started instantly that morning.

'Lunch, then? We thought we'd try the village pub. Is it all right? Would you join us? Perhaps you could tell us about Audrey's life there.'

'I can't,' said Yvonne. 'I'd only just met her. She seemed to be a rather private person.'

Rupert nodded.

'It's kind of you to suggest lunch,' Yvonne added. 'I don't think the pub does more than toasted sandwiches, but in any case I'm afraid I must get on with my work.'

'What do you do?' asked Felicity.

The gaze that Yvonne turned towards her was so frosty that Felicity could almost feel a physical chill.

'I make soft furnishings for an interior decorator,' said Yvonne.

'And you've lost several precious hours already. We mustn't keep you, then,' said Felicity.

'No. I'll get off, if you'll excuse me,' said Yvonne.

To avoid the traffic in the town centre, she took a route round the outskirts. Her way led through streets of houses and, pausing at a junction, she noticed the sign *Birch Street* on a wall. Surely that was where Denis lived? She had missed him on Friday. He had been coming to Ford House for only a few weeks but she had grown used to his difficult, ungracious company over their morning break. Last night Charles had said it was a pity she had let him go; the boy could have begun clearing the weeds from the former tennis lawn which Charles meant to restore, chiefly to attract his daughters. Denis, employed casually, would be cheaper than getting a firm in to raze the lot and re-sow it, and he might be just as competent in the long run.

Yvonne had not felt cooperative. She had muttered that she would try to find him when she had the time. Now was her chance. If he was out, his grandmother could give him a message. She turned into Birch Street and began looking for Number 7.

She soon found the house, one in a semi-detached row dating from the thirties and now mostly turned into flats or bedsitters, though a few were still occupied by families. Some had been renovated; this district would soon be on the way up.

There were various bells by the door.

Yvonne rang one marked *Crow* and after a long delay a

very old woman wearing a pinafore appeared. She smelled of stew and tobacco, and other things Yvonne preferred not to identify. Rather dismayed, Yvonne put on her best smile.

'Good morning, Mrs Crow. I wonder if you would give a message to Denis?' she said. 'I don't suppose he's in now.'

'Denis? Denis who?' asked Mrs Crow irritably. She had been watching television. Those educational programmes in the mornings were very interesting and she did not care for interruptions.

'Denis Crow, of course. Your grandson,' Yvonne answered, startled.

'I don't know no Denis,' said Mrs Crow. 'My grandson's in America with his dad and I haven't seen none of them for twenty years, nor will now, likely enough.'

Yvonne stared.

'Are you sure?' she asked.

'Course I'm sure. I know about my own family, don't I?'

'But he's been working for me. He said he lived with his grandmother at this address and his name's Denis Crow.' Yvonne knew she had the right number because it was the same as Emily's age.

'He was having you on,' said Mrs Crow, sucking at her dentures.

'Well, who is he, then?' Yvonne demanded. 'Does a boy live here – about seventeen? Round red face and short brown hair. He has a Walkman.' She put her hands to her ears to demonstrate.

'Oh, that's the young lad as sleeps in the van,' Mrs Crow said. 'Brother of the girl upstairs at the back. And they're not married, neither.'

'Who aren't?' Yvonne's head was spinning.

'The girl upstairs and the young fellow, Alan. Some sort of builder, he is. Has his own van – a blue one –

keeps it outside in the road. This lad's been sleeping in it.'

'Well!' Yvonne didn't know what to make of this information. Why had Denis lied to her about his name? Was he just teasing, as Mrs Crow implied? If so, he had an odd sense of humour. 'If you see him, perhaps you'd tell him that Mrs Davies came round and there's more work for him, if he wants it.'

'I'll make a point of it, dear,' said Mrs Crow, who had mellowed enough to start enjoying this encounter.

Yvonne drove home feeling cross and bewildered. Denis had told her a pack of lies about his circumstances, but she would hardly have engaged him if she had known he was living rough. Or would she? Perhaps all he needed was a chance to get on. He had worked well and he was healthy and strong. He wouldn't get into the Marines if he tried to deceive them, that was certain. Perhaps that had all been a fairytale, too.

She did not expect to see him again.

20

After the inquest, Detective Superintendent Hawkes sent a sergeant to Ivy Lodge with Rupert. The police had finished in the house and were going to hand the keys to the solicitor, who had been unable to get over to Leckerton in time for the brief inquiry.

He had not arrived when they reached the house. He had to travel from Sussex, where Audrey had lived before.

Detective Sergeant Dale unlocked the door and led the way inside. Treading reluctantly, Rupert and Felicity felt they were intruding on the dead woman's privacy as they entered her home. The police had been through some of her papers but they had no need to inspect everything; they had wanted to look at her insurance policy in case specific items of value were mentioned, but little was separately listed and Rupert had already supplied a description of what might have been stolen.

When Mr Gray, the solicitor, arrived, Dale handed him the keys and said that before he left there was a matter on which he wanted advice. The two went upstairs leaving Rupert and Felicity looking uncomfortably round the room, where they recognized pieces of furniture Audrey had brought to Tettlebury after Ford House was sold. Felicity pulled her coat collar closer, shivering slightly although the house was warm; the police had left the heating on low to prevent things getting damp. Rupert fretted about leaving the house empty; would Gray ask someone local to look after it? Not that it mattered now Audrey would not be returning.

Mr Gray and Detective Sergeant Dale came back, and Gray spoke to Rupert.

'Could I ask you to come and see what the police have found? You may know something about Mrs Bannerman's interests,' he said. 'You too, Mrs Bannerman, if you wouldn't mind. We men are at sea over this.'

A tall, thin man with fair greying hair, he led the way to a bedroom. There was a patchwork quilt on the bed, and the room was painted white with flowered curtains on a yellow ground at the window. There were china ornaments displayed on shelves, and a number of books. It was Hesther's girlhood room re-created in miniature.

Rupert had scarcely taken this in before Dale was showing him the contents of a drawer in a mahogany chest which had come originally from Ford House. It was full of knitted garments carefully sealed in plastic bags. A second drawer, then a third, was opened, similarly filled.

It was Felicity who examined them more closely and saw that the garments ranged from baby jackets to sweaters and dresses for first a toddler, then a larger girl, right up to teenage size. In the end they opened some of the bags to make certain of their contents.

'They were for Jenny,' said Rupert, and he felt as if a bar of ice had entered his soul. He turned to the two men. 'We had a daughter who died. You both know that. She became very depressed after a miscarriage. The child was a girl and she – my daughter – spoke of her as Jenny. It seems she didn't die for her grandmother either.'

'Oh!' Felicity turned away, her hand to her mouth.

'She'd have been fourteen by now,' Rupert said.

Felicity wondered why Rupert had not guessed what Audrey was knitting before they parted, for many of these things went back that far. Had they discussed nothing? She kept silent, waiting for someone else to speak.

Dale had seen plenty of strange things in his time and so had the solicitor, but this was a new experience for them both. Macabre, thought Gray, but she had been a strange woman.

'I'm the sole executor,' he told Rupert. 'But I'd like your advice about disposing of these.'

'Some charity for children?' suggested Rupert, surprised that he could utter at all.

Gray nodded.

'She left everything to an organization for the rehabilitation of prisoners, specifically for women. The house is to be offered to them as a hostel, for women who need care rather than incarceration, with the freedom to sell it and use the money to buy a property elsewhere if that seems more appropriate.'

Coxton would be glad to know that, thought Felicity. The village had had enough contacts with convicts already, from what she had heard lately.

'I see,' Rupert said.

'Before she came down here, she worked among women offenders,' said Gray. 'Maybe you didn't know that. She travelled to London, but in the end it became too much for her. Her heart wasn't too good latterly, though she ignored it.'

Dale, listening to this exchange, chose not to mention some other knitting, pale yellow wool, work in progress, found in a workbag in the dead woman's desk. Gray would come to it in time.

It was decided to ask the vicar to hold the key for the present, in case it was necessary to enter the house. Dale had found it hanging on the back of the door. The heating oil tank was full; Audrey would, Rupert knew, be too well organized to let it run low. He could not bear to think of the place getting damp and musty and was relieved when Mr Gray decreed that the heating should be kept on at a low temperature. The legatees would not want a sodden house and possibly, later, frozen and burst pipes.

'I hope you won't give Audrey's clothes to a jumble sale,' he told Mr Gray as they went out to the cars which were in the road.

'Oxfam, I thought, or the WRVS,' said Gray.

Rupert nodded. He did not want the inhabitants of Coxton fingering Audrey's skirts and sweaters in the village hall.

Detective Sergeant Dale drove back to Leckerton, and the others went to the vicarage.

Felicity thought she had never spent a more harrowing day in her life.

Back at headquarters, Dale told Detective Inspector Wright who, under Detective Superintendent Hawkes, was heading the inquiry, about the collection of knitted garments, and Wright decided that they had better learn the facts concerning the daughter's death, though it was not relevant to the case. He ordered a report to be made.

The police were not the only ones to express interest in the past. A reporter of the *Swalton Weekly Herald* had suspected that the victim was the former wife of one of the town's retired magistrates. When Rupert and Felicity arrived back at Tettlebury Manor, he was waiting for them.

Apart from saying that he was shocked and saddened by the tragedy, Rupert refused to comment, but this did not deter the reporter. On his way back to the office, he stopped off in the village and asked about the family. Soon he learned about the daughter, and when he checked the files he found the report on Hesther Bannerman's death. Because she had died in London, the inquest was held there, but the *Herald* had recorded the verdict and much of her story.

When he could, the reporter acted as stringer for a London daily. Soon the news was on its way.

*

Denis thought about trying school again on Monday morning, but instead he wrote his letter to the Marines. Tracy had got him an envelope and a sheet of paper; letter-writing did not feature in her life or Alan's, but she had begged them from Mrs Dove in the front flat.

Denis gave the Birch Street address and wrote the letter out in rough first, on the back of a bill. Then he went into town to buy a first-class stamp and post it. After that he went to the Pizza Parlour, where some youths he knew ribbed him, saying that they had heard his father had been to the school to answer questions about his absence.

'That's a lie,' Denis said. 'My mum's very ill and I'm looking after her. She'll probably die.'

The boys, who had made their assertion in order to bait him, were not sure if he was telling the truth. He had a reputation for invention, but he had been seen at school with a bruise on his face which he alleged had been caused by walking into a door, and one or two of them felt awkward about adding to his possible problems. After a few more taunts they grew bored with goading him, but when Denis left the Pizza Parlour he telephoned the emergency services and said that the school was on fire. Then he went back to Birch Street where he could lie on the bed watching television until Tracy came home.

He was just going upstairs when Mrs Crow came out of her ground-floor room and called him.

'You come here, young man,' she ordered. 'I want a word with you.'

Denis hesitated. He could ignore her; the old bag wouldn't come upstairs after him. He knew she rarely made it to the bathroom and had her own place at the back.

'Come on down,' she repeated.

Denis found himself turning to face her, staying half-way up the stairs where he could look down at her. She was such a little person. One good shove and she'd topple over.

'What did you mean by telling that Mrs Davies that I'm your grandmother?' Mrs Crow demanded.

Denis gaped at her.

'Yes, you may well look like that,' said Mrs Crow. 'She came round, Mrs Davies did. Thought you lived with me and that I'm your gran.' The old woman gave a sudden cackle. 'I can tell you, if I was, I'd send you about your business fast enough. Idle, you are.'

'I've done good work for Mrs Davies,' said Denis.

'Hm. So you say. Well, she's got more for you to do, if you're interested,' said Mrs Crow. 'That's why she came round. You're to go over there.'

'Did you tell her you're not my gran?' Denis came down a step.

'Course I did.'

'What did she say?'

'Bit surprised,' said Mrs Crow.

'She'd still give me work?'

'Seems so. I hope you behave yourself round there,' said the old woman.

'I must do, mustn't I, or she wouldn't be so keen to get me,' Denis retorted.

'What's to become of you?' asked Mrs Crow, shaking her head. 'Sleeping in that van's not right.'

'I'm joining the Marines,' Denis declared.

'Think they'll have you, do you?'

'Why shouldn't they?'

'You been in trouble with the law?'

'No.'

'Then why're you hiding out here?'

'I'm not hiding. I left home, that's all,' said Denis. 'Tracy did, too, but she was going with Alan anyway.'

'Hm. Well, if I was you, I'd go round to Mrs Davies and get myself fixed up, before she changes her mind,'

195

said Mrs Crow, tiring now and ready to conclude the interview.

'I'll think about it,' Denis said.

He slept a while on Tracy's bed. It was so warm and soft, and there was that smell. He was still there when she came home and she was none too pleased to find him lying on the duvet in his jeans.

He went out then and stole a bicycle, cutting the chain that secured it to a railing with some pliers he'd taken from the shed at Ford House. He put them in the bike's saddlebag and rode off. It was a good bike, with seven gears. As he went through the town he passed a gang of youths who had been drinking; they were scuffling together on the pavement, spoiling for a fight. Denis swerved away from them, pedalling past so that none was tempted to pick on him and pull him from the bike. Drink did bad things to you. He meant to keep away from it.

He put the bike round at the back of the house, beside Mrs Crow's private washroom. He'd tell her that he'd bought it from his wages.

He'd sell it when he went off to the Marines, and give the money to Tracy.

21

It was a long time since Jim had been so comfortable.

He had a deep, steaming bath and strolled round his hotel room examining the various refinements. There was a leather folder containing leaflets about various local attractions and instructions on how to view the house video, obtain laundry service, dial overseas calls, summon room service and even a doctor. There was also writing paper. The sheets were large and white. He fingered one, making up his mind. Then, with a razor blade, he cut the headed address from two of the sheets. On one blank page he printed his name and the words ALIBI. WHITE HONDA PICK-UP TAKEN WEST OF LOCKLEY PRISON WEDNESDAY EVENING. BEIGE ANORAK TAKEN FROM THE COACH AND HORSES. VAN LEFT IN READING STATION CAR PARK.

He folded the paper in three sections, like a circular, tucking one fold into another, and addressed it in capital letters to POLICE HQ, LECKERTON. They would check it for prints and find that it was genuine, but if he posted it in Birmingham, they would know where to look for him. Now came the gamble of the second letter.

Dear Maureen, he wrote. *I didn't kill Mrs Bannerman. She's the one who came to see you. Someone else did it but they will pin it on me unless he's found. Please post the enclosed and don't tell anyone. DESTROY THIS. Am OK. Jim.*

She'd know that the letter genuinely came from him, but if it were to be found by the police it said nothing to indicate that he had seen her. He put the message and the note to the police in an envelope, addressed it to her in capitals and went down to the foyer where he bought a first-class stamp from the hall porter, who barely glanced at him. He dropped it in the box provided for guests. He had probably missed the evening clearance but that didn't matter. Now he must will Maureen to do as he had asked. The name of the hotel was printed on the envelope and he must trust her not to make use of that information to betray him.

He hoped the man, her lover, would not see the letter and ask questions.

Jim ordered a meal from room service, soup, then steak with chips and vegetables. He ordered some wine, too. Why not? He would not be paying. When the meal arrived, he made himself busy in the bathroom, calling out to the waiter to leave it. He didn't want too many people looking at his face.

There was nothing on the television that night about the crime. Audrey Bannerman was not a missing child or pretty girl, nor even a brave inner-city ancient fending off a mugger. She was not the stuff, for long, of headlines.

Maureen did not receive the letter until Wednesday. The post came before she left for work and she opened it at once, puzzled by the address on the envelope and not recognizing Jim's writing from the capitals. As soon as she read the contents, her heart seemed to plummet. Then she rallied. So he was in Birmingham. Well, that, at least was a long way from Reading. She had seen a television interview with the stout woman who had sat next to him on the bus to Oxford, and had breathed more freely knowing he had left the area.

She hadn't recognized the dead woman as her visitor. The press had only a passport photograph of Audrey to use and it was not a good likeness. Fancy thinking she was from the welfare! What was she doing, interfering in things that were not her business?

Jim hadn't put a stamp on his weird message addressed to the police. She read it and believed what was written, so she stamped it and posted it on the way to work. She tore up his note to her, and the envelope, and burned the pieces in a saucer, much to the amazement of Nicola. Then she flushed the ashes down the lavatory. They failed to disappear at first, and she waited for the cistern to re-fill. This time, helped by a shove from the brush, they were swirled away.

Wednesday morning's tabloids told Hesther's story and brought Audrey's murder back to the front pages.

CONVICT DAUGHTER'S SUICIDE read one headline, and there was a picture of Hesther, her hair cropped short, face gaunt and lined. The paragraph below revealed that she had been sent to prison for stealing three items worth less than ten pounds. The act had been a cry for help, said the piece, but instead of giving it to her, by means of hospital treatment, she had been sentenced to eighteen months detention from which she had emerged so depressed that eventually she had killed herself.

Rupert read only a small paragraph in *The Times*; it was Felicity who was curious enough to see what the popular press had to say. One paper went far enough back to recount that before her lapse Hesther had lived in a flat in Pimlico and worked for a wine merchant. Felicity remembered how interested she had become in viniculture after a trip to France, and how pleased and amused Rupert had been as he discussed vintages with her and asked her advice about what to buy. Then her visits home had become less frequent. Her parents supposed she was involved in a romance and because she brought no man home, Rupert feared that she might be mixed up with someone who was married. He had tried, on one of her rare visits, when she was obviously unhappy and looked ill, to get her to confide in him, but she had closed up into mulish silence. After that she did not come for six months, always making excuses when they tried to press her. Then she arrived one day without warning and was clearly unwell. Audrey realized what was wrong at once: she had had an abortion, a late one, as they discovered afterwards, but since Hesther refused to discuss it with her, it was only much later, when she was in prison, that the full truth was acknowledged. Long before her arrest, Hesther had given up her job and was drifting along, eating little and smoking too much – not drugs, just tobacco – unable to sleep. She had money enough to live on, had she chosen to use it, for her father gave her an allowance and her parents, between them, had bought her the flat.

After she was released from Holloway, she was like a stranger, refusing to talk either to Rupert or Audrey who had both visited her regularly, sitting in silence with her because she could find nothing to say and was patently uninterested in the small stories they dredged up in attempts to amuse her. She spent a short time at home before going as a voluntary patient to a psychiatric hospital. One day she disappeared and went to London, where she took her own life.

Even now, Rupert liked to think that the loss of her baby had been a natural event. Neither he nor Audrey could accept the truth, and now Audrey, knitting for the infant that never was, working with other offenders, had met her own death at the hands of a convict she had employed. It would never end, thought Felicity sadly.

Hesther's crime was so trivial. She had taken a few items from, of all places, a cosmetic counter in a big store, she who by now was plain and unattractive and used no make-up. She was twenty-eight years old when she died. There was something very wrong about a society which incarcerated among hardened criminals a sick woman who had stolen goods worth only a trifling sum and which allowed drunken motorists who killed people to go free.

Hesther had needed love and had not allowed those who wanted to cherish her the chance to do so. Now the past had been resurrected to haunt her father.

Leckerton police's current preoccupation was their murder, but other crimes continued to be committed. There were stolen cars, drunken brawls, burglaries, motoring offences, failures to pay fines and taxes, neighbours' disputes and accidents, plenty to keep them busy.

Audrey's nightdress and dressing gown had been sent for analysis. The discovery of traces from the killer's person or clothing would be useful when Jim Sawyer came to court, as he would in time. Because the victim had had a minor heart condition, the defence might go for manslaughter; indeed, Sawyer would be wise to admit to that as such a plea might be accepted, but nevertheless the prosecution must mount a case.

An irritation for the police was the number of hoax emergency calls there had been in recent weeks, one naming the cinema, one McDonald's, and one the comprehensive school. The last one indicated a disaffected pupil and perhaps they were all linked. The matter must be investigated; public time could not be wasted in this way and one day there might be a genuine alarm which could not be answered because of another false call.

Jim Sawyer's letter arrived on Thursday. Checks on it for fingerprints proved that it genuinely came from him.

'So he went to Reading after all,' said Detective Inspector Wright, examining the good quality paper, cut along one edge. 'He's removed the heading. He's holed up in a hotel spending Mrs Bannerman's money.'

The only flaw in this theory was that they now knew that her credit card had been used in Bristol. A great many things had been bought, ranging from alcohol to telephones.

'He's stocked up to make a sale,' said Detective Sergeant Dale. 'He'd have learned about that in the nick.'

They found the Fiat in Bristol, in a multi-storey car

park, with several sets of fingerprints inside, none of them Sawyer's.

He had never touched Audrey's car. He had not even washed it when he worked for her.

The stolen Honda pick-up had not been recovered. In fact it had been stolen by someone else, repainted and sold. Its owner never got it back.

Hotels in Reading and around the area had to be checked out.

'He may be hanging about hoping to see his wife and the kiddie,' Wright declared. The wife had denied seeing him but she could be helping him secretly. She would have to be watched.

The small church in Coxton was well filled for Audrey's funeral. Julian Parker, the vicar, was agreeably surprised to see faces familiar and unfamiliar ranged before him as he read the lesson, Revelations XXI, always appropriate. People had been so shocked by the violence in their midst that those who could make the gesture of attending had done so.

Rupert and Felicity sat near the back of the church, and as they moved out to the graveyard, rain started to fall from the leaden sky. To Felicity, it seemed as though every day, this autumn, had been wet.

A large spray of white flowers had rested on the coffin throughout the service. They bore no card, for Rupert had not known what to write. Several bunches of chrysanthemums and a few late dahlias had been left at the church, and Yvonne had brought a small posy of anemones. On her way to buy them, she had had her hair cut in a bob to just beneath her ears. Felicity, sitting in the pew behind her, thought it a big improvement.

Yvonne did not stay for the interment, but Detective Inspector Wright and Detective Sergeant Dale were there to observe who remained. It had been known before for killers to attend their victims' funerals.

This one did not.

'Didn't you see anything that night, Charles?' Yvonne asked over dinner.

'What night?' Charles had been enjoying the chicken casserole which Yvonne had taken from the freezer for their meal. Lately, they had had a lot of casseroles. Not so long ago she had taken much more trouble over meals.

Now she'd had all that hair, which had reached to between her shoulder blades, lopped off. It made her look different: older, assured. He wasn't sure that he liked it.

'Wednesday night, last week. The night poor Audrey was attacked,' said Yvonne impatiently. 'You were very late home. I hadn't thought about it before but you could have seen something as you came through the village. Did you?'

'No, not a thing,' said Charles. He ate two more mouthfuls. She'd put almonds in the sauce, which was a nice touch. Then he remembered. 'There was a van parked across the road from our gate,' he said. 'Some couple necking, I suppose.'

'What sort of van?'

'A blue one. A Bedford or Ford, I think it was. I didn't take a lot of notice.'

'That might be important, Charles,' said Yvonne.

'Why? It was nowhere near Ivy Lodge, and he took her car, didn't he? The convict?'

'I know, but you don't usually see blue vans outside our gate when you come back late, do you? Have you ever before?'

'No.'

'You should tell the police,' said Yvonne.

'Why? They know who did it. It's just a matter of picking him up.'

'Yes, but suppose the van was involved. They could look for it. It could be important. Where is it now?

Maybe he had an accomplice who met him outside the prison.'

It was this last theory that swayed Charles. Tiresome though it would be, he must do his duty.

Detective Sergeant Dale came out straight after he had telephoned, though it was after nine o'clock. He listened to what Charles had to say and then they both went to examine the spot where the van had been pulled off the road on to the grass verge.

More than a week later there were still faint tyre marks visible, but they were too indistinct to yield useful impressions.

A Bedford or Ford van was not what Jim Sawyer had mentioned in his note, and the Honda pick-up stolen that night had been white. The blue one was nothing to do with the case and could be discounted.

No one was looking for Jim Sawyer in Birmingham. He had moved from the first hotel to another on Thursday, walking quietly out through the rear entrance, leaving his bill unpaid. The new one was just as comfortable. He'd go on to Coventry next, then, perhaps, Leeds. He could keep this up indefinitely, he had decided, as he passed the quiet days. He had been on the run for more than a week, and his moustache was a definite structure on his short upper lip. He could see it from the corner of his eye when he peered downwards. He touched it up with dye every day.

He was more confident now, walking round in his smart suit, but the days were long. He still read a great deal. David Copperfield had married his Agnes, and because the book had been so solid, Jim had bought *Great Expectations*. He wandered round busy stores playing the game of Let's Pretend by picking out things Maureen would like. He chose a doll for Nicola, and almost bought it, but then realized that her mother would not allow her to keep it if it had come from him.

Most evenings he ate in his room, watching television. Room service was efficient and it was wiser to charge up his meals to his bill than go outside to a restaurant where he would have to use Lesley Wilson's card. He always ordered half a bottle of wine with his dinner, and he had put on weight.

On Saturday afternoon he went to the cinema. He had visited several during the week. It made a change from television and he had to get out of the hotel to allow his room to be cleaned. Fresh sheets every day were a treat, and the towels were large and soft.

When he came out of the cinema it was raining hard. His anorak covered only his upper half and, by comparison with his suit, it was very shabby. He needed a proper raincoat.

The shops were still open and, on impulse, Jim decided to buy one. Making his choice, he presented the bank card which he had used before for minor purchases. He forgot that a sanction was required for more than a certain sum.

He was arrested there in the shop. The assistant, going away on the pretext of folding the coat before packing it into a bag, asked someone else to call the police and delayed the unsuspecting Jim long enough for them to arrive.

They did not realize who he was for some time, since at first Jim would not utter a word.

22

Bet learned about Jim's arrest on the radio on Sunday morning.

'Got that bloke,' she told Len, relieved. Len was still in bed while she had been giving Bruce and Sharon their breakfast. She took Len a cup of tea and told him what she had heard. Now she could stop wondering where Len had been at the time of the crime.

'How? Where?' Len sat up in bed, alert.

'In Birmingham, it seems,' Bet replied. 'They didn't give any details.'

'Hmph.' Len lay back against the pillows. 'He'll be for it now,' he said.

He would lose no sleep over Jim. It was his bad luck, picking the same night to break out. Now he, Len, was safe. The police wouldn't go looking for evidence for the defence.

Bet was going to say that Sawyer deserved all he got for doing in a defenceless old woman, but decided to keep her opinion to herself. Len could be violent; he had just served a sentence for manslaughter and he had struck her before now, though never the kids. He knew that would mean curtains. Since he'd been home this time he'd been soft with them all, which was nice, but it might not last.

He'd be inside again before long. She knew that. He couldn't resist easy money.

As soon as he had finished his tea, Len got up and dressed and went down to the shop to buy a paper.

The arrest made headline news in the tabloids and he read how Jim had been caught using a stolen bank card. The silly sod; you needed to be careful with those, keep the purchases small, not be greedy.

Now he dared not risk using Audrey Bannerman's card again because to do so would show that whoever had taken it was still at large and was therefore not Jim Sawyer. When Bet was busy, he cut it and her cheque book into small pieces and dropped them in the litter bin. Then he took the bag down to the large bins in the basement, a task he rarely undertook. Bet noticed that their own bin had been emptied and a new plastic liner fitted. It had not been full and she thought it wasteful; however, as Len had been so helpful she made no complaint, but thanked him and asked him to peel the potatoes for the roast they were going to have at midday. Len was good about the place when he was at home; he did not find household tasks demeaning.

Peeling away, Len thought about the kid who had been with him on the job. He didn't even know his name. Perhaps it was just as well, though the kid knew him as Len. The blinds had been down in the kitchen and the kid wouldn't have seen a thing, but he knew Len had been there. Suppose he grassed? He was a wild kid and might get into trouble on his own account. Then he'd split on Len and get himself off the hook.

Len decided that something would have to be done about him.

Jim admitted who he was as soon as a constable looked from him to a poster on the wall in the police station to which he was taken after his arrest.

'Changed yourself quite a bit, haven't you?' said the arresting officer, and his manner hardened. Until then, he had thought that the prisoner was merely a thief; now he knew that he was a killer, one who mugged old women.

He didn't look much of a menace, standing there in his smart suit, but some of the most merciless murderers in history had been mild-looking men.

Jim was charged with using a stolen bank card. That

would do for the moment, while the police team investigating the crime in Coxton were told that their hunt was over and took charge of the prisoner.

He was driven to Leckerton that night.

Jim was left alone in a cell for a long time before anyone spoke to him. He was given no cup of tea, nor any food.

At some stage it was his right to be fed; it was also his right not to talk, and to be represented by a solicitor. All this was very different from his first arrest, but even then he had not been allowed bail, although the prisons were bursting at the seams and he was no threat to public safety. In the end, he had decided it was just as well, because Maureen was so bitter and unforgiving. She could not understand why he had done what he had; all she could think of was the disgrace.

He should have realized that an appeal to her would be useless. Mrs Bannerman had said that her mind was made up and she had been right. Now she – his one friend, as it seemed to Jim – was dead, and he was banged up again. At least he wasn't responsible for what had happened to her; that was a separate matter, whatever the law might decide. If he went down for her murder, it wouldn't be like his last conviction, when he was a category C offender. This time he would be sent to a maximum security prison where there would be hard men, terrorists and multiple murderers, real villains who should be locked away for the rest of their lives. Jim might be sentenced to twenty years, and unless he admitted his guilt he would never be considered for parole. Sitting there, chilled and hungry, Jim's not very vivid imagination delivered up to him dire scripts of the future.

He was too tired and depressed to consider how to establish his innocence, but he remembered advice from old lags in Lockley. Say as little as possible and press for your right to a brief.

At last he was taken to an interview room, where Detective Superintendent Hawkes and Detective Inspector Wright came to see him. They asked him what he had done after leaving the prison, and he told them the truth. When he said he had gone straight to Reading, they suggested that, on the contrary he had gone out to Coxton after taking the pick-up.

'Why would I do that? It was near the prison and I had my bike, if that was what I meant to do. I could have hidden up somewhere till it was dark,' Jim dredged up some defiance.

'You only thought of it after you'd got the pick-up,' said Wright.

'Haven't you found it? The pick-up?' Jim asked. 'I left it in the station car park in Reading.'

'So you said in your note, but it wasn't there when we looked, and it's still missing,' said Wright.

'I'd still got the key,' Jim said. 'You've got it now, with my things.' All his possessions had been surrendered, put in bags and listed.

'That proves nothing. You could have left it in Coxton, preferring the Fiat, and some kid could have taken it to get home,' said Wright.

'Where's the Fiat key, then, or Mrs Bannerman's cheque book and such?' Jim asked.

It was true that although the Fiat had been found its key was missing.

'You got rid of them,' Wright suggested.

'It's not true,' said Jim. 'None of it's true. You should be looking for somebody else.'

Naturally enough, they didn't believe him and they kept him there for most of the night, going over and over the ground and asking him what he had done with the stolen jewellery.

Jim stuck to his story.

'I've told you what happened. I went to Reading to see my wife. I left the pick-up and cycled out towards

Calcot. I found a boiler room behind some offices and spent the night there. Then I went home the next day but Maureen – ' he choked, mentioning her name – 'was out and I had to give up.'

'You took the Fiat and drove to Bristol, where you did a good bit of shopping,' said Hawkes. 'Then you spent time in Reading before moving on to Birmingham.'

'Bristol? I've never been there in my life,' said Jim.

At some stage in the proceedings he was given sandwiches and tea, and after that he simply repeated that he had told them the truth and had nothing more to say. He was reeling with fatigue, and eventually he was sent back to his cell for what was left of the night.

'It's all down to forensic, now,' said Hawkes. 'Let's hope the lab comes up with something good.' He'd have probably worn the anorak at Ivy Lodge, though he wouldn't have had the suit by then. 'He can't prove he was anywhere else.'

'I suppose he wasn't?' remarked Wright.

Hawkes gave him a look.

'He couldn't have been driving to Bristol in that Fiat while he was on a bus going to Oxford,' Wright stated.

'A wrong identification,' said Hawkes. 'That's the explanation. The woman made a mistake.'

Witnesses had made such mistakes before. Identification was not always easy.

A solicitor came in the morning. He spent a long time with Jim, who had been given a good hot breakfast. He was safely locked up now and could murder no more old ladies; correct procedures must be followed; no one wanted complaints about the prisoner's treatment. The solicitor, Gordon Stone, a young man who had not minded losing his Sunday's golf because he was interested in criminal law, spent a long time with Jim.

'What time did you break into the house in Coxton?' he asked, and 'Where did you leave Mrs Bannerman's car?' He tried plenty of trick questions and was not satisfied with all that Jim told him, but he was also not convinced that he had committed the offence for which he was being held.

When Jim was originally arrested for fraud, he had soon seen that the game was up and had been frank in admitting what he had done. This time, he declared that he was innocent of murder although he had stolen a purse and used the Marks and Spencer's charge card and the bank card as well as the cash it contained. He also revealed where he had stayed in Birmingham and that he had left the first hotel without paying, and the second, though not voluntarily. The police had checked this and had collected his things from the second hotel. He was hardly a skilful criminal, the solicitor decided, surveying his blond client who now had the grizzled stubble of overnight beard on his chin.

'I dyed my hair,' Jim said sadly.

'Yes.' Gordon Stone saw a broken man who must always have been weak, like so many whom he found himself attempting to defend. 'Why did you abscond?' he prompted.

'I wanted to see my wife. I wanted to sort things out with her. I knew she'd found someone else.' Now the words poured from him. He had been alone for over a week, a period in which he had spoken only minimal sentences to do with obtaining food or the few other things he had needed. He had fought against being loquacious with the police, aware of the danger, but this man was on his side. 'There's not much to think about in prison,' he explained. 'I knew it was all up, really – she didn't visit or write – but I couldn't accept it.' He sighed heavily.

'Go on,' Stone urged.

'When I went to work for Mrs Bannerman, she was nice,' said Jim. 'She treated me very well and she knew about prison. I wondered if she'd been inside herself, as a

211

matter of fact. Of course, I know now that it was all on account of her daughter.' He had read every report. 'I asked her to find out how Maureen was, and Nicola, my daughter.'

'Did Mrs Bannerman visit you at the prison?'

'No. We spoke on the telephone.'

That was a pity. A visit would have been recorded, but though a telephone call would have been noted, if Sawyer paid for it, the number might not have been registered. He would check it. The man's wife would have to admit meeting Mrs Bannerman, if challenged. Still, proving this part of his story to be true did not disqualify him from having carried out the robbery.

'I'd stopped working for her by then, you see,' Jim went on. 'I wouldn't have hurt her, Mr Stone. Whoever did it should be strung up.' He looked fierce as he said this.

'Who do you think it was?'

'How should I know? Anyone passing. But why her? Her place isn't all that big.'

'Because they knew an old lady lived there?' suggested Stone.

'She wasn't that old,' said Jim. 'Just getting on a bit. She kept the place herself and did the garden, except the heavy stuff. That's why she needed me, to plant a hedge and then lay some stones on the pat – on the terrace. And I painted the kitchen.'

'And you left your fingerprints there.'

'I suppose so,' said Jim.

'There's a lot of circumstantial evidence against you,' said Stone.

'I can see that.'

And there was no obligation on the police to look for evidence against Jim's complicity: none at all.

'You stole the pick-up and coat,' Stone confirmed. Jim had described his night on the run and his misery as he huddled in the boiler room. Such a tale had to be true.

Most men on the run would have hung on to the stolen vehicle, parked it in a field or copse somewhere out of the way and spent the night in it, but not this ineffectual muddler.

'You never saw your wife?'

Jim did not hesitate.

'No,' he said. 'She was out. Must have gone to work.'

'You didn't wait till she got back?'

'No. I thought her bloke might turn up. Mrs Bannerman said he was on nights.'

'You could have gone to her work place.'

'Too risky.'

'You gave up very easily.'

'Yes.' Jim could not let Maureen down by telling Stone what had really happened.

Stone knew that it made no difference whether he was speaking the truth or not: he could have committed the crime in question and gone to Reading afterwards.

'So you caught a bus to Oxford and sat next to a woman who later reported seeing you?'

Jim nodded.

'Then what did you do?'

'I was thinking of going back to Lockley or giving myself up at a police station, but then I read about what had happened to Mrs Bannerman and that I was being blamed, so I decided to run for it,' said Jim.

He described his theft of the car in Oxford and his journey to Banbury where he had bought the hair dye and a razor.

'What about the car?' asked Stone.

'I left it in a street in Stratford-on-Avon,' said Jim.

'Have you told the police that?'

'I'm not sure – I don't think so. What difference will it make?'

'Not a lot, but they might make sure its owner gets it back, if he hasn't already,' said Stone mildly.

'I stole a purse in Stratford,' said Jim. 'At a pub. I was

using the card from it when they took me. There was a Marks and Spencer's card, too. I bought this suit with it.' For the first time a faint smile appeared on his face. 'I felt good, doing that.' He said this with some complacence.

'I can imagine,' said Stone drily. 'I expect you practised the signature first.'

'Yes,' said Jim, looking surprised at this perspicacity.

'You dumped your prison gear?'

'Yes. In a litter bin. I left my jacket in the Honda.'

There was no point in trying to locate the clothing. It could be proved that Sawyer was where he said he was after the crime was committed. If the real perpetrator had been using Audrey Bannerman's bank card, and maybe passing her cheques elsewhere while Jim was known to be in Birmingham, it might help his case. In France, such a line of investigation would be followed as a matter of course; in Britain, no such duty rested with the police but he, Stone, could set inquiries in train.

They would not necessarily prove that his client had not killed Audrey Bannerman. The prosecution would argue that he had panicked and dumped the car, cheque book and bank card and someone else had found them and used them.

It was going to be very difficult indeed to prove that Jim Sawyer had not been in Coxton on Wednesday night.

Len thought about that odd kid while his family enjoyed their roast pork and crackling. To follow, there was apple tart and custard. Bet was a really good cook when she put her mind to it.

'When I retire, we might run a pub, with you doing the grub,' he said, spiking a crisp roast potato on his fork and running it round his plate to mop up the gravy.

'When you retire? Don't make me laugh,' said Bet.

He shrugged.

214

'One bit of luck and we'd be set up for life,' he told her. He went into a dream of robbing a bank and gaining half a million pounds.

'Like winning the pools?' mocked Bet.

'Right.'

He was planning something now, she could tell. He'd never go straight, whatever he said, but the trouble was that he was too ambitious. He'd done loads of small jobs and never got caught, but as soon as he had tried something big, it had gone wrong.

They went to the park in the afternoon, so that Bruce and Sharon could play on the slide and the swings. It was pleasant there, a mild late autumn day, but after a time it began to rain and they hurried home.

Bet put on the kettle to make some tea. Len drank his quickly and then he went out.

'I may be late back,' he said. 'Don't you worry, love, if I am.'

It wasn't another woman. She knew that. It was a stronger attraction, the lure of getting something for nothing, and perhaps the spice of danger attached to the way it was done.

Len needed a car.

He walked round the town looking for one that had been left unlocked or that one of the keys in his collection would fit, and he still had the key of Mrs Bannerman's Fiat. He looked out for another Fiat: it stood to reason a car of the same make was the most likely one to suit.

It took him nearly an hour to find one, but he succeeded. The key needed a bit of jockeying before the engine would start, but it worked. He found he couldn't withdraw it again, or not without using a lot of force, but that didn't matter. He'd go and attend to the boy, then put the car back somewhere near the place where he had found it.

He took his cosh.

23

Denis knew that Jim Sawyer had been arrested.

He lay in the van, zipped into his sleeping bag, his earphones silent so that he could think.

The guy hadn't done it, so he'd get off, wouldn't he? Be able to prove he was somewhere else? But people did get nicked for things they hadn't done. Everyone knew that. Even for murder.

He could go out and make a phone call, tell the police they were wrong. He could say that the real killer was a man called Len who had been in Lockley Prison up to a few weeks ago. They'd be able to trace him, then. But if Len was caught, he'd split on Denis, because he'd know who had tipped off the cops, and if that happened, he wouldn't get into the Marines. The papers had come already and needed a lot of studying, but you'd no chance if you'd got a record, or not until years afterwards. He'd understood that much. He and Tracy had looked at them together.

She and Alan had been good to him this weekend. The night before, Saturday, they'd taken him to the cinema and then a meal, paying for him, and today he'd had the use of their room while they were out. He knew they felt bad because Alan had said he couldn't go on sleeping in the van after the end of next week. He must look for a place of his own, like a bed in a hostel for homeless people, and try for a regular job.

'I can go back to Mrs Davies,' Denis told him. 'She sent a message. Can't do without me.' He grinned defiantly. 'Trust me, Alan. It'll work out.'

He could ride to Coxton on his new bike. He'd been out for a spin that afternoon. Mrs Crow had seen it and said it was all right to keep it round the back. She wasn't so bad, after all.

He didn't want Tracy or Alan to find out he'd got it. They'd know he wouldn't have had enough money to buy it.

He'd ride out to Ford House in the morning and see what Mrs Davies wanted. Then he'd find digs.

Falling asleep, Denis wove a fantasy in which Mrs Davies offered to take him in as a lodger, in one of those fancy rooms upstairs in the big, comfortable house.

Len opened the door of the van and shone his torch full on Denis's face.

'Come on, lad, we've work to do,' he said, catching hold of the end of the sleeping bag and giving Denis's foot a hard tweak.

'What –?' Terrified, Denis sat up. When he realized who had woken him, he was still more afraid.

'Ran out on me, didn't you?' Len said. He spoke pleasantly. No sense in getting the kid's back up. He was a strong young chap and Len didn't want to cosh him here, where he'd have to get rid of the body. He wanted the kid's cooperation in his own destruction, for destroyed he must be. Len had decided that he had no choice in the matter.

'I – I –' Denis did not know what to say.

'I expect you wanted to get your hands on the van, try a bit of driving yourself,' Len suggested.

'Yes, that was it,' gasped Denis.

'Well, get up kid. Get your clothes on,' said Len. 'We're going out.'

'I – I don't want to,' said Denis feebly.

'You don't want to, eh? Too bad. I'm afraid you've got to come,' said Len. He slid the cosh down his sleeve and into his hand. The kid might try yelling, but not if he was sufficiently afraid. Folk never realized how a good yell might save them. Women faced by rapists were too polite; a good scream might make the man run off, but they didn't like raising their voices. 'We're going out to the place you got the key for,' he said. 'It's a pity to waste it.'

'But – but –' Denis spluttered.

Len let him see the cosh.

'If I hit your hand with this, you won't like it,' he said conversationally. 'It'll break your bones. Them bones in your hand aren't strong, you know, and they don't mend easy. You and me are in this together, my lad. We're mates, remember? If I go down, so do you. A lad like you was hanged years ago when he was out on a job with another fellow who killed a guy. He didn't do it, mind, the one that was hanged. His mate did, but he swung for it.'

'They don't hang no one now,' said Denis. He trembled as he began climbing slowly out of his sleeping bag. He slept in his sweater; it got cold in the van.

'No, they get sent down for life instead,' said Len. 'Sometimes they get out quite quick. Sometimes they're in for twenty years. It depends. Now, hurry.'

Denis slowly pulled on his jeans, then reached for his trainers. He felt sick with fright as he got out of the van, pulling his anorak on. Perhaps he could run away once he got into the road.

But Len had thought of that. He took hold of the boy's arm and twisted it up behind his back, forcing Denis to go where he was bidden.

He thought that perhaps Len wanted to use the van again. If so, and Denis had to get the keys, he'd wake Alan and Tracy no matter how much trouble he got into afterwards.

But this wasn't what Len had planned.

'I've got wheels,' he said, pushing Denis along the road to where a yellow Fiat was parked. Denis noticed that it was the same model as Mrs Bannerman's. For a wild moment he thought that it might be her car,

218

resprayed, but as soon as he was bundled inside, he saw that the upholstery was a different colour.

'Now, don't get any fancy ideas about running away again,' said Len. 'You got nothing out of that other job. That was stupid of you, wasn't it? If you'd stayed, you'd have had some loot.'

'You – you killed Mrs Bannerman,' whispered Denis.

'No, I didn't. She slept sweetly all the time I was there,' said Len. 'Jim Sawyer came along later and did for her. Funny, that, wasn't it? Him breaking out the same night.'

If Denis hadn't seen for himself what had really happened, he might have believed Len.

Len bundled him into the back of the car and gave him a hard rap over the knuckles as he did so. The heavy cosh hurt and Denis smothered a whimper of pain.

What if he yelled for help?

Len seemed to read his thoughts as he got into the driver's seat.

'No good shouting,' he said. 'You'd be in just as much trouble as me. You took the van that night, after all. I can say I wasn't there. It'd be your word against mine. I didn't leave any prints.'

He was wearing gloves now. Denis saw the cosh held in one stubby hand. Perhaps it was the very weapon that had killed Mrs Bannerman. He shuddered.

'What you need's a drink,' Len said kindly. He put the cosh down.

Denis was wondering if he could somehow get out of the car and run, but if he tried to tip the front passenger seat forward to open the door, Len would have time to pick up the cosh and hit him.

Len had picked up a bottle from somewhere in the car. He undid it and passed it to Denis.

'Have some of this,' he said. 'It will make you feel better.'

'I don't drink,' muttered Denis.

'Don't know what you're missing, then,' said Len. 'Go on. Drink it down.' He lifted the cosh threateningly. Denis raised the bottle to his lips and Len tilted it so that he was forced to swallow some of the whisky it contained. It took his breath away but almost at once a warm glow seemed to spring up inside him. Len made him swallow some more, and this time Denis was less reluctant.

'There,' said Len, when he was satisfied. 'That wasn't so bad, was it?' He hadn't reckoned on the kid not drinking. The scotch would have quite an effect on him, more than he'd expected when he thought of giving him alcohol. The right amount would make him easier to handle; too much might make him aggressive.

He started the car and drove off down the road.

Denis sat in the back, hugging his arms across his body. What was going to happen now? Were they really going to Coxton? Len was driving through the town, heading towards the country. If only a police car would come along and stop them! Denis would say he had been abducted. When the police saw the cosh, they'd believe him.

After a few more miles, Len stopped the car again and made Denis swallow some more whisky. He had none himself; that was for later.

Denis felt rather swimmy now but much less afraid. Something would happen to save him. He peered out of the window, recognizing various landmarks as they drove through the countryside. The night was dry, with fitful interludes when clouds blew past the moon and a pale silver light shone down. Soon they reached Coxton, passing the shop and Ivy Lodge.

Len had had a look round earlier, before darkness fell. He remembered cycling over a narrow bridge crossing a small river when he came from the prison. It was near the big house, and he'd seen, today, that after so much rain the river was in spate, its dark water rushing towards the bigger river which it joined further on. He'd

220

decided to tip the kid in, then go on to Ford House and do the job that had failed before.

They met no other traffic. Len stopped in a small parking bay by the river, where fishermen and picnickers left their cars. Then he turned off the lights and got out.

'Want to do a bit of driving, kid?' he asked.

Denis had been very relieved when they drove past the gates to Ford House. Perhaps Len was only having him on. What now, though?

'Get into the front and have a feel of the wheel,' Len urged. That would get the kid's prints all over it. The fact that he could not have stolen the car locally, since Len had travelled sixty miles in it, was not important. If he managed to take the BMW, he would abandon the Fiat and the police would think the kid had been joyriding.

Denis blundered out of the car, the world swaying around him, and Len pushed him towards the driver's seat. Denis's legs stuck out of the car but his hands gripped the wheel as he tried to keep his balance. Then he struggled out to stand beside Len, holding on to the car to stop himself falling over.

Len twisted Denis's arm up behind his back again and pushed him towards the river bank, meeting little resistance because the boy's head was spinning.

As they reached the water's edge, Len let Denis go and gave him a push, but, fuddled though the boy was, he realized what was happening and thrust himself back against Len, who raised the cosh to strike him. They grappled in the darkness, two blurred shapes who could barely distinguish each other. Denis sensed the man's movement and lifted an arm to ward off the blow that was aimed at his head. The cosh struck his forearm hard and knocked him off balance into the water. There was a loud splash, then silence.

Len leaned over to discover the fate of his victim but

could make out nothing. The water was swirling by. He went to the car and got his torch, which he shone at the point where Denis had fallen in and towards the small bridge, but the boy had vanished. He crossed the bridge and looked in the water there, the cosh ready to use, but he saw nothing, and all he could hear was the sigh of the water rushing past.

It was time for him to hurry, too. Len turned back to walk the short distance to Ford House, the key for which Denis had provided the mould in his pocket.

The door might not be bolted tonight.

Earlier that night, Philip lay in bed thinking about the day that had ended. On the whole it had been a good one. Charles had finished painting the drawing room and had allowed Philip to help, giving him a small brush and telling him to crawl round and do the skirting boards. Philip had concentrated on the task, doing his very best and not making a single smudge on the pale walls. Charles encouraged silent working, saying Philip must pay attention to what he was doing, but at the end he praised what had been done.

'It's nice to have help,' he said. 'You did a good job.'

Philip understood Charles's problem. They were not father and son, and it was rough on Charles to have to put up with him and Emily when he would much rather be living with Rosalind and Celia. When they came, the whole family tended to have treats, go on an excursion somewhere, maybe the cinema or swimming in Swindon, things there wasn't time for in the ordinary way because Mum had to work so hard to pay their share.

Now, in the darkness, he wondered if his own father, out in Australia, had married again and had more children. If so, they'd be half related, like Robin. The thought had never occurred to him before but he supposed it was highly likely. It was tough, living alone.

Mum had said so when Charles moved in and had explained that he would help her look after them. It was only much later, because of something Celia had said, that he realized Charles had left that other family because of Mum.

If he'd done that once, he could do it again. Suppose he met someone else in London? Philip couldn't imagine Charles finding anyone nicer than Mum, but it might happen. In a way, he almost hoped it would. Then they'd be on their own again, though this time with Robin, too. Perhaps it would be rather hard on Robin. He was too little to understand these things.

Philip wasn't sure that he understood them, either. Puzzling about it, eventually he fell asleep.

They had all tried hard that Sunday. Yvonne had kept the children out of Charles's way while he got on with the painting, and she had appreciated the gesture he made in requesting Philip's help. During a fine spell in the afternoon, they had all gone for a walk over the fields to the river, squelching in their boots because the ground, after so much rain, was waterlogged. If it went on, the river would burst its banks and the fields would flood. Audrey Bannerman had told her that she had skated on the frozen flood water during the war.

They might have become friends, if she had not died. They had got past the first hurdle of Audrey's defensive shyness and her own reluctance to spread her energy beyond the family. Yvonne knew that friendship across the generations could be very rewarding. What a waste it all was.

After tea, with the painting done, they had played Racing Demon with Robin and Charles as invincible partners. Emily had cried because she had not managed to win a single game, but she stopped quickly when Charles told her that you had to take the rough with the smooth. She didn't like making him angry and, indeed, rarely did so; she was a child who had learned early in life how to stay out of trouble.

It had all been rather a strain, thought Yvonne, gazing into the darkness after Charles had fallen asleep. Even making love had become an effort. Where was the fun and laughter? Surely there had been plenty of both in those first years?

Things would improve in the summer, when the children could play outside in the sun, if there was any. After all, they had come here to enjoy the peace of country life.

It hadn't been very peaceful in recent days, since the attack on Audrey. Yvonne's thoughts kept returning to that. Still, the man Sawyer had been arrested so he wouldn't be hurting anyone else.

It was odd about the blue van that Charles had seen in the road on the fatal night. She would like to know what it had been doing there.

Someone else had mentioned a blue van to her lately. Who was it?

The water was bitterly cold, and the shock of it, when his head went under, jerked Denis out of his immediate torpor. Automatically, he thrashed out with his arms and kicked with his legs, and while he struggled to gather his fuddled wits, the thick padded anorak spread out on the water and kept him afloat as the fast-running river carried him under the bridge and out of Len's sight.

Len could not have known that when Denis and Tracy had stayed with their grandparents they had both learned to swim. Denis had loved it and lamented that there was no public pool in Leckerton. Discussions about building one had been going on for years but each new scheme came to nothing.

He bumped into the stonework under the bridge and, still spluttering, clutched at it, shaking his head, trying to clear it, taking in the fact that Len had tried to kill him. Still affected by the whisky, it was instinct rather than reason which told him to stay still and make no noise. Len might come after him. He saw the torch beam flashing beyond the bridge as Len crossed it to look over the far side, then it disappeared.

Denis waited under the bridge for several minutes. He did not hear the car start up, nor any other sounds. After a while he struggled on and worked his way towards the bank. When he got there, groping among the reeds, it was an effort to pull himself up, but he managed it and staggered to his feet. He was promptly very sick, shuddering and spluttering, vomiting river water and whisky. The taste in his mouth was vile and he thought he was going to die, but at last the retching was over.

He turned and trudged wearily back over the bridge, his one thought to find help. He was cold and felt ill and more frightened than he had ever been in his life. He'd go to Mrs Davies. She would look after him.

He had forgotten that Len had said they were going to finish the job abandoned before.

Then he saw the Fiat, parked by the river.

Denis was past using caution. He did not look to see if Len was hanging about but tottered towards the car, opened the door and slid into the driver's seat. It was a little while before he had recovered enough to try to start it, and then the key didn't seem to connect very well and he had to twiddle it to get it to work. After that he had to find the light switch. His teeth were chattering and he was sobbing as he managed to swing the car round without driving it into the river. He headed back the way they had come.

Somehow he turned between the gates of Ford House, gripping the wheel, peering ahead and bouncing from pothole to pothole along the drive, travelling fast in second gear.

Then he saw a man on the gravel sweep in front of the house.

Len turned and began to run when he saw the lights. The front door key he'd had made hadn't worked before and it didn't work now, and he was looking for a window by which to enter. He was caught like a dazzled rabbit in the headlights of the approaching car, and he froze for several seconds before dashing round to the yard where he and the boy had hidden before.

The car came after him.

Afterwards, Denis said he hadn't known what he was doing when he drove straight at Len, who had been caught by the car's wing as he tried to leap to one side, and in a way it was true. It had all seemed to happen in slow motion. Had he reached for the brake with his foot, or had he stepped more firmly on the accelerator? All that was certain was that Len was pinned against the wall of the house as the car struck it, and Denis collapsed over the wheel in a shower of shattered glass as the windscreen splintered. The headlights went out and in the sudden darkness his bulk caused the horn to sound, and it went on echoing into the night until Mrs Davies arrived in a blaze of light from the rear of the building.

She opened the driver's door, leaned in and pulled Denis back from the wheel, then switched off the ignition because although the engine had stalled, there could be a risk of fire. Later, she was surprised that she had done this automatically before she helped Denis clamber out of the car. There was blood on his face and he held an arm to his side.

Somehow it was no great shock to discover his identity.

'What have you been up to, Denis?' she asked him calmly. Nothing good, that was certain, at this time of night, and where had he found the car? Had he been joy-riding round the district? Was this how he spent his spare time? The answer to something that had been puzzling her came into her mind like a revelation and she said, 'It was your van that night. You sleep in a blue van.'

Denis wasn't listening.

'There's someone – ' he gasped. 'A man – Len – '

'Don't try to talk,' Yvonne instructed. 'It'll keep. Let's get you indoors and look at the damage.'

Denis was shivering, and as Yvonne put her arm round him, she realized that his clothes were sodden. He groaned as she led him into the house, limping along, a hand to his chest.

'You're soaking wet,' she said.

'I've been in the river,' said Denis. 'He – ' and he tried to point back towards the car but the effort made him groan again.

'Well, never mind now,' said Yvonne, coaxing him into a chair. He was not complaining of being unable to see, so the cuts on his face and head might be superficial; head wounds bled freely, she knew. He had not been wearing a seat belt so he had been lucky not to be catapulted through the windscreen, but only the side of the car had struck the house; it had not been a head-on collision.

She had poured warm water into a bowl and was beginning to dab the boy's forehead below his bristle of brown hair when Charles appeared in his blue towelling robe.

'What on earth's going on?' he exclaimed.

'It's Denis,' said Yvonne. 'He's smashed up some car outside, and himself, too, but I don't think he's too bad.'

'Oh Christ,' said Charles. He had taken only vague notice of Yvonne's sudden departure from their bed, thinking she was going to one of the children, although she had shaken him awake and muttered some urgent words. It was sounds from downstairs that had roused him properly and brought him to investigate.

'There's someone out there,' Denis managed to say at last. 'A man.'

'What? You weren't alone?' Charles snapped the words.

'He pushed me into the river – Len did. He tried to kill me,' said Denis, and added, 'He killed Mrs Bannerman.'

'Do you mean there's some murderer prowling about outside? Charles demanded.

'I don't think he's prowling now,' said Denis, and uttered a curious croak that was almost a laugh. 'He got in the way of the car.'

'I'll take a look round,' said Charles. 'Can you cope here?' he asked Yvonne.

'Of course,' she replied. 'But be careful. Hadn't you better take something with you, just in case? A stick or something?'

Charles picked up a heavy torch that was kept on the dresser and Yvonne continued dabbing at Denis's face. She had just decided that it was more important to get him out of his wet clothes than to deal with his injuries when Philip came into the room carrying a small cricket bat upraised like a weapon.

'I heard noises,' he said. 'But it isn't burglars, is it?' He had armed himself when he found Yvonne and Charles were not in their room.

'It's only Denis,' said his mother, as if such nocturnal visits were nothing out of the ordinary. 'He's had an accident and got very wet. It's a good thing you've come – you can be a help. Could you pop back upstairs and get a blanket from the spare room?'

'Right, Mum.' Philip, trailing the bat, went away and Yvonne started to help Denis out of his clothes. Blood was still oozing from several of the cuts on his head but it was starting to clot and she thought the wounds were best left until a doctor could see them. She was afraid some of them contained fragments of glass.

'So you ran into this man, did you?' she asked.

'He was in the way, wasn't he?' Denis repeated. 'He

was going to break in,' he added, remembering, and uttered a wail of protest as she drew off his jacket.

'Your chest hurts, does it?'

'Just here.' Denis clutched his side again.

'I expect you've cracked a few ribs,' said Yvonne. 'They'll mend. You've been lucky.'

Somehow, between them, they got his sweater off, Denis reluctant to lift his arm. Perhaps he'd broken his collar-bone, she thought. Then Philip appeared with the blanket.

'Oh thanks, Philip,' said his mother. 'Now, could you make Denis some cocoa? I think he'd like a hot drink before we get him off to hospital. You might like one, too.' She began extracting Denis from his heavy sweater.

'We must get the police,' said Charles, coming back into the room clearly in a highly charged condition. 'There's a dead man out there, pinned under a car.'

Philip, already carefully pouring milk into a saucepan, almost dropped it at these words.

'You're sure he's dead?' Yvonne shot Charles a sharp look.

'Certain,' said Charles grimly.

Yvonne was unlacing Denis's trainers. She felt the smooth soles at the same time as she felt Denis himself become less tense.

She was silent for a moment. Then she said, 'I expect Denis's foot slipped on the brake. Is that what happened, Denis? It can, with wet shoes.'

Denis stared at her, still shivering.

'Stand up and take off your jeans. We've got to get you warm and dry,' Yvonne ordered. 'It did slip, didn't it? Your foot?' she repeated as he obeyed.

'Yes. Yes, it did. It must have,' said Denis.

'Don't forget that, Denis,' Yvonne said. 'When you're telling the police what happened. We must telephone them now. You understand that, don't you?'

she added, as she wrapped the blanket round the boy's sturdy naked form.

Charles had gone out of the room and now he returned with a bottle of brandy.

'The boy needs picking up,' he said. 'Give him a tot.'

'No,' said Yvonne sharply. 'Not with the police coming. They'll breath-test him.'

'Have you been drinking?' Charles asked Denis.

'He made me. Len did. I've puked up most of it,' Denis muttered.

Husband and wife exchanged glances. Then Charles astonished Yvonne.

'Best if he has some brandy now. Then we can tell the police we gave him some to pull him round and the test will be invalid,' he said. 'Pour it into his cocoa or whatever you're giving him.'

By this time Philip had regained his calm and was solemnly watching the pan of milk which he had put on the stove. A mug stood nearby. Yvonne silently held it out towards Charles who slopped in some brandy.

'I won't be able to join the Marines now, will I?' Denis asked mournfully as he sipped his drink. A warm glow began to spread from the centre of his body to his extremities and his shivering eased.

'I don't suppose you will,' Yvonne agreed.

What would happen to him? He'd be up for careless driving, maybe manslaughter. Where had he got the car? And what did he know about Audrey's death? He'd said the man Len lying dead outside had killed her. Denis must have been there with the blue van, an accessory. Surely he couldn't have had anything to do with the actual murder?

'How old are you, Denis?' she asked. 'Are you really seventeen?'

'I'm almost sixteen,' he mumbled.

A liar, too. She sighed. Would he be treated as a juvenile offender and get off more lightly than someone

230

older? Yvonne didn't know, but it was a fact that if he hadn't knocked Len down with the car that had crashed outside, the man might have broken into the house and attacked them, and that was a terrifying thought.

'What about your parents?' she said. 'You told me that old woman, Mrs Crow, was your grandmother, but that was another of your lies, wasn't it?'

'I've left home,' Denis said. 'My dad beat me up once too often so I walked out. They didn't bother. Glad to get rid of me.'

That sounded much more like the truth, and if it was, what sort of future waited for him after he served the punishment he was sure to receive for this night's work?

Yvonne became aware of Philip listening in fascination to all this.

'Off to bed,' she told him. 'I'll come up as soon as Denis has gone.' For the moment it seemed very important not to abandon Denis. 'Take your cocoa with you.'

'I'll tuck you up, old man,' said Charles, putting a hand on Philip's shoulder and propelling him away.

'Your sister.' Yvonne spoke to Denis. 'She'll stick by you.'

He shrugged.

'Maybe,' he said.

'I'm sure she will,' Yvonne declared. 'I'll go and see her. I'll explain.'

'Will you?'

She nodded.

'You can trust me, Denis,' she said. 'Just tell me what really happened when Mrs Bannerman died.'

Somehow he managed to do so, leaving out only the part about the key to Ford House whose impression he had obtained. Most of the rest was the truth, though he said that Len had insisted on taking the van, not that he had offered it.

Charles met the two constables whose patrol car had

231

been the nearest to Coxton when the call was received. He led them to where Len's body lay dark and unmoving beneath the car.

'We have a young lad in the house who was driving the Fiat,' said Charles. 'He told us this man – Len, he called him – killed Mrs Bannerman.' Charles had mentioned this on the telephone.

'We're holding someone for that. An escaped con,' said one of the officers.

'Seems you've got the wrong man, then, doesn't it?' Charles remarked.

The men soon radioed in for help, and it was a long time before they all left Ford House. A doctor had to be summoned to pronounce Len definitely dead, and Denis described how Len had taken Alan's van on the night of the original crime.

'Keys in it, were they?' asked one of the officers.

'He'd got one that fitted. Had a whole bunch,' said Denis, inspired.

Later, the police found signs of a scuffle on the river bank and marks further along showing where Denis had climbed out of the water. His sodden clothes, which could be tested for corroborative evidence that they were drenched with river water, were borne away in polythene bags.

Denis was also removed.

Len was identified when the police learned that he had recently been a prisoner in Lockley who worked in the village. They found the key to Ford House in his pocket among various other keys and paid no particular attention to it, deciding that it was simply part of his burglar's collection of useful accessories. They did, however, connect the key in the crashed Fiat with Audrey, and found her door key with it, linked together on a ring with a worn leather fob stamped with her initials.

Charles and Yvonne, curled up warmly together in

bed for what little was left of the night, were unable to sleep.

'Denis never meant to kill that man,' Yvonne reassured them both. 'He just meant to stop him breaking into the house. That's why he came here when he got into the car after climbing out of the river. Otherwise he'd have driven back to Leckerton. The man must have told him he was going to rob us.'

'Mm. Maybe.' Charles felt sure of nothing now. 'How did he ever get mixed up with such a villain?'

'He didn't say,' answered Yvonne. 'I suppose the man saw him about the village and got talking, and then it was chance when they met in Leckerton the night Audrey died and he needed transport.'

'I wonder why they parked outside here?' Charles remarked. 'We never asked Denis that.'

'They were probably waiting until Audrey was asleep,' Yvonne said. 'They must have been in the van when you came back that night.'

'I didn't notice if anyone was in it,' Charles said, and yawned. 'I never liked being so near that prison,' he added.

'They'll let Sawyer go now, anyway,' Yvonne said, not sure herself how she felt about it now.

'They won't. He stole bank cards and walked out of hotels without paying, and he broke out of gaol. Stole cars, too, didn't he?' Charles reminded her.

'Well, at least he won't be charged with killing Audrey when he didn't,' said Yvonne. 'That's something.'

'I suppose so.'

'I wonder how Denis really feels,' said Yvonne. 'After all, he has killed a man, even if it was an accident.'

'Shouldn't think he's really taken it in,' said Charles, who was at last beginning to feel sleepy though it would soon be time to get up. 'Too busy with his bad ankle and his ribs and his cuts and bruises.'

'Too shocked,' said Yvonne. 'I'll go and see his sister tomorrow.'

Charles wished she wouldn't, wished she would walk away from it all, avoid further involvement, but he was beginning to learn not to expect indifference from his wife. 'Try not to promise to visit him in gaol,' he urged, and she laughed.

The police, having made a full identification of Len, went to see Bet, taking a search warrant. They found Audrey's jewellery stashed under a floorboard but they did not discover the ring Bet had hidden in the flour. She would sell it later when all the fuss had died down; it was her only insurance. The television set and radio were removed; Audrey had marked them, as advised by the police, with an invisible pen.

When Mrs Crow heard what had happened to Denis, she waited until it was dark, then wheeled out his splendid new bike. Of course the boy had stolen it; she should have known as much. She pushed it down to the end of the road where she propped it against a wall.

Someone else would soon ride it away. Denis had trouble enough.

Bestselling Crime

☐ No One Rides Free	Larry Beinhart	£2.95
☐ Alice in La La Land	Robert Campbell	£2.99
☐ In La La Land We Trust	Robert Campbell	£2.99
☐ Suspects	William J Caunitz	£2.95
☐ So Small a Carnival	John William Corrington	
	Joyce H Corrington	£2.99
☐ Saratoga Longshot	Stephen Dobyns	£2.99
☐ Blood on the Moon	James Ellroy	£2.99
☐ Roses Are Dead	Loren D. Estleman	£2.50
☐ The Body in the Billiard Room	HRF Keating	£2.50
☐ Bertie and the Tin Man	Peter Lovesey	£2.50
☐ Rough Cider	Peter Lovesey	£2.50
☐ Shake Hands For Ever	Ruth Rendell	£2.99
☐ Talking to Strange Men	Ruth Rendell	£2.99
☐ The Tree of Hands	Ruth Rendell	£2.99
☐ Wexford: An Omnibus	Ruth Rendell	£6.99
☐ Speak for the Dead	Margaret Yorke	£2.99

Prices and other details are liable to change

ARROW BOOKS, BOOKSERVICE BY POST, PO BOX 29, DOUGLAS, ISLE OF MAN, BRITISH ISLES

NAME...

ADDRESS..

....

....

Please enclose a cheque or postal order made out to Arrow Books Ltd. for the amount due and allow the following for postage and packing.

U.K. CUSTOMERS: Please allow 22p per book to a maximum of £3.00.

B.F.P.O. & EIRE: Please allow 22p per book to a maximum of £3.00.

OVERSEAS CUSTOMERS: Please allow 22p per book.

Whilst every effort is made to keep prices low it is sometimes necessary to increase cover prices at short notice. Arrow Books reserve the right to show new retail prices on covers which may differ from those previously advertised in the text or elsewhere.

Bestselling Thriller/Suspense

☐ Skydancer	Geoffrey Archer	£3.50
☐ Hooligan	Colin Dunne	£2.99
☐ See Charlie Run	Brian Freemantle	£2.99
☐ Hell is Always Today	Jack Higgins	£2.50
☐ The Proteus Operation	James P Hogan	£3.50
☐ Winter Palace	Dennis Jones	£3.50
☐ Dragonfire	Andrew Kaplan	£2.99
☐ The Hour of the Lily	John Kruse	£3.50
☐ Fletch, Too	Geoffrey McDonald	£2.50
☐ Brought in Dead	Harry Patterson	£2.50
☐ The Albatross Run	Douglas Scott	£2.99

Prices and other details are liable to change

ARROW BOOKS, BOOKSERVICE BY POST, PO BOX 29, DOUGLAS, ISLE
OF MAN, BRITISH ISLES

NAME...

ADDRESS...

....

....

Please enclose a cheque or postal order made out to Arrow Books Ltd. for the amount
due and allow the following for postage and packing.

U.K. CUSTOMERS: Please allow 22p per book to a maximum of £3.00.

B.F.P.O. & EIRE: Please allow 22p per book to a maximum of £3.00.

OVERSEAS CUSTOMERS: Please allow 22p per book.

Whilst every effort is made to keep prices low it is sometimes necessary to increase cover
prices at short notice. Arrow Books reserve the right to show new retail prices on covers
which may differ from those previously advertised in the text or elsewhere.

Bestselling Fiction

☐ No Enemy But Time	Evelyn Anthony	£2.95
☐ The Lilac Bus	Maeve Binchy	£2.99
☐ Prime Time	Joan Collins	£3.50
☐ A World Apart	Marie Joseph	£3.50
☐ Erin's Child	Sheelagh Kelly	£3.99
☐ Colours Aloft	Alexander Kent	£2.99
☐ Gondar	Nicholas Luard	£4.50
☐ The Ladies of Missalonghi	Colleen McCullough	£2.50
☐ Lily Golightly	Pamela Oldfield	£3.50
☐ Talking to Strange Men	Ruth Rendell	£2.99
☐ The Veiled One	Ruth Rendell	£3.50
☐ Sarum	Edward Rutherfurd	£4.99
☐ The Heart of the Country	Fay Weldon	£2.50

Prices and other details are liable to change

ARROW BOOKS, BOOKSERVICE BY POST, PO BOX 29, DOUGLAS, ISLE OF MAN, BRITISH ISLES

NAME...

ADDRESS...

....

....

Please enclose a cheque or postal order made out to Arrow Books Ltd. for the amount due and allow the following for postage and packing.

U.K. CUSTOMERS: Please allow 22p per book to a maximum of £3.00.

B.F.P.O. & EIRE: Please allow 22p per book to a maximum of £3.00.

OVERSEAS CUSTOMERS: Please allow 22p per book.

Whilst every effort is made to keep prices low it is sometimes necessary to increase cover prices at short notice. Arrow Books reserve the right to show new retail prices on covers which may differ from those previously advertised in the text or elsewhere.

Bestselling General Fiction

☐ No Enemy But Time	Evelyn Anthony	£2.95
☐ Skydancer	Geoffrey Archer	£3.50
☐ The Sisters	Pat Booth	£3.50
☐ Captives of Time	Malcolm Bosse	£2.99
☐ Saudi	Laurie Devine	£2.95
☐ Duncton Wood	William Horwood	£4.50
☐ Aztec	Gary Jennings	£3.95
☐ A World Apart	Marie Joseph	£3.50
☐ The Ladies of Missalonghi	Colleen McCullough	£2.50
☐ Lily Golightly	Pamela Oldfield	£3.50
☐ Sarum	Edward Rutherfurd	£4.99
☐ Communion	Whitley Strieber	£3.99

Prices and other details are liable to change

ARROW BOOKS, BOOKSERVICE BY POST, PO BOX 29, DOUGLAS, ISLE
OF MAN, BRITISH ISLES

NAME..

ADDRESS...

....

....

Please enclose a cheque or postal order made out to Arrow Books Ltd. for the amount
due and allow the following for postage and packing.

U.K. CUSTOMERS: Please allow 22p per book to a maximum of £3.00.

B.F.P.O. & EIRE: Please allow 22p per book to a maximum of £3.00.

OVERSEAS CUSTOMERS: Please allow 22p per book.

Whilst every effort is made to keep prices low it is sometimes necessary to increase cover
prices at short notice. Arrow Books reserve the right to show new retail prices on covers
which may differ from those previously advertised in the text or elsewhere.